THE PRIVILEGED DEATH

Also by Susan Jane Wright:

Box of Secrets

The Glass Lake

Fortune Favors the Dead

Murderous Dreams

THE PRIVILEGED DEATH

SUSAN JANE WRIGHT

ROAN IMPRINT

ISBN 978-1-7390380-6-9 (Paperback Edition)
ISBN 978-1-7390380-7-6 (eBook Edition)

Characters and events in this book are fictitious. Any similarity to real persons, living or dead, is coincidental and not intended by the author.

Editing by Roan Imprint
Front cover image by Valeria Dubych
Front cover design by Roan Imprint
Map icons from flaticon.com users caputo (hen, pig), freepik (compass, garden, greenhouse, plane, spa), iconic artisan (hotel), made by me premium (stables), prosymbols premium (staff), rahul kaklotar (parking), smashicons (archery, trees), vectoricons (horseriding), victor turchyn (falls)

Published by Roan Imprint
PO Box 86091 RPO Marda Loop
Calgary, AB T2T 6B7
Canada

Printed and Bound in Canada

Visit www.SusanJaneWright.ca

*To my mother who taught me
the meaning of resilience*

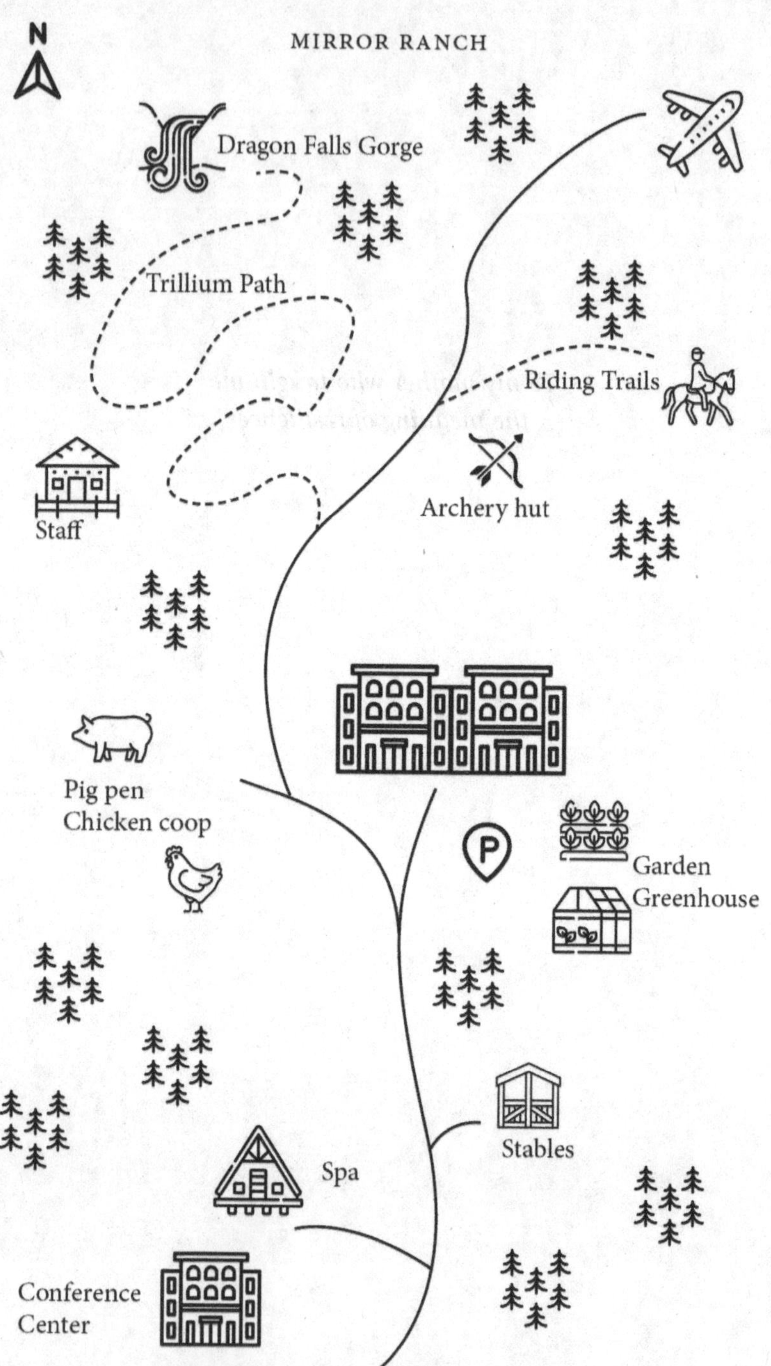

N
MIRROR RANCH
Dragon Falls Gorge
Trillium Path
Riding Trails
Archery hut
Staff
Pig pen
Chicken coop
Garden
Greenhouse
Spa
Stables
Conference
Center

JOURNAL

A famous British actor once said he preferred playing the evil Shakespearean kings to the good ones. "Bad kings have no moral compass. Their drive for power and wealth knows no bounds. That relentless hunger lets me dominate the stage."

He pontificated for twenty minutes about creativity and catharsis—actors can be such windbags—but he was right about the relentless hunger.

You're a perfect example. It doesn't matter how much you have, how many houses, how many planes, how many yachts, it's never enough.

Your greed and your arrogance demand more.

So here's the thing about bad Shakespearian kings: in the end they get slaughtered.

You'd be wise to remember that.

CHAPTER 1

Friday

I'm a city girl through and through and I was about to be trampled to death by a gigantic black horse.

"Step off! Step off!" the woman shouted, her coppery-red hair flying and her body low on the horse's back. A flurry of pounding hooves and creaking leather.

At first I thought the horse was out of control, that he'd caught sight of the barn and in typical dude-ranch fashion, was charging home and there was nothing his hapless rider could do to stop him. But no, she was urging him on.

We dove off the trail into the coarse grass and they flew by. Just before they reached the stables, the horse swerved sharply to the right and came to a shuddering stop under a gigantic pine tree. Laughing, the woman dismounted, coming around to face him, to look into his eyes and touch her forehead to his.

She was Katie Moore and she had to be in her mid sixties is she was a day. Surely too old to be tearing around the countryside on a horse, especially *that* horse. But I'm a city girl. What did I know?

"That's what we should be doing," AJ said as he climbed back onto the path and bent down to pick a twig out of his shoelaces. "Enjoying the clean mountain air, basking in the sunlight, not stuck in a dinky conference room plotting"—this in air quotes— "our future."

"You two all right back there?" Keith was well ahead of us on the pine-needled path.

AJ, Keith and I are lawyers. We came to Mirror Ranch to sort out the future of our law firm, Braxton, Lawson and Valentine. AJ is Braxton, Keith is Lawson and I'm Valentine. Two of the three of us thought BLV's future as a boutique (read: small) environmental law firm was just fine; one of us, that would be Keith, disagreed.

My sister Louisa says BLV is the unlikely partnership of Eeyore (Keith), Tinkerbell (me) and Peter Pan (AJ). AJ and I inhabit the same fairytale universe because we're both quick and intuitive whereas Keith is so risk averse he seizes up like a rusty engine when confronted with the unexpected. It's a bizarre combination, but it works.

"A little help here, please." I extended a hand to AJ who reached down and pulled me out of a prickly wild rose bush.

"You've got to look before you leap," he said.

"Yeah, I'll bear that in mind the next time a crazed woman on a massive horse tries to run me down."

I released AJ's hand and fell in step beside him. "I think we're driving our facilitators nuts." Mick and Lucy, two bright young things with Harvard MBAS, had experience launching tech start-ups into the stratosphere, but we were a law firm, not a tech company and by Day Two I knew the stratosphere was not where I wanted to be.

AJ grinned. "That's why they booted us outside. My mom

did that when I started to get on her nerves. She wouldn't let me back in the house until the streetlights came on."

"You lived on a farm AJ, there wasn't a streetlight for fifty miles." The thought of living in such isolation in the middle of the bald prairie made the hairs on the back of my neck stand straight up.

He dismissed my comment with a wave of his hand and said, "These consulting firms sell the same cookie-cutter package to all their clients; unfortunately for them BLV doesn't fit the Harvard MBA playbook."

"So you're saying it's not us, it's them. They're to blame for why we're not getting it."

Up ahead, Keith stopped walking and turned to face us. The sun was in his eyes and when he squinted he looked like a real, weather-beaten cowboy, which he was in his own way now that he'd moved to an acreage outside the city.

"It would help if you two took this seriously. I swear sometimes you're worse than children." Keith was only half kidding. He's forty-three, four years older than me, five years older than AJ, and sometimes treats me like his little sister.

He's a nice guy, but I didn't need any more siblings. I had Louisa. She was driving out to join us for the weekend. "I figure you'll be in desperate need of my calming presence by then," she'd said.

"You just want an excuse for a long weekend getaway." I'd replied. She's a neuro nurse and the last three months had been particularly brutal.

At first it was going to be just the two of us, then Keith's wife took their daughter to Victoria to visit her mom and AJ decided he wanted to enjoy the full dude ranch experience. So they both decided to stay.

The cool spring breeze tugged at the flipchart paper

rolled up under Keith's arm. Mick, our facilitator, referred to it reverently as The Blueprint. It would reveal our future. His colleague, Lucy, shot me a grin when I snorted in disbelief, I liked Lucy, she was a pragmatist.

"That's what I'll be doing tomorrow," AJ said with a backward glace at Katie who was now leading her horse into the barn. "Tearing all over the countryside with the wind in my hair."

"I don't know, AJ, it's been years since you left the farm, perhaps trotting quietly down a path on a pony would be more your style."

"Bite your tongue, Ms. Valentine." He feigned shock. "Once a farm boy always a farm boy." AJ was raised on a farm north of Calgary but he'd left right after high school. He was no more a farm kid than I was.

We traded jibes all the way past the large kitchen garden. It was late May and delicate green shoots destined to become carrots and cabbages tentatively poked their tender heads out of the dark soil.

"I like this place," Keith said, leaning down and pulling a long, squeaky blade of grass out of the ground and popping the white end into his mouth. "How'd you find it?"

"Madeline suggested it." Madeline's our paralegal. I'd met her on my first day of articles at Gates, Case and White. She'd sized me up with her cold green eyes and decided I wouldn't last until Christmas unless she took me under her wing. Until then I'd thought guardian angels were gentle celestial beings who nudged you out of harm's way, but Madeline proved to be the ruthless, Machiavellian kind.

Mirror Ranch was a luxury dude ranch and spa. It offered rustic accommodations at ridiculously high prices, but Madeline finagled a special deal. That's one of her superpowers. If we came just before the May long weekend and were prepared to rough it—the ranch didn't officially open until the first of June and the summer staff had not yet arrived—they'd drop our rate by twenty percent. Other than the skeleton crew staff and a group of MMG executives we'd have the place to ourselves.

It seemed like a good idea at the time.

CHAPTER 2

AJ, Keith and I climbed the trail searching for a quiet place to sit down and review The Blueprint. Eventually we reached the Staff HQ building and I dropped down onto the wooden steps leading up to the veranda.

AJ settled on the step below me. His sandy brown hair and his brilliant blue eyes give him an innocent 'aw shucks' demeanour, it's particularly effective when he's cross-examining a recalcitrant witness.

"Right," Keith took a deep breath, "let's get to it." He slapped the sheet of flipchart paper down on the wood plank deck and anchored the corners with his wallet and his phone and we stared at the multicoloured lines and circles that were supposed to be a roadmap to our future.

"I don't see it," AJ said, squinting at the hieroglyphics on the page.

"Neither do I." I turned to Keith. "Care to elucidate?"

While Keith pulled a small notebook out of his jeans pocket and flipped through his notes, AJ turned to me and asked if I knew anything about the other guests who would be arriving soon.

"Yep." I couldn't hide my excitement. "Charlie Moore and his family are coming."

A few days after Madeline had booked us into the Ranch, Parker Moore called to say her family—she called them the Moore clan—would be at the Ranch all weekend and she was looking forward to catching up. I was surprised I hadn't made the connection. MMG: Moore Management Group, owned by billionaire Charlie Moore. Parker was his daughter. We'd articled together at Gates and kept in touch after she'd left the firm.

Keith glanced at us. A small muscle twitched in his jaw. "Have you two heard a single word I've said?" I shot a *busted* look at AJ and we both snapped to attention while Keith reexplained what all the squiggles and circles meant. "By my reading, the inputs suggest we should expand."

Inputs? Those weren't inputs. They were scribbles on a fluttering piece of paper, no better than chicken bones and sheep's entrails, to be interpreted any way you liked. How could Keith who agonizes over big decisions—his wife Wendy was signing the purchase contract on their acreage while he was still pacing around the conference room questioning the wisdom of moving out of the city—interpret the runes as saying BLV should expand?

AJ, who was as skeptical about expansion as I was, frowned and asked Keith to take us through the squiggles one last time. Keith let out an exasperated sigh and went back to the beginning. I smiled at AJ. *Good move.* With any luck, by the time Keith was finished he'd have talked himself into doing nothing.

As Keith droned on I leaned back on my elbows and lifted my face to the sun. Down at the stables Katie Moore was closing the broad barn doors. They rolled along an overhead rail and bumped closed with a satisfying thunk.

Then a younger woman rushed around the corner of the barn, her arms extended, squealing like a teenager.

"Mom!" Parker's voice carried up to us on the breeze, "It's so good to see you."

Katie crushed her daughter in a long, long hug, before holding her out at arm's length to take a good look at her. My mom used to do the same thing, telling me I looked tired and was working too hard. I'd reply I was getting old, and she'd say thirty-something wasn't old. She could never remember my age.

From this distance, you'd think Parker and Katie were sisters; it was their hair, thick and shining like a copper penny in the bright morning light. They linked arms and strode up the path to the Lodge.

The entire Moore clan would be here by dinner time. Not all of them would go home.

CHAPTER 3

When I first met Parker Moore, I didn't know she was rich. Out of this world, insanely rich. To me she was just one of the ten articling students milling about the 45th floor boardroom at Gates, Case and White. We'd finished law school and had been offered articles by Gates, one of the best law firms in the country. Or so we'd be told, repeatedly, by the partner who hired us.

Seven men and three women, all smartly dressed, chatty, nonchalant even—'of course I expected to land here, didn't you?'—eying the competition out of the corners of their eyes, wondering who'd be still standing at the end of the year.

No one recognized Parker. Like movie stars, the rich often look smaller and less imposing when you see them in real life. It's only when you remember they can buy and sell you a thousand times over that they grow to be the size of Goliath.

Clad in the standard female lawyer's uniform, a fitted navy jacket, slacks that were neither too tight nor too baggy, her attire was exactly what you'd expect...until you got to her shoes which were blood red leather and high, not vampy TV-lawyer high, just high enough to look daring and expensive. She was listening to a reedy young man who looked more like an IT geek than a lawyer. She had a polite smile on her face. Then he said something that made her laugh. Her eyes flashed—she had unusual eyes, brilliant green, and slightly tilted up at the corners—and instantly I was drawn to her.

In the coming months I discovered there was more to Parker Moore than her pedigree. Not that the hiring committee cared, they'd have offered her a job if she was as dumb as a sack of hammers, anything to get their hands on even a tiny sliver of Charlie Moore's business. The Moore Management Group, MMG, was like a fat, overripe peach, every law firm in the city wanted a taste of the action.

Gates professed to value work/life balance. What a joke. Our articles were a trial by fire, intended to weed out those who didn't bill enough to ensure the partners at the top of the pyramid took home big fat payouts at the end of the year.

This didn't cut it with Parker who quit after three years to go work for her dad at MMG. "I don't mind working hard," she'd said at the time, "but I expect to be paid for it." She said if you divided our annual compensation by the number of hours we worked, we made less than plumbers and electricians.

I sighed as the memory faded. "We were so naïve back then."

Keith looked up from the black sharpie marks on the large white sheet of paper. "Back when we started BLV?" The sheet fluttered in the slight breeze, struggling to fly away.

"No, I was thinking about our time at Gates."

AJ glanced at me. "Best move you guys ever made was leaving that place. The second best move you made was inviting me to join the partnership."

It *was* a smart move. Our partnership was perfect. So why did Keith want to ruin it?

CHAPTER 4

The lobby was abuzz with activity when we got back later that afternoon. Suitcases littered the hardwood floor in front of the reception desk, children were shrieking, and the call bell was banging away as if someone's life depended on it.

"All right, all right." Charlotte swept into view and took up her position behind the reception desk. We'd met her two days ago when we checked in. She was young and very pretty with sparkling green eyes and thick auburn hair. She slung her floppy straw hat into a corner on the desk and squared her shoulders in front of the computer.

"Robson, you flew in, right?" Charlotte asked the man glaring at the boy tormenting the call bell. Mirror Ranch had its own private hanger located at the edge of the property.

Robson, as thin as a whippet and just as twitchy, leaned across the front desk. "Of course we flew in." He turned to the woman standing behind him and snapped, "Elise, get him under control before he sets Amelia off."

The woman, a compact, well-maintained blond, flicked her hair off one shoulder and gave the little girl standing next to her a reassuring smile. The child blinked, as if wondering whether she'd missed an opportunity to get into mischief.

Elise approached the desk, turning her attention to Charlotte. "Honey, be a dear and send someone to the hanger to fetch Teddy's backpack. He left it under his seat." The small boy paused for a moment at the sound of his name, then continued to abuse the call bell.

"Stop." The bell made a muted *bing* when Robson snatched it away, whippet eyes flashing as he placed it firmly on the front desk out of reach.

With a bang of the double mahogany doors, Parker and her mother entered the lobby. The little girl ran to them, throwing herself into Katie's arms. "Grandma," she squealed. The boy kicked a pink Barbie rollie bag out of his way and strolled over to his grandmother, bouncing on his toes, impatient for his share of hugs and kisses.

The resemblance was uncanny. Upturned green eyes and auburn hair. Parker, Charlotte and Robson were Katie Moore's kids, although Robson was a good four inches shorter than the Moore women. I'd assumed they all worked for their father at MMG but apparently Charlotte, the youngest, ran Mirror Ranch.

AJ glanced at me, thinking what I was thinking: Where was Charlie Moore? We'd been here for two days and not once had we caught a glimpse of one of the richest men in the country.

Keith disappeared upstairs with the rolled up piece of flip chart paper under his arm and AJ and I wandered over to the bar, strolling past the trophy wall, scanning the photos of Charlie with presidents and kings and the big money men from Bay Street and Wall Street. Sometimes he wore a suit, other times he was dressed in khakis with a hunting rifle cradled by his side. Always standing tall and self-assured, comfortable in their company.

"Look," AJ pointed to a photo of Charlie with the pope and whistled. "This guy knows everybody."

He pulled open the bar fridge, it was an honour bar, and selected two bottles, beer for him, a pink grapefruit seltzer for me, and we settled in the squishy leather armchairs grouped around the massive river rock fireplace and watched the mayhem at the reception desk.

Robson was grousing, he wasn't satisfied with the rooms he'd been allotted. Charlotte replied she wasn't moving Katie again—shortly after we'd arrived we discovered their mother usually stayed in one of the rooms Charlotte had set aside for BLV.

Katie was trying to distract the little boy who demanded that she force his father to hand over his bell immediately.

AJ set his beer down on the coffee table and said to me. "Remind me to never have kids."

I took a long swallow. It was warm in the lobby and the bottles were beading up. "I think you need a significant other first." I'd known AJ for five years and other than a very serious relationship in university, none of his girlfriends seemed to stick. My sister's voice sounded in my ear: *Pot meet kettle. When was the last time you went on a real date?*

"You two okay over there?" Charlotte called out from behind the registration desk. We smiled and held up our bottles. "Don't mind them." She waved a hand at the Moores who were making their noisy way up the central staircase to their rooms on the second floor. "The clan has a habit of making their presence known." Yes, I thought, being billionaires and heirs to billionaires gives you a certain insouciance the rest of us don't share.

"Hey, listen," Charlotte continued, "the family dines at

6:30. You're more than welcome to join us." She sounded sincere, but I hesitated. For the last two evenings we'd had our dinner in the snug just off the bar. The cozy space was preferable to rattling around in the large, wood panelled dining room.

"Oh no, we wouldn't want to intrude."

"Please," Charlotte said, "it's no bother and you'll finally meet Jay."

When we'd checked in she tapped the photo of her husband in the Mirror Ranch brochure, saying if we needed anything, anything at all, we should tell her or her husband— "You can't miss him, he's the Indian guy charging around all over the place"—except he was either locked away in his office or traipsing around the 640 acre property fixing trails or mending fences or something. Jay was as elusive as a shadow.

CHAPTER 5

The little girl pranced into the sun filled dining room with her hands curled under her chin. She was making whinnying noises. Reminding me of when I was small and used to gallop all the way home from the library. Her frilly yellow dress bounced up and down and her shiny, patent leather shoes tip-tapped across the pine floor.

When I bumped into her and her mother in the corridor earlier that afternoon, Amelia announced she was named after the lady who died in a horrible plane crash and that she was five years old and her brother was eight and his real name was Robson Moore Junior after his father, but everyone kept getting the two of them mixed up so they called her dad Robson and her brother Teddy because he didn't want to be called Junior. There may have been some logic there but I couldn't follow it.

Teddy almost mowed his little sister down when he charged into the dining room and flung himself into a chair at our end of the long table. The cutlery rattled and I caught my wine glass before it tipped over. It was large and very round, like a fishbowl. Madeline, my paralegal, would approve. She believes wine glasses should be as big as your head.

I'd invited Madeline and Bridget, our legal assistant, to participate in our strategy off-site and in less than an hour Madeline came back to me with a long list of reasons why they should stay home. *Somebody's got to keep the office open* appeared as Reason #10, well behind *We'd be bored to tears* which clocked in at #1 and *It's a colossal waste of our time (and yours)* which was #2. I suspected the real reason Madeline was loath to participate was she'd made plans with Antonio, he was some kind of money manager, to fly to Mykonos for the long weekend. Madeline moved in circles the rest of us could only dream of.

"What did I tell you about running?" Elise scolded Teddy as she pulled him out of the chair. "Now take your place up there, close to Grandpa." Teddy scowled. "Family at the top, guests at the bottom," Elise said, gripping Teddy's shoulder and frogmarching him away.

Guests at the bottom? I bristled at the sound of that.

The minute they took their seats Teddy slumped and flopped around and Amelia's patent leather shoes began to tap rhythmically against the legs of her chair. Elise settled herself, smoothing her skirt and patting her hair before turning to stare at the entrance to the dining room.

Keith glanced at his watch. "The Great Man is late." He'd no sooner said the words than Charlie made his grand entrance.

Part of it was his imposing appearance. Charlie was a big, barrel-chested man, with a full head of silver hair and a thick walrus mustache. He'd attract attention even if he weren't a billionaire. Following in his wake came his wife and Robson and Parker. *Where are his bodyguards?* I thought about it for three seconds and decided Mirror

Ranch was so remote that even a super rich man would feel safe here.

"Evening, folks." Charlie shook our hands and greeted Keith by name as he strolled down the line of chairs to the head of the table. He didn't bother to introduce himself, there was no need.

Teddy held out his fist and Charlie gave his 'little man' a fist bump, Amelia beamed when he planted a noisy kiss on top of her head. Katie gave us a polite smile as she sailed by and settled next to Elise on Charlie's left. Parker and Robson arranged themselves to his right. There was no fuss with the seating, everyone seemed to know their place.

Robson picked up the bottle of red wine, examining the label carefully before reaching for the corkscrew and deftly removing the cork.

When Charlotte entered the dining room from the kitchen and told her father the chef was ready to serve dinner, Charlie said he hoped it wasn't Bernard's signature dish. As much as he liked stuffed tomatoes, that last time Bernard served them he was sick as a dog. "Too rich. I'm going to lay off for a while."

"No, not tonight Daddy." Charlotte took her seat next to Robson. "The kids don't like tomatoes. Bernard is serving something that will appeal to them too." My first thought was Kraft mac and cheese, but the Mirror Ranch website said Bernard was a celebrity chef so macaroni slathered with buttery orange powder was unlikely.

A well built young man emerged from the kitchen and sat down beside Charlotte who introduced him as her husband, the elusive Sanjay. He flashed a very white smile and said, "Please, call me Jay."

Chef Bernard and his assistant, a middle-aged Asian woman named Opal, appeared carrying heaping plates of grass-fed beef and heritage carrots and parsnips. Bernard didn't say much but when he did it was with a distinctive New York accent. Opal, on the other hand, sounded British. The whole thing, out here in the middle of the Canadian wilderness, was slightly disorienting.

Over dinner Charlotte explained that after she and Jay had left MMG, they'd scoured Canada and the US looking for a large acreage. It was Jay's dream to open a luxury dude ranch and spa.

Jay interrupted, speaking quickly as he described the frustrating year they'd spent crawling through one decrepit, broken down barn after another until they discovered Mirror Ranch. "It was well worth the wait. We absolutely love this place, don't we Char, it's paradise on earth, Shangri-La—"

"Jay, stop." Kindly, Charlotte patted his arm, "You're rhapsodizing again. Suffice it to say we're very happy with how Mirror Ranch is coming along."

At the head of the table, Parker and her brother were debating about business strategy—God, we'd just spent two days arguing about the same thing, can't we talk about something else, the state of the world perhaps—while their father sat back, arms crossed, with a slightly amused expression on his face. He turned his eyes away from his children and called down the table to Keith.

"Keith, you're a smart man running a successful small business, what's your opinion? You'd agree that a business must grow or die, am I right?"

Keith set down his fork. A dark red blotch appeared on his neck, just above his Adam's apple. He cleared his throat. "It depends." The red blotch crept higher, spreading across his face. I've known Keith for over a decade. He only flushes when he's angry. It's his tell, warning others to stay clear.

Puzzled I glanced back at Charlie who stared at Keith for a long moment, then turned to Robson and asked him the same question. Robson reeled off a long list of reasons why prudent CEOs leapt at the chance to grow their companies. Parroting the same buzz words we'd heard from our facilitators, Mike and Lucy, two lovely people I hoped never to meet again.

By the time I looked back at Keith he was hunched over his plate, sawing at his beef as if it were a chunk of rubber.

Across the table one of the children was grizzling.

"Please," Elise said to Amelia, "just one tiny bite, darling. For Mommy."

Flushed with heat, her yellow dress wilting like a spent daffodil, Ameilia declared she was a vegetarian and could not possibly eat a cow. Immediately I felt a surge of sympathy. There's nothing more off-putting than a gigantic slab of rare beef bleeding off the edge of a white plate.

Magically, Chef Bernard appeared from the kitchen. He reached over Amelia's shoulder, whisking away her plate and replacing it with a small bowl of gourmet mac and cheese. Amelia speared a noodle with her fork and noisily sucked off the cheese sauce.

At Charlie's end of the table, Robson and Parker's voices grew louder. Then Charlie raised his hand and said, "That's enough."

The room fell silent, but for the sound of Amelia slurping her macaroni.

Slowly Charlie dabbed the corner of his mouth with a red check napkin, then rose to his feet. He was going upstairs. He had work to do. "Charlotte, please tell Bernard the meal was excellent, as always."

Charlotte and Parker tried to convince their father to

stay a little longer, at least have some coffee, but Charlie's jaw was set. He said he'd made up his mind.

After Charlie left Robson sat back in his chair. With a thin smile on his lips he said, "Hear that Parker? Dad's made up his mind."

"Don't be such a jackass," she replied.

The children looked stunned, then giggled. "Parker swore, Parker swore." But none of it registered with Katie who was toying with her wine glass, tipping it back and forth as if she were trying to see how close she could come to the rim without spilling wine all over the red and white tablecloth.

CHAPTER 6

When we were little, Louisa and I didn't go on vacation. Dad was building his accounting practice and we didn't have the money to rent a cabin on a lake. I told Dad I preferred splashing around in the local swimming pool because there was no chance I'd step on something squishy on the muddy lake bottom. Dad thought I was being diplomatic but I meant it, even today wading into wild water unnerves me.

I had that feeling now, a whisper of dread as I watched Charlie leave the dining room.

Amelia had finished her mac and cheese and was working on her chocolate mouse. She pushed it aside, half-finished. Her little face was red and tendrils of fine blond hair clung to her forehead. Elise brushed them away as she leaned over to tell Teddy it was time for bed.

The boy stiffened. "No, I won't, it's not fair." Then hopped out of his chair and ran around the table to stand at his father's elbow. "Daddy, just because she's tired, doesn't mean I have to go to bed!"

Robson shot a cursory glance at the boy, then stared at

his wife who said it had been a long day and the children were exhausted. "Please, Robson. It's time for bed."

He replied he had business to discuss with Parker. Teddy whined louder and did that jerky, floppy, wiggly thing kids do when they don't get their way. Then yanked his father's elbow.

"Stop that!" Robson wrenched his arm away. "Just stop it." Teddy's eyes filled with tears. Any minute now he'd fly into an epic temper tantrum.

"Oh for pity's sake, Robson," Parker said as she rose from her chair, "we can do this tomorrow." By then Katie was leading Amelia out of the dining room. Robson glanced at his son who was rooted to the spot, then pushed back his chair and marched out of the room. Wailing, Teddy raced after him.

Opal emerged from the kitchen and began to clear away the dinnerware. The sun had set and in the dim light from the deer antler chandelier the smudgy wine glasses and sticky mouse plates looked tawdry.

AJ and Keith pushed back their chairs, preparing to head upstairs. I was about to join them when Parker asked if I would like to go for a walk.

Outside, the air felt cool and the breeze was soft. Stars sparkled overhead, tiny pinpricks in the indigo sky, and pine needles cushioned our footsteps on the illuminated trail.

Parker didn't say much until we reached the paddock fence where she directed me to the adirondak chairs arranged in a circle around a firepit. She pulled a bundle of newspapers and small dry branches out of the long wooden box sitting on the ground beside the paddock gate and set to work building a fire. Flicking her lighter a couple of times—she didn't smoke, but Parker was always ready for anything—until the edge of the newspapers curled yellow and black and burst into flame.

The adirondak chair was so deep I didn't dare sit back, choosing to perch on its edge I watched Parker poking at the fire. They say patience is a virtue, but it's never been one of mine, and after a minute I asked her what was going on.

The flames fluttered in the night breeze, throwing strange shadows across her face and turning her green eyes black.

"Did I mention that Mirror Ranch is Charlotte's baby?" Parker asked.

"Charlotte said something about it at dinner."

"They've done wonders with the place and they're not finished yet. Jay has what we in the business would call 'ambitious' plans." She gave a wry smile. "He wants to add glamping and zip lines, maybe even a mini rodeo." She shook her head. "The boy dreams big, I'll give him that."

As she stared into the flames her voice took on that dreamy quality of someone whose thoughts were far, far away. "Good old Sanjay Azeem. Charlotte fell for him hard when she joined the firm. He was in our financial analysis group and she was convinced he'd go all the way. But working for Charlie—it's not easy. Charlotte was livid when Jay got the boot. They were married by then, she quit on the spot and didn't speak to Dad for months."

When Parker left Gates to work for MMG she had no qualms about working for her father. The company was professionally run, she'd said. It utilized the best practices (some would argue the worst practices) of the big investment banks and consulting firms. Employees worked 24/7, the rumours of sleeping on the couch in their offices were true, but surviving a brutal work ethic wasn't enough in MMG's up-or-out culture. At the end of the year you were judged by what the clients and those higher up in the hierarchy thought of you. If they liked you, you stayed, if they didn't you were gone.

Likeability. It's a fuzzy metric, not easy to cultivate. You either had it or you didn't. And if you didn't, even being married to Charlie Moore's daughter wasn't enough to save you. Jay's last-day march to the elevator clutching a cardboard box jammed with his personal items must have been mortifying.

A smoldering ember popped like a gunshot and landed on my runner. I shook it off and crushed it, watching the sparks float up into the stary darkness as I listened to Parker's soft voice.

"Dad loaned them the money to buy this place and sends our clients here when they need to go on an off-site. I think he's trying to make it up to Charlotte for firing Jay. And the family comes here all the time." Her face softened. "Mirror Ranch is Mom's real home. She rarely goes into the city anymore."

When I told her that Katie and her beast of a horse practically mowed us down that morning, she laughed. "That would be Shadow, isn't he stunning. He's Mom's horse and God help anyone who tries to ride him."

The breeze rustled through the treetops and an owl hooted softly in the black woods on the edge of the clearing. Owls are the only birds that make no sound when they fly, silently swooping down on their prey. One could be circling overhead right now and we'd never know it.

"How old is your mom, mid sixties? She seems to be very confident on a horse."

Parker nodded and said Katie took up riding three years ago, after Charlotte bought Mirror Ranch. Soon she became an accomplished rider, equally comfortable in an English or Western saddle. Parker gazed down to the stables just beyond the paddock fence. But for a single light over the barn door, it was shrouded in darkness.

"You know, Evie, I didn't think they were serious about this place. Jay was such a prissy, button-down accountant. Spreadsheets and analytics, that's his forte, I couldn't see him rolling up his sleeves and fixing fences and clearing paths and yet, he seems to like it.

"And Charlotte, that girl was transformed. One day she's wearing designer clothes and zipping around the world in the corporate jet—she was incredible at marketing, much better than Robson or me—the next she's mucking out the stables and running the front desk. Turns out she's one of those people who's great at everything she touches, even taking care of the livestock. Sometimes I think she should have been a vet."

"It's good they found their calling," I said. The fire was dying down but Parker showed no sign she was ready to leave.

"What about you, Parker, are you glad you switched from law to business? Working for your dad can't be easy."

"It's got it's ups and downs." She glanced up from the fire and looked at me, becoming animated for the first time since we'd come out here. "Can I tell you something in confidence?" She blurted it out before I could reply. "He's going to retire."

"*What*?" This was huge news. Charlie was MMG personified, like Elon Musk and Tesla. The stock market would go wild when he announced he was leaving, unless…

"I assume you're getting Charlie's job."

She became very still. "Well, it's either me or Robson. That decision has yet to be made."

"But it has to be you. You'd be perfect—"

She stood up, shaking her head. "Forget it, Evie, please. I shouldn't have said anything."

She kicked some dirt onto the fire, then walked over to the wooden box and pulled out a large jerrycan and sloshed water over the embers until they were waterlogged and dead.

JOURNAL

*C*harlie and I met at a party in one of those huge glass houses in Hollywood Hills. A friend of a friend was producing a film and needed investors. Hot shot investment bankers were easy targets. They loved rubbing elbows with movie stars.

I was an actress, a starlet, one of those pretty young things scattered around the room pushing booze and drugs to get the money men to open their wallets. Hoping to be noticed by someone who mattered.

Right from the get-go, Charlie bowled me over with his looks, his energy, his charm. He was working at McKinsey then and boasted he'd be running the place in five years.

He whispered that from the moment he laid eyes on me, he knew he had to have me. What Charlie wants, Charlie gets and eight months later we were married.

He was very busy at work but we managed to squeeze in a five day honeymoon in Bermuda. The resort was fantastic, white umbrellas dotted the pink sand beach, the skies were cobalt blue. I stepped through every moongate I could find, making the same wish over and over again. Charlie had a terrible sunburn, his skin peeled off on the sheets. But he *indulged me, asking what I had wished for. I wouldn't tell him—please love me forever—it sounded so banal.*

When we came back home to San Francisco, he was stunned I wanted to keep my little apartment in Los Feliz. It was a cool neighbourhood, close to auditions, close to my friends.

Our "unorthodox" living arrangements made him uncomfortable, he said. He wanted his wife to be at home with him. But Charlie, I said, you're constantly on the road, overseeing big files in New York, Toronto and Dubai. It made no sense to me to give up my place.

Reluctantly, he relented. Then one day when we were staying in my place in LA, it all came out. He was desperately worried about my safety. We were in the middle of Griffith Park. He looked out over the rough terrain, there wasn't a soul around, and said if I tumbled down the hill right here, right now, and was seriously injured, no one would know where to find me.

It's too dangerous for you to live here alone, he said, if something terrible happened I couldn't bear it.

He begged me to give up my little apartment and stay in San Francisco with him.

I said I'd think about it.

CHAPTER 7

When Parker and I returned to the Lodge, the post and beam lobby was deserted except for Charlotte and Jay who were enjoying a quiet drink in front of the towering stone fireplace. They waved us over, but I begged off.

Upstairs, small stained glass uplights brightened the dim hallway and a sliver of light slanted across the floor from AJ's room. He'd wedged the door open with a wastepaper basket. The air was cooler in the hall.

I tapped on the door frame. AJ and Keith were talking quietly on the small plaid sofa in front of the empty fireplace, a miniature version of the river stone fireplaces in the lobby and the dining room below.

AJ waved me in and the sooty smell of the firepit wafted in behind me. He asked if I'd been camping and whether I wanted a drink.

"No and yes."

By the time he returned with my gin and tonic, I was draped across a small armchair with my feet propped up on the coffee table.

"How's Parker?" AJ asked as he settled in the armchair kitty-corner to the sofa.

"I'm not sure. We had a pleasant chat—"

"Charlie seemed a little testy at dinner. Did Parker say anything?" Keith asked with a frown.

She had said something, something huge, but Charlie's retirement plans were confidential and I couldn't tell them. "You know what these executives are like." I rolled my eyes. "Ours is not to reason why, ours is but to do or die." The fact that this maxim was true irritates me to no end and I shuddered.

AJ asked if I was cold and crossed over to the window, pulling the billowing curtains to one side and cranking it shut.

That sense of dread came back, like I was about to step into a lake full of leeches. "Have you ever had the feeling something bad is going to happen?"

Keith pulled his feet off the coffee table, set his beer bottle down with a soft clunk and stared at me for a few seconds. He used to dismiss my hunches, but over time learned that when I get a 'feeling' it merits attention. I inherited my sense of intuition from my mom. That woman was amazing, able to predict what a self-serving politician would do well before the pundits caught on.

"What exactly did Parker say?" Keith's face was wary.

"Nothing. That's what's bothering me. Clearly she wanted to talk or she wouldn't have asked me to go for a walk, but when we got to the firepit she just prattled on about Charlotte and Jay and the Ranch—"

"Did she talk about me?" Keith asked.

AJ was back at the minibar and stopped rummaging long enough to look at Keith. "Why on earth would Parker talk about you?"

"Yeah," I added, "she doesn't even know you."

Casually, Keith picked up his beer bottle and took a gulp. "No particular reason. Just curious."

AJ continued poking around in the minibar until he found what he was looking for. Two Kit Kat bars. He tossed one to Keith and snapped the other one in half and handed me a piece before dropping into his armchair.

Keith unwrapped his chocolate bar, lay the red wrapper on the coffee table, then broke the bar into four pieces and lay them on the wrapper. He was arranging the ends so they lined up when he said, "So I've been thinking about the future of our firm."

My sense of dread spiked.

"You're kidding," AJ said with a groan. "After two solid days of listening to those MBA types spew mumbo jumbo, the absolute last thing I want to talk about is our future." He yawned. "Sorry, bud. That's not happening, not tonight."

I took a bite of my Kit Kat. "I second what AJ said."

Keith sagged back into the corner of the couch and stared at the label on his beer bottle as if it were a brand he'd never seen before. "Fine, but we're going to have to talk about it sooner rather than later. We're at different stages of our careers—"

"Hold on." I pulled my feet off the coffee table and turned to look at him. "We're at exactly the same stage in our careers—equal partners in a lucrative law practice. In fact, we're doing so well we can't figure out how to handle the workload." *What the heck was he prattling on about?*

"Stop," AJ rubbed one eye, then yawned again. "It's late, we're tired, we're not discussing this now. It is the May long weekend. We're officially on a mini break. There will be no more work talk until Tuesday morning. Period."

For a guy who uses farm boy charm to get his way, this was pretty strident. AJ caught my eye and flashed a tiny smile as if to say, yeah, I know, you didn't think I had it in me, did you.

CHAPTER 8

Later that evening I stepped out of the shower and was toweling dry my hair when my phone binged with a text:

You said you'd call. You didn't call. FT me!

Madeline. She had no interest in attending the offsite, in fact she was supposed to be in Mykonos with what's his name, but she'd insisted I call her with our decision—were we expanding BLV or standing pat? I glanced at my watch, what time was it in Greece anyway?

Tightening the belt around my bathrobe, I tucked myself into the armchair by the balcony, pecking at my phone. When she appeared on the screen she said, "You forgot, didn't you?"

"Absolutely not," I lied. "We've been extremely busy. Why are you calling? Aren't you supposed to be sunning yourself on a yacht in the Aegean Sea?"

"Oh that." She waved a hand dismissively. "It's over. Poor Antonio, he's much too clingy for my liking." Madeline is a woman of a certain age, I've known her decades, everyone she dates is too *something* for her liking.

Behind her came the squawk of birds and the barking of

dogs and I realized she was calling from her living room. She lives in a magnificent Georgian style house and lets the menagerie have free rein. One day there will be a monkey swinging through the bougainvillea in the conservatory.

"Forget about Antonio," she said. "How did it go? Was it a typical off-site, lots of eating, drinking, and carousing around?"

"Listening the Moore family bickering is more like it. Okay, we decided—"

"Stop." she interrupted me. "Bridget, get in here."

Madeline disappeared off screen, then reappeared with Bridget, our admin assistant, in tow. She's worked for me for years and she still reminds me of Rosie the Riveter, curly blonde hair, bright blue eyes, and nice broad shoulders. She was carrying Quincy, my sister's bull terrier, in her arms. Bridget refused to let Louisa put him in a kennel for the long weekend and would pamper him to the point where he'd be intolerable when we got back. Quincy's ears popped up when he heard my voice.

Bridget laughed. "Awww, look at him. Isn't he cute. He hears your voice, but he can't figure out where you are."

"What on earth are you doing there?" I asked. Then it hit me, if Madeline was concerned about the firm's future, Bridget must be frantic. She'd recently married an IT consultant and was nowhere near as wealthy as Madeline. Now that I think about it, most people aren't as wealthy as Madeline who has a legion of admirers who give her lavish gifts and, more importantly, investment advice. It's true what they say about the rich getting richer.

"Say hi to Mommy," Bridget said, waving one of Quincy's paws at me. "We're having fun with our friends in the menagerie."

In the background Madeline's cockatiel, Rupert, was

screeching Quincy's name—Rupert learned this trick when Louisa and I stayed with Madeline during the Great Flood— Quincy wriggled and tossed his head about and Bridget disappeared off camera to set him down on the floor. There was a scrabble of claws on tiles, then Bridget popped back into view. "Well, what's the verdict? Are we all fired?"

Where did they get these ideas? "No," I said, "no one is getting fired. Unfortunately, we couldn't agree on a path forward so we're going to continue visioning"—I put the word in air quotes— "when we return to the office."

There was such a long pause at their end I thought the connection had frozen. Then Madeline turned to Bridget and said, "See, I told you we'd have to do it for them. They're hopeless."

"Hello? I'm still here, I can hear you."

Bridget giggled. Good Lord, they'd been drinking. Madeline can drink a Marine under the table, but Bridget is a sweet, country girl, one drink and she's done. I told Bridget she was over the limit and should spend the night with Madeline and she replied that had been the plan all along.

In the background Evangeline, Madeline's tiny, long-haired, very strange dog, began to yip. This set Quincy off, which set Rupert off. Madeline told Bridget to see to the dogs and picked up her phone and said, "I'm taking you into the bedroom."

How many men have longed for Madeline to whisper those words? I'd always assumed her bedroom would look like a Victorian boudoir, packed with gold flocked wallpaper and red velvet drapes, but when we moved in for a couple of weeks during the Great Flood I discovered it was a pale, elegant room, filled with light that bounced across the tall mirrors. It had a lot of mirrors, now that I thought about it.

She arranged herself in the slipper chair by the dark window. "I know what the problem is. You guys are distracted by the Moore clan. Charlie's retiring and they're up there talking about succession, aren't they?"

So much for confidentiality. "Why would you say that?"

She laughed. Madeline was on a first-names basis, well, let's be honest, an *intimate* first-name basis with some of the most powerful men in the city. If they'd heard Charlie was retiring you'd think they'd have the brains not to pass it on to their paramour. But Madeline has her ways. She could wheedle information out of a Russian spy if she had to.

"As a matter of fact—and you're not to repeat a word of this to anyone, Madeline, promise me—Charlie is stepping down and, as you'd expect, there are only two contenders for his job, Parker and Robson."

She crinkled her nose in disgust. "Robson is a joke. Word on the street is that Parker is smarter and tougher than her brother, not that it will do her any good. She's got one too many X chromosomes."

"What?"

"She's a woman, two X chromosomes. He's a man, X and Y. So despite his iffy education and his lackluster work ethic, rumour has it he'll get the job."

The image of Robson pouring wine into his father's glass came to mind. If you're dumber and lazier than your female competition, what else would you do but ingratiate yourself with the boss.

Madeline pulled the gauzy curtain away from her window and looked out into her garden. The tall weeping willow shimmered in an uplight.

"Apparently, when Robson was still in university Charlie got him a summer job at one of MMG's subsidiaries and Robson, being the arrogant prick that he is, showed up on

Day One in shorts and flip flops and told his manager to drop him off at the mall."

"You're kidding. What did his manager do?"

"What do you think he did?" Madeline shrugged. "Robson was the boss's son; he wanted was to go to the mall, so he drove the kid to the mall."

This reminded me of a conversation I'd had with Parker over dinner a few years ago. She said her father expected his kids to work as hard, if not harder, than everyone else on the payroll. They wouldn't get any special breaks just because they were the Moore kids. When I pointed out that no one else had a direct line to the corner office or the power to make or break someone's career by dropping a few choice words in Daddy's ear, she took offense. Nepo babies hate to be told they're nepo babies.

"Evie," Madeline brought me back to reality, "has Parker found a way around the Arrangement? From what I've heard, it's a serious, perhaps fatal, impediment to her moving up."

The blank look on my face gave me away and immediately she changed the subject. Glancing into the hall where the dogs were making an unholy racket, she said, "Look, I've got to rescue Bridget. I'll talk to you later—"

"What Arrangement?"

She bit her bottom lip and said she'd spoken out of turn. "Forget it, it's nothing."

"It's got to be something if it presents a serious, perhaps fatal, impediment—your words, not mine—to Parker replacing Charlie. Madeline, you have to tell me. Maybe I can help her." This was one of a lawyer's worst character flaws, the ridiculous notion that since they know the law they can fix their friends' problems.

Madeline narrowed her eyes as she weighed her loyalties.

Me? Or her rich friends who'd passed along this juicy bit of information? She sighed and resigned herself to giving me a crumb.

"Look, all I can tell you is the Arrangement is a contract that's automatically triggered under certain circumstances and gives Robson the top job."

"What circumstances?"

"I can't tell you that."

"You can't or you won't?"

"Evie, please."

There was an uncomfortable moment where we both wondered how far I was going to push this, then I relented. "All right, forget I asked. I'll get to the bottom of it myself."

"There's no need to get huffy." She sounded huffier than I did. From the hallway came a blood curdling yelp and Evangeline darted into the bedroom, whimpering as if she'd lost a leg. Madeline propped her phone against something on her table and I found myself FaceTiming her prickly rodent of a dog and hung up.

CHAPTER 9

Saturday

It was eight o'clock the next morning and already the day was going sideways. The doors to the dining room were locked and through the glass panes I could see that the mahogany table and sideboard were bare. Was I too early for breakfast or heaven forbid, too late? I was halfway to the kitchen to beg Chef Bernard for a coffee, praying that he was nothing like those ill-tempered, egotistical maniacs you see on TV, when someone called my name.

Charlie and Parker were huddled in a quiet corner at the far end of the lobby, the coffee table in front of them covered with laptops, file folders, papers, and coffee mugs. The only thing of interest to me at this hour were the coffee mugs.

I tossed them a quick wave and continued in the direction of the kitchen but Charlie rose to his feet. He towered over his daughter who glanced at me, harried, no smile. Charlie waved me over and I sat down beside Parker on the crowded loveseat while Charlie spread himself across the long red leather sofa across from us.

"Evie," he said with a slow smile, "I was just telling my daughter that BLV is the perfect example of what I'm talking about."

"He wasn't," Parker said, turning to look at him. "Dad, we weren't talking about BLV."

Charlie rolled over her as if she hadn't spoken. "Your firm is doing so well you've hit an inflection point. You need to make a decision. Do you expand or die?"

"Expand or die?" I looked at him. "What about the third option? Stand pat. Growth for growth's sake isn't necessarily a good thing."

Casually, he crossed one ankle over the other knee and stretched his long arms along the top of the sofa, taking up as much of the sofa as possible.

"Oh come now, standing pat is the same as dying. You, Keith, and AJ have invested your expertise and more importantly, your cash, in BLV. You don't want to risk it all now by doing nothing."

My heart skipped a beat. It does that when I'm stressed. Why were we having this conversation? BLV was much too small to ping on Charlie Moore's radar. But he kept on talking.

"I don't know what they taught you in law school—"

"Law is what they taught me in law school."

"Then they were negligent in their duties, they should have taught you the fundamentals of business."

As he prattled on about the importance of growth, revenue, and profits, I remembered the one business course I had to take to pass the bar—Accounting 101. It almost killed me. I tuned back in when he said something about the virtuous circle (presumably growth, revenue and profits) leading to the good life.

I make it a rule never to argue with people I don't know or care about. Especially not before my first cup of coffee, but it was such an inane thing for him to say.

"No, Charlie"—it felt strange saying his first name— "I'm an environmental lawyer, I've seen the harm unchecked growth can do to the environment and the people affected by it."

Under that walrus mustache, he frowned. Leaning forward, Charlie rested his arms on his thighs and stared at me for a moment. "I don't deny that some regulation is necessary to keep the bad actors in line, but that's no reason to shackle growth. Just because folks are afraid of change."

"Dad," Parker interrupted, "I think Evie was on her way to the kitchen, you're looking for breakfast, right, Evie?"

It felt like she was trying to shove me out of the conversation by sheer force of will, but it was too late, I was stuck into the debate now. My mom used to say I was too stubborn for my own good, Dad put it down to tilting at windmills. It was neither. I just have a hard time walking away when people say stupid things.

"Charlie, this isn't about the fear of change, it's about corporations dumping aviation fuel into rivers and oil seeping into lakes. It's the role of government is to curb the excesses of capitalism."

That made him laugh. Loud and long. "It goes without saying that the bad actors have to be stopped from destroying the planet, but that's no excuse for interfering with the free market."

If it goes without saying, why do people like me have to keep saying it to people like you?

"Evie." Parker touched my arm. "You'll have to excuse us, we're in the middle of a business meeting."

I hopped up, grateful to make my escape, but Charlie wasn't finished with me yet. His eyes gleamed like two hard blue marbles, and he said, "You and Parker are young, you have much to learn, but know this: Some men are horses, others will ride. One day you will understand that some men, and women—got to be politically correct here—are born to rise to the top where they'll direct the labour of others. That's the way it is and the way it will always be."

The voice in my head said, *leave it,* but I couldn't walk away.

"Charlie, this is a serious discussion and you're resorting to memes, so let me counter with this: Success is a combination of skill and luck"—Charlie's parents were high school teachers, he didn't start with nothing—"some people are dealt a better hand than others, your children for example. They've had opportunities kids born in the ghetto can only dream of."

A thin smile played about his lips and he said, "Ah yes, opportunities, that's something you may wish to discuss with Keith."

What's Keith got to do with this?

I told Parker I'd catch up with her later and threaded my way through the overstuffed chairs and occasional tables until I reached the kitchen. Where I was hit by a wall of sound. Classic rock and Chef Bernard's deep baritone belting out *American woman, stay away from me-e-e-ee!*

Bernard was everywhere, pulling eggs out of the enormous stainless-steel fridge, chopping onions with a long, razor-sharp knife, hauling frying pans down from a shelf. His head bobbing. *American woman!*

Then, as if he sensed my presence in the doorway, he

became still and turned his hooded eyes on me. The pale morning light softened the fleshy contours of his face making him look less like a Mafia don. His gleaming knife pointed at me.

"You're hungry, am I right?" With his New York accent and the noise pouring out of the radio I could hardly understand him. I nodded, muttering something about toast and coffee. He turned down the music. A small frying pan appeared in his hand. "You look like a cheese omelette kind of girl."

Perched on a stool at one end of the stainless steel island, I discovered Bernard was one of those people who can cook and talk at the same time—it's a skill I greatly admire; every time I've tried it something goes up in flames—and I asked him how he came to be at Mirror Ranch.

With a faraway smile he explained that he'd met a beautiful woman who lured him out west. "After twenty years in New York City I was ready for a change."

"You're an awfully long way from home."

"This is home." His knife pointed to the view out of the small square window inset in the back door. In the distance the Rockies reflected the rising sun with delicate hints of blue and yellow and orange. "Just look at that, will ya, it's like a painting. Nothing beats that view."

Opal, his assistant, passed him a small cutting board on which lay two perfectly sliced white mushrooms. They were tipped into the frying pan to join the onions sizzling in butter. My stomach growled.

"So this beautiful lady…?" I nudged him for the rest of his story.

"She was a real charmer. Shimmering green eyes and long red hair."

Of course, Charlotte. The best marketing executive MMG had ever had.

"Every time Charlotte came to town she'd stop for breakfast at my place. I had a small diner back then. We got to know each other. Then one day she leans over the counter and says she's got a proposition for me. An offer I couldn't refuse. She's left Daddy's company and is setting up Mirror Ranch. Wants yours truly to be the head chef." He chuckled as he slid my omelette onto a plate, nudging the sliced avocados aside to give the eggs centre stage. Opal buzzed around behind him pouring orange juice.

"Did you even know where Mirror Ranch was?"

"Hell no, I figured it was a fancy-ass spa in Colorado." He eased his bulk onto the tall stool across from me while Opal went over to the back counter to fold napkins.

The omelette, light and buttery, melted in my mouth and I made a *mmfff* sound. Bernard smiled and explained the workings of Mirror Ranch. Unlike him and Opal, most of the staff weren't permanent. They came from all over Canada, the US and Europe, stayed a season or two and then moved on.

"They're young. For them it's an adventure. Take the wranglers. Sophie's from Corsica and her partner's from southern France. They'll all be here on Tuesday rested and ready to kickoff the summer season. Until then it's just Charlotte, Jay, Opal and me; but don't worry, we'll take good care of the family and you three —"

"Four, three of us lawyers and my sister Louisa." She'd texted me late last night to say she'd checked in. I couldn't wait to see her.

"Yeah, the family decided at the last minute to make it a family weekend. Too late to cancel you guys"—Bernard's tone became vague, as if he'd been distracted by a random thought— "never mind, we'll take good care of you."

"Morning." Charlotte's cheery voice floated over the sound of Queen belting out *Bohemian Rhapsody*. "Bernard, is this a kitchen or a rock concert?" She said it with a smile and Bernard crossed to the Bluetooth device sitting on the counter and turned it down another notch while she poured herself a steaming coffee and joined me at the stainless steel island. She closed her eyes and inhaled. "That omelette smells fantastic."

Bernard turned to me and said, "I'd make her one, but she won't eat it. Always rushing around. Too busy."

She smiled at him over the rim of her mug. The corners of her eyes tipped up, making her look mischievous.

"Gotta run," she said, "I've got places to be and horses to see." It sounded like something she said every morning before she disappeared out the back door. Her coppery ponytail bouncing. From this distance she looked incredibly young.

Bernard watched her with paternal pride. "That one is special. Beautiful like her mother, cunning like her father."

I was mulling that over when Jay strode into the kitchen looking for Charlotte. His hair was combed back, but an unruly lock had fallen forward into his eyes like a Superman curl, and I realized that Jay's good looks pushed people away, like a model who's too perfect to be real. But last night as I watched him striving to please Charlotte's family I realized that he was just an insecure man hoping to be accepted by these people who lived a life so different than his own. This made him more endearing somehow.

Bernard pointed at the back door and Jay disappeared without another word.

"Now *that's* a city boy," Bernard said, gazing after Jay.

"Charlotte runs around all day tending to the animals and the gardens, that's on top of dealing with the guests and staff, and he's holed up in his office, staring at his computer."

Opal stopped stirring a pot on the stove. "Now Bernard," she said in her clipped British accent, "Jay pays the bills and takes care of the Ranch, fixing fences and whatnot."

Bernard shrugged, grudgingly admitting Jay might be good for something.

Setting down my knife and fork I said, "If Jay worked in finance at MMG, I'm guessing he also does the books."

"Yeah." Bernard said, "I'm not knocking egg heads but Mirror Ranch has more than enough bean counters with Jay, and now Charlie and Robson, poking their noses in."

There was a metallic racket at the other end of the island. Opal was dumping some cutlery into a metal cannister and it had tipped over sending a handful of forks across the metal countertop. She shot Bernard a long cool look and he reddened, as if he realized he'd said more than he should.

Bernard was fiddling with the coffee machine when Keith and AJ strolled in. Keith was apologising for sleeping in and AJ smacked his arm with his iPad, saying. "Buddy, it's the May long weekend, relax." His eyes darted around the kitchen, registering my demolished omelette and the empty frying pan resting on the stove.

"You ate already? Why didn't you bang on my door on your way down?"

"AJ, I'm not your mother. Besides it would be hopeless, you sleep like a hibernating grizzly bear." I glanced at my watch. "I've got to go wake up Louisa."

"You're waking her, but you won't wake me?" AJ looked pained.

"She's my sister. You're not."

As I was leaving, Keith asked AJ how I knew he snored like a grizzly bear.

"She said slept, not snored," AJ replied.

"I stand corrected," Keith said. "How does Evie know you *sleep* like a hibernating grizzly bear? Anything you want to tell me?"

I didn't wait around to hear AJ's reply. As I knocked on Louisa's door I glanced at my weather app. Sunny and warm right through to Monday. The long weekend was going to be glorious.

What's that saying about best laid plans?

JOURNAL

---

*H*e said he was going to save me from a tawdry career in Hollywood.

I should have seen it coming but he was so contrite after every argument, sending me heaps of flowers and ridiculously expensive presents, that I treated his words as a joke.

Everything came to a head after I landed a decent role in a Todd Field film. Charlie made it crystal clear: he resented me being away on location, the long hours, my actor friends, the business. All of it.

What do I have to do to make you understand? he said. And presented me with his 5 year plan. On the right side of the page were his personal goals, on the left side were his business goals, each with its own monetary value rounded up to the next million.

I said, you've lost your mind. He said, let me take you through it.

Personal goals: Get married, have two kids, raise family, K (that was me) joins charity boards, C joins business boards and private clubs. Value of K and C: $$$$.

Business goals: Go from Young-Turk-Who-Delivers-Value

to Global Management Partner and Chairman of the Board. Value of C: $$$$.

Timeline: 5 years.

Charlie, I protested, there's no allowance here for me or my career. I can't continue acting if I'm a brood mare and spend all my time volunteering and being one of those ladies who lunch.

Darling, he said, look at the monetary value. The role of being Charlie Moore's wife and the mother of his children is literally a million times more valuable that being a middling actress in middling films. Surely you can see that.

This was during the third or fourth wave of women's lib. We could have it all, a family and a career if we worked hard enough. I would find a way to do both.

CHAPTER 10

Louisa and I met Charlotte on the trail on our way down to the stables. She'd just finished mucking out the horses. Whatever that was, it sounded messy. Not that you could tell judging by Charlotte's appearance. Her soft blue chambray shirt set off her burnished auburn hair, she looked radiant, like a wood nymph darting through a magical forest.

When we said we were going riding, she told us Katie was already at the barn with Shadow. "Mom's good at picking horses. She'll put you on one that's best suited to your skill level."

This was reassuring because my skill level was minimal and Louisa's was non-existent. My little sister is terrified of horses, not that she'd ever admit it. The last time we went riding she picked the tiniest horse, Flicka, who was so outraged that Louisa dared hoist herself up into the saddle that she pinned Louisa's leg against a fence post for ten minutes.

Katie was at the far end of the barn when we entered, sweeping a stiff brush across Shadow's broad shoulders. In the soft, gold-flecked light he shone like polished ebony.

She must have misheard me when I said we wanted to go

riding, because she snapped that no one was allowed to ride Shadow. He whinnied and tossed his head at the sound of his name and her face softened. "It's okay, my darling boy."

After assuring her that we wouldn't dream of taking Shadow out, she relaxed. Soon we were up on two lovely chestnuts, a smaller one for Louisa and a bigger one, Diablo, who was as broad and solid as a couch, for me.

Katie made us promise to stay on the trail. "No wild galloping across the meadow and whatever you do, stay clear of Dragon Falls. The path is treacherous up there and I don't want the horses getting hurt."

She explained she was unable to join us because it was time for Shadow's training session. "He likes his routine." She put him into position, walked to the other end of the barn, then blew two shrill blasts on a tin whistle. And I'll be damned if Shadow didn't gallop right up to her.

"That's what we need for Quincy," I said to Louisa as we clip clopped away. "A tin whistle."

"Nah, he's hopeless." Louisa was right. Poor Quincy failed obedience school twice, although the last time Louisa came home with the most improved handler ribbon. It did nothing to improve her mood.

The morning sun was warm on our backs as we ambled around the stable and set off on the riding trail, weaving our way past the sign pointing to the spa, in search of the large meadow behind the conference centre.

We'd been riding at a leisurely pace for about an hour when we spotted Parker in a small clearing. She was perched on a fallen tree trunk, bent forward with her elbows on her knees and her head in her hands. I glanced back at Louisa and tilted my head in Parker's direction. Louisa nodded and clicked her tongue, urging her little horse forward, but startling it instead. The horse shied and lunged sideways.

Louisa shrieked and her horse came to an abrupt stop, almost pitching her to the ground. I don't know what it is about that girl, but she brings out the worst in horses.

Parker jumped to her feet, looking around. Spotting us, she waved for us to join her.

"Sorry," I said as we dismounted and settled on either side of her on the log. "We didn't mean to disturb you. You looked like you were a million miles away."

Without warning, tears welled up in her eyes. She blinked rapidly but couldn't stop them from rolling down her cheeks. For a moment, I wondered if she was upset about my disagreement with her father. *Born to ride and born to be ridden*. What nonsense.

"Shit," she said, using both hands to brush her tears away. I pulled a tissue out of my pocket and handed it to her. Louisa's eyes met mine. *What the heck is going on?* I gave a small shrug. I had no idea.

Parker leaned into me as I slipped my arm around her shoulders, her copper hair falling forward to shield her face. Louisa murmured that it was fine, everything would be fine.

"No," Parker twisted away to glare at Louisa. "It's not fine. Nothing will ever be fine again."

Between brave sniffs she explained that the Moore family had decamped to Mirror Ranch to make a critically important decision. "Dad is stepping down. Resigning as executive chair. And this time he really means it."

"Yes," I said, "you told me last night at the firepit." Had she forgotten she'd sworn me to secrecy?

"Oh yeah, that's right." She blotted her tears with the tissue. "He's threatened to retire so many times in the last five years it's hard to take him seriously. He sets a departure date then something 'unforeseen' happens, nothing we couldn't handle mind you, and"—she snapped her fingers— "he changes his mind because only the great Charlie Moore could possibly fix it. The arrogant bastard."

"But this time is different?" I asked. It had to be, otherwise she wouldn't be sitting out here in a field crying her eyes out.

Her face hardened. The tears dried up. "This time, he pulled a fast one. He's resigning as executive chair but staying on as a director so he can *oversee* the transition to his replacement. In other words, who ever replaces him will be his sock puppet. It's a clever move, don't you see?"

I shook my head, I didn't see.

"He'll still be in charge. If things go well at MMG, the great Charlie Moore gets all the credit, but if things go sour, it will be his successor's fault."

A gentle breeze rolled across the meadow in a grassy wave and the grass turned a darker shade of green. I understood. Charlie would never relinquish power.

Louisa shifted on the log, tipping her head away from her horse, he was nuzzling her neck. To her credit she didn't leap off the log and run screaming across the meadow. "If Charlie's still going to be active in the company why is he bothering with the charade?"

"Because he's ill. Dad's had two heart attacks. The last one almost finished him off. He doesn't want to retire, but the doctors put the fear of death into him and he's agreed to ease up on the day to day stuff." She blew her nose and stuffed her crumpled tissue into her pocket. "He says he wants to spend more time with the family, what a joke that is. He can't stand being around the grand kids for more than ten minutes and he and Mom, well…let's just say theirs is not the happiest of marriages."

My horse snorted and dropped its soft muzzle onto my shoulder. I reached up and stroked his cheek.

Parker smiled. "Diablo's my favourite. Evie, you've got a friend for life."

She prattled on for a few minutes about the horses, there were six in the barn, each with their own unique personalities. You didn't have to be a psychiatrist to see she was trying to get a grip on her emotions.

Louisa furrowed her brow and I knew what she was thinking. I always know what she's thinking. We're only fourteen months apart and have that twin-like ability to read each other's minds.

"Parker," she said gently, "I understand this transition could be difficult, but you seem awfully destressed. Is there something…what I mean is, is there more to this than…" She trailed off.

Parker's face froze. For a moment it felt like time had stopped. Then she said, "Ever since Charlotte quit, it's just been the two of us, Robson and me, competing to fill Dad's shoes. Both of us want it—God knows we want it—even if Dad's going to be on the Board for a while, it's not as if he's going to be around forever.

"For the last three months things have been intense. He's been testing us, judging us, trying to figure out which of us is worthy."

Maybe, contrary to what Madeline said, Parker did have a shot at Charlie's job.

"Surely, there's no contest," I said. "It has to be you. Parker you're smarter than Robson, your experience is more varied and you're way better with people. I don't see how Charlie could seriously consider anyone but you for his job."

"Brains and track record. Yeah, that's what I thought when I started working at MMG twelve years ago. If I kept my head down and my nose to the grindstone, I'd get what I deserved." She gave a mirthless laugh.

"My lawyers called yesterday. Some new information has come to light. A couple of years ago Dad signed a document that says if he dies before he names a successor, the job would automatically go to Robson"—Madeline's source was right, this was the Arrangement— "Dad's made my life a living hell pretending I had a real shot at his job when he was going to give it to Robson all along."

"You don't know that."

"Evie, get real. If he thought I was a serious candidate he'd have cancelled the Arrangement long ago."

"Maybe he forgot—"

"Oh please." She took a deep breath before continuing. "It's not me. It was never going to be me. Just when I thought I'd gotten him over the primogeniture issue…"

Louisa shifted closer to Parker on the tree trunk. Her little horse murmured and shifted along with her. "What's the primogeniture issue?"

"Dad insists MMG will never leave the family. It must be passed on from generation to generation. Preserving his legacy, I guess. That's why Elise keeps shoving those kids in his face all the time. If I'd known bearing heirs was a job requirement I'd have had IVF years ago." I had the feeling she was only half-joking.

Louisa said, "What if the grandchildren don't want to run the business? What then? That old Chinese proverb about rags to riches to rags in three generations pops to mind."

"It doesn't matter anymore." Parker straightened her shoulders and sat up a little straighter. "Mom, bless her heart, has been funnelling intel to me for months. She didn't believe for a second he was seriously considering me. It's funny, Dad doesn't think she picks up half of what he says, but she's heard him and Robson scheming. She says he's going to name Robson his successor at dinner tomorrow night."

She smacked her hands down on her thighs and stood up so fast the horses snorted in alarm. "Damn it. It's not over till it's over. My slack-assed brother is not going to take this away from me. Not without a fight."

Tough words, accompanied by an artificially bright smile.

CHAPTER 11

By the time Louisa and I returned to the barn Katie was gone and Shadow's stall was empty. We wandered down the centre aisle, our restless horses trailing behind us.

"Wasn't Katie going to show us how to cool down the horses?" Louisa asked. We waited a couple of minutes and then did what everyone does when they haven't a clue what they're doing, we looked it up on YouTube. There's a video for everything nowadays.

We uncinched and removed the horses' tack and gave them water and settled them in their stalls, then headed back up to the Lodge. A cool breeze whipped through the treetops and the Rockies, which were morning-sun pink a couple of hours ago, had disappeared under heavy clouds. Voices floated on the wind from the large kitchen garden. Jay was pointing at something down by the greenhouse while Bernard gazed at him, arms crossed and impassive.

Inside the Lodge Amelia squealed as she raced down the staircase and flung herself into the red leather sofa in front of the fireplace. Teddy barreled down the stairs right behind her. As he passed Louisa, her hand shot out, catching him in mid sprint. "There will be no more running," she said in her best nurse voice. That voice stops grown men in their tracks and Teddy deflated like a day-old party balloon.

Where are their parents? I wondered as I approached the reception desk where Parker and Charlotte were talking quietly to each other. Their faces grim.

"Is everything all right?" I asked.

"Mom's missing." Parker replied.

"No," Charlotte said, a little cross. "Not missing per se. We just don't know where she and Shadow are at this precise moment."

I didn't understand what all the fuss was about. Obviously Katie had gone for a ride and from what everyone said she was an excellent horsewoman.

Parker explained it wasn't Katie's horsemanship that worried them. It was the weather. She glanced out the window. "The wind is picking up and those clouds look bad."

The sky had turned a mottled gray. A puff of wind blew the front door open, we hadn't shut it properly, and we flinched when it banged against the wall.

"Shadow is a big powerful horse," Parker said, "but he's afraid of thunder—"

"And lightening, and loud noises, he's just a big baby." Charlotte shook her head, then her cell phone chimed. "It's Dad." She picked up, nodding a few times before hanging up. "She's fine. He found her in the stable, putting Shadow away."

Thirty minutes later Charlie and Katie came through the main doors. Katie was stiff with anger. Charlie had a smug smile on his face. When he touched Katie's elbow, telling her it was time for a nice nap, she wrenched her arm away and snapped she could decide for herself whether she needed a rest or not, then marched off into the kitchen and told Bernard to make her a sandwich, she would take her lunch upstairs in her room.

Charlie's smile faded when he spotted his daughters. Eyes hardening, jaw tight. "I thought I told you girls to keep an eye—"

"Don't you dare start that crap with me." Parker's voice was strained. "Why is it always us girls? What about you and your precious son? Oh wait, what am I saying, men aren't born with the caregiver gene. How lucky for them, they're too busy running the world and making a right mess of things to lift a finger at home."

The tips of Charlie's ears had turned a deep shade of red. He opened his mouth but Charlotte cut him off before he could utter another word.

"Keep your voices down!" she hissed. "Mom's in the other room…and we have guests."

Everyone turned their eyes to Louisa and me.

"Right," I said with a polite smile. "Louisa and I were just going to get some lunch—"

"Bernard!" Charlie bellowed as he pushed past us, yelling into the kitchen, "Where's Katie's lunch. Get your lazy ass in gear." The minute Charlie entered the kitchen Katie marched out and went upstairs. A few minutes later Opal appeared with a tray and followed her up to her room.

Charlotte stammered an apology for her parents' behavior but Louisa cut her off. "Don't give it another thought. Every family has a little bit of drama."

Louisa and I would know. Our mom was a volatile Hungarian and our dad was a reserved Englishman. Often they didn't see eye to eye. But they'd never glared at each other with such loathing.

JOURNAL

The first time it happened it took me completely by surprise. It was just before the kids were born.

Charlie had soured on McKinsey. The Five Year Plan had stalled. If they didn't promote him immediately, he'd quit. They called his bluff and he marched out, taking five McKinsey guys and two lucrative files with him, and set up MMG. They worked at our dining room table until they could afford to rent office space.

He was so stressed he was vibrating. So just before the big move from our dining room to Bankers Hall, I took him on a ski weekend in the French Alps. We stayed at La Folie Douce Hotel. The name means sweet madness.

The mountain air was as cold and crisp as an apple caught in an early frost.

We carved lines in the snow all day and danced to loud, techno music at night.

It happened on our last night. We were watching a guy in a pork pie hat howl into a microphone when I ordered drinks in French from a charming young bartender who could toss loaded shot glasses into the air without spilling a drop.

Charlie hauled me back up to our room. He gripped my arms and shook me so hard I thought my teeth would fall out.

Stop trying to be something you're not, he shouted in my face. You're too old for this crowd. Act your age.

I was twenty-seven. He broke my heart.

La Folie Douce.

The sweetness is gone. Only the madness remains.

———

CHAPTER 12

You can't sit through a yoga class, how on earth are you going to survive an afternoon at the spa?" AJ shook his head in disbelief, then took a huge bite of his ham and Swiss cheese sandwich. He and Keith were eating lunch at the island in Bernard's kitchen, debating whether the weather would hold long enough for them to try their hand at archery.

"What makes you think I can't sit through a yoga class?" I asked. It's amazing how much personal information AJ knows about me.

"Louisa told me."

"Oh." No point in denying it then. Last year Louisa conned me into taking a yoga class with her. While everyone was chilling to the sound of Tingsha bells, I was riveted by the jingle of car keys out in the hall. On the other side of the door some lucky sod was heading to the parking lot and I desperately wanted to go with him.

AJ laughed. "Look at you, you're getting twitchy just thinking about it."

When Louisa invited the guys to join us at the spa, Keith

went pale and AJ laughed so hard I thought he'd choke on his sandwich.

"Right," Louisa said to me, "I guess it's just us then."

Thank God. For some reason the thought of prancing around half naked in front of AJ made me feel self conscious.

An hour later Louisa and I were strolling down the north-south trail looking for the fork that would take us to the spa building which, according to Charlotte's cartoon map, was a little A-frame building nestled in a clearing under some gigantic pines.

When we entered the wood and glass structure we were greeted by whale song. What, I wondered, were the whales saying to each other: *Come here my lovely. Get out of my ocean. Es-cap-e?*

Opal, a woman of many talents, appeared behind the reception desk. "Just to be clear," I said as she checked us in, "I draw the line at full body mud baths." I've never understood the allure of lying in a pile of wet dirt.

Opal stopped tapping on her tablet and glanced at Louisa whose face was a mask of innocence.

"Are you sure?" Louisa asked. She's been trying to get me into a mud bath for years. "It will sooth your aching muscles, admit it, you're sore from our morning ride, and, bonus,"—she picked up the pamphlet lying on the countertop— "it'll draw the impurities in your skin."

I raised an eyebrow. "You're a nurse. You of all people should not be spouting such malarky."

"Okay, okay, forget about drawing out impurities. I'm sure Opal can suggest something else for us, can't you Opal?"

Opal smiled, handed me a fluffy white bathrobe to wear over my bathing suit and practically shoved me into the change room. By the time I emerged, flip flops slapping my heels and my terry rob pulled tightly under my chin, Louisa had changed and Opal informed me that the mud bath had been replaced with a beer bath hydrotherapy session. The rational part of my brain said beer wasn't much better than mud but it was too late to make a fuss.

The beer spa room looked like a normal spa room except that the deep, cedar tub was filled with hot bubbling beer. "It's watered down." Louisa said, shrugging out of her robe and dipping her hand in the frothy liquid. "No yeast. Just hops, barley, and herbs curated for maximum hair, skin, and mind benefits."

"Mind benefits? From sitting in a vat of beer?"

"Just don't drink it."

"You don't seriously think I'd—" I glanced at her face, she was grinning— "never mind."

As we climbed up the pale wooden steps and slowly lowered ourselves into the vat, I thought this was one of the strangest things I'd ever done. Five minutes later my eyelids were drooping and Louisa's voice faded into the background. It turns out there's something hypnotic about being immersed in a vat of bubbling beer.

I was bobbing closer to Louisa to tell her this was a brilliant idea when Parker appeared. She slipped out of her bathrobe, revealing a lithe swimmer's body in a red speedo and asked if we'd mind if she joined us.

"Come on in." Louisa jiggled away from me, the vat was deep and we were very buoyant, making a space for Parker in the middle.

Parker twisted her thick coppery hair into a loose bun on top of her head and with an appreciative sigh lowered her long, pale body onto the bench between us. She leaned back, resting her head on the cedar ledge. It didn't look terribly comfortable, but her eyes were closed and she had a faint smile on her lips.

We were lost in our thoughts in the warm scented haze of the beer bath, when out of the blue Parker said, "It's going to be much worse this time."

My eyes popped open. She sounded so forlorn it was gut wrenching. "What's going to be worse?"

She looked startled, as if she hadn't meant to say it out loud, then pulled herself up straight on the bench seat and reached behind her head for a towel. "Nothing," she said, dabbing the sweat from her brow. She was very flushed, it could have been the heat.

I was prepared to let it drop but Louisa swivelled around, picking up her towel and wiping her face. "No, Parker, what did you mean?"

Parker looked at Louisa, then at me, and sighed with the resignation of someone who has set down a heavy burden knowing full well that they'll have to pick it up again.

She repeated what she'd told us that morning, that despite the fact Charlie favoured her brother for the top job, she was going to fight Robson every step of the way.

"Trust me, this is going to be brutal."

She explained that throughout their childhood she and Robson were rivals, constantly competing for their father's affection. "Charlotte was lucky. She was born seven years later; she was too young to be a serious threat."

Threat? As children Louisa and I competed with each other for silly things like the biggest slice of cake or who got to ride shotgun in the car, but never for our parents' love.

"Parker." I edged a little closer, "what do you mean by rivals?"

"Dad used to set up these little contests. Who could jump the highest, who could hold their breath the longest. That was a weird one. I was eleven and Robson was ten and he won, Dad said it didn't count because Robson passed out.

"One summer Dad had us racing laps in the pool. It was our own mini-Olympics. He had a starting pistol and a stopwatch, it was all very official. I was pulling ahead of Robson when he grabbed my legs and dragged me under. The little prick kneeled on my back, pressing me down to the bottom of the pool. I was so tired my arms were like spaghetti, I just couldn't fight him off. I remember thinking, that's it. I'm going to drown.

"Suddenly Mom dove in. She dragged Robson off and towed me, spluttering and wheezing, to the edge of the pool. The whole time she never stopped screaming at Dad that Robson almost killed me. Dad said she was being melodramatic, it was just a game."

"Robson tried to drown you?" Louisa's eyes were round with disbelief.

Casually, Parker adjusted the strap of her swimsuit. "Well, I don't think it was intentional"—he'd pulled her under and wouldn't let her up, it sounded pretty intentional to me— "I was older and bigger than he was, he was a shrimpy little kid, and he was sick of losing. Anyway Mom wouldn't let us compete after that."

Parker dragged her hand through the rapid bubbles. They fizzed and popped and swirled away. "This is nice, isn't it." She stretched her arms over her head and said it was time for her to return to the Lodge. Louisa and I crawled out of the vat on rubbery legs and followed her into the showers.

With a tsk, Opal said we had ten more minutes left, but the tranquil mood had been broken. The fight to replace Charlie as the head of MMG was the biggest competition the Moore siblings would ever have. As the favoured son,

Robson was in the lead, but Parker was determined to win. How far would she go to vanquish Robson once and for all?

CHAPTER 13

Keith was giving AJ a hard time when we found them later that afternoon hunched over the pine coffee table playing an energetic game of checkers. It was like a scene from a Norman Rockwell painting but instead of a rosy cheeked little boy and his wise old granddad, there were two grown men loudly bouncing checkers all over the board.

When I asked if they'd tried their hand at archery, Keith said AJ couldn't hit the broad side of a barn with an arrow if he tried.

"I did try," AJ replied without lifting his eyes from the board. "Crown me."

Keith fumbled with the stack of red checkers and they clattered onto the board.

"Great," AJ said with a laugh. "Crown them all." Then he turned to me. "You should have seen this guy out there on the range. He'd put Robin Hood to shame."

Keith shook his head. "And you my friend aren't fit to carry Friar Tuck's quiver, heck even Maid Marion would have had better aim."

AJ hopped a checker piece diagonally across the board

then threw both hands in the air and whooped, "Did you see that? I won!"

"*Even* Maid Marion?" I took a chair. Behind us Louisa was rummaging in a low deep bookcase looking at the games. "Why does everyone assume Maid Marion was just a scullery maid, cooking and cleaning for Robin Hood and his band of merry men? I'll bet she was an excellent archer or Robin Hood wouldn't have brought her along in the first place."

The guys looked at me but neither was prepared to engage in the debate.

Louisa returned with three beat up board games and two decks of cards. "Look, *Clue*, I haven't played this in ages." I took the cards out of her hand and started to shuffle. They were so old they stuck together.

"I take it you guys spent the afternoon at the archery range?" Louisa asked.

Keith nodded as he scooped a handful of cashews out of a glass bowl and popped them into his mouth. Dinner was an hour away and they'd already demolished two large bags of potato chips.

It turned out Charlotte had been reluctant to let them onto the archery range because the archery instructor, who also happened to be the Corsican wrangler, was spending the long weekend in Vancouver with her partner.

"Yeah, that's right," I said, rapping the bottom of the card deck on the tabletop to align the cards. "Bernard mentioned Mirror Ranch was down to a skeleton crew. Poor Opal is doing everything from house keeping to running the spa."

Keith nodded at AJ and said, "AJ turned on the farm boy charm and before you could say 'hayseed' Charlotte was pressing the keys to the archery hut into his hand."

AJ grinned and said all you had to do was be nice and

everything would fall into place. "Also, I promised her I wouldn't shoot anyone, not even Keith."

I chuckled. "Thank you for that. I'd hate to have to change the letterhead again." We'd dithered so long trying to rename the firm after AJ became a partner that Bridget, our admin assistant, made the unilateral decision that we'd be known as Braxton Lawon Valentine. Someone had to make a decision, she'd said, before we ran out of stationary.

AJ glanced at Keith and said, "He was ready to drill Charlie right between the eyes."

Keith made a sound; I thought he was choking on a cashew but it was a snort of derision. "Riding?" he said. "I don't know what Charlie thought he was doing behind the archery range, but it sure as hell wasn't riding."

Then Keith, the man who never swears, went off on a rant about Charlie yanking his horse around like a madman. "That big black one. It put up one hell of a fight. Bucking, and wheeling, trying to throw Charlie off. He's damn lucky I saw him before I let my arrow fly."

I stopped shuffling the cards. "A big black horse? Shadow? No one's allowed to ride Shadow but Katie."

Keith's neck was blotchy, a sure sign he was angry. "Isn't the great Charlie Moore supposed to be a man's man? The poor boy from the wrong side of the tracks who made good—"

"That's a myth," I said, "before he made all his money he had a nice middle class life."

"An accomplished sportsman? Big game hunter? Sports fisherman?" Keith pressed on as if I hadn't interrupted. "Even a novice rider knows that screaming at a horse doesn't get you anywhere. He's lucky I didn't lay him out like Saint Sebastian."

AJ glanced up from the checkerboard. "Did you know

Saint Sebastian survived the arrows but later was beaten to death?"

I shook my head at AJ's tidbit of trivia and gestured to Louisa to cut the cards.

"That's strange," she said, her hand hovering over the deck. "Shadow is very sweet as far as I could tell."

I dealt out two hands while Keith and AJ set up the checkerboard for a rematch. Louisa and I were playing a Hungarian card game similar to Gin Rummy but with some idiosyncratic rules. I swear Mom would change them when she started to lose.

The room grew quiet but for the slap of playing cards hitting the table and the click, click, click of checker pieces hopping across the board. Outside the wind grew louder, testing the windowpanes one by one.

Ten minutes later Bernard appeared. With a gentle cough he suggested we might like to move to the dining room as Charlie and the rest of the family would be along shortly. We'd just seated ourselves at the table when Opal emerged from the kitchen and drew Bernard aside.

"Don't worry," he told her, "Charlotte would have told me if they weren't dining in." Opal nodded and the two of them hustled back into the kitchen.

A few minutes later Bernard returned. "Apéritifs?" Before we could demur, four Negronis materialized before us.

We clinked our glasses. *Cheers! Salud!* Trying to outdo each other with toasts in different languages when Katie, Elise and the kids arrived.

They settled in their usual places at the other end of the table. Katie fiddled with her cutlery, arranging it so the ends lined up perfectly with the edge of her placemat and Elise brushed Amelia's bangs out of her eyes and put her hand on Teddy's shoulder in a futile effort to stop him from fidgeting. The kids amused themselves by flinging insults at each other.

From the kitchen came the sound of low, urgent voices. Charlotte and Jay were huddled with Bernard while Opal darted back and forth behind them.

"Are you eavesdropping?" Louisa whispered with a theatrical wiggle of her eyebrows as she leaned closer to me.

I nodded. I had a direct line of sight into the kitchen. That's the trouble with these open concept kitchens. There's not a lick of privacy.

"Charlotte wants Bernard to hold off serving dinner until Charlie shows up. Bernard says if he waits any longer, the meal will be ruined. Jay told him to hold off anyway and Charlotte told Jay to watch his tone."

AJ leaned across the table and touched my arm. "What's the holdup?" he whispered, glancing over his shoulder into the kitchen. "Keith is starving and we all how ornery he gets when he's hungry."

"Ha, ha." Keith doesn't care when he eats, whereas I go snaky if I'm kept waiting more than ten minutes. It's a blood sugar thing.

In the kitchen, Jay was pacing around while Charlotte talked quietly to Bernard, trying to convince him to give Charlie another ten minutes.

"Oh for heaven's sake!" Katie flung her checkered napkin down on her plate and marched into the kitchen. Emotions flashed across Charlotte's face when her mother joined them. At first irritation, then relief.

Katie made no effort to keep her voice down. "I don't care where the hell they are, they're late. Bernard, start the dinner service. The children are famished." Then she strode back into the dining room and told the kids to behave themselves, dinner was on its way.

Midway through the salad course Parker hustled into the room, nodding at us and apologising to her mother for being late.

"Where's your father?" Katie's tone was harsh.

Parker shrugged and smoothed her napkin across her lap. When she reached for the breadbasket, her fingers trembled.

Bernard appeared with a very large platter of beef and set it in the centre of the table before disappearing back into the kitchen. There was a ripple of hesitation, we'd finished the starter, was it safe to dig into the main course without Charlie's blessing?

"Please, everyone, help yourselves," Katie said. "Texas-Style Barbeque is Bernard's speciality. It would be a crime to let it get cold."

Elise was sawing off a tiny sliver of beef for Amelia when Charlie's voice boomed across the lobby, followed by a high pitched giggle from Robson. They ambled into the room with the studied care of someone who'd had one drink too many.

Charlie performed his usual routine, greeting Amelia with a showy kiss on the top of her head and giving Teddy a fist bump which almost missed. As he passed behind Katie's chair he bent down to give her a kiss on the cheek.

She waved an irritated hand in his face and turned away. "Sit down, you're drunk." Unfazed he sidled into his chair.

Robson dropped into the chair opposite Elise and the kids. Her eyes were huge, searching his face for clues. *What's going on?* Robson tossed her a bleary-eyed smile, then jolted everyone by bellowing into the kitchen. "Bernard, what's the hold up? We're starving in here." I glanced down at my plate heaped with beef and corn. We'd been served. Not that Robson noticed.

Louisa's eyes met mine. After "the incident" at Gates, Case and White, loud aggressive drunks unnerve me. I try not to think about the attack; a year of therapy helped, plus the fact the firm gave me a hefty settlement when I threatened to sue, but even now being around belligerent, out of control men sets me on edge.

She reached across the table and squeezed my hand. *You good?* I nodded, *I'm fine,* and she turned to Keith and asked him to tell us about life on the farm. A distraction.

Grateful, I listened while Keith told a delightful story about his daughter Claire's startling discovery that fuzzy yellow chicks don't stay that way for long.

At the other end of the table Charlie droned on about the sad state of government in this country. "So much waste. I say it's time to fire the slackers, focus only on what is absolutely necessary. Things would be so much better if government was run like a business."

I leaned over to AJ and whispered, "Now, there's an idea. Let's pay cabinet ministers multimillion dollar salaries, give them private jets and lavish expense accounts so they can wine and dine the lobbyists looking for favours for their clients."

He shushed me with a shake of his head, but it was too late. Charlie had heard me.

"Evie," his voice boomed down the table, "I take it you don't agree. You like fat governments sticking their noses into everyone's business."

Great, now I'm arguing with a drunk.

Parker and Charlotte looked down at their plates and Robson stared at me. Daring me to respond. I decided to make it quick.

"Charlie, I hate waste as much as the next guy. All I'm saying is I've seen my fair share of executives who bring nothing to the table but still keep their jobs because they're buddies with the CEO or their brother-in-law is a cabinet minister who might prove handy one day."

I bit my tongue to stop myself from adding: *Or they're the CEO's deadbeat son and their future is golden.*

There was a moment while Charlie digested this and I was unsure which way he'd go. Then he leaned back and laughed, *har, har, har,* and slapped the table. Raising his glass to me he said, "Good one, Evie, good one."

Taking his cue from his father, Robson laughed. Parker caught Charlotte's eye and held her gaze for a moment, making me wonder how many drunk-Daddy episodes they'd witnessed over the years.

Charlie's smile vanished when he spotted the two empty wine bottles sitting on the table in front of him. Robson, ever the attentive son, raised his arm and snapped his fingers. Bernard was in the kitchen and Opal was standing at the sideboard with her back to Robson, stacking used plates on a tray. When she didn't turn around, he snapped his fingers again and shouted, "Christ, woman, are you deaf?"

Startled, she turned to face him. Charlotte was halfway out of her chair when Robson shouted, "More wine. Hop to it."

Opal scuttled off to fetch more bottles from the bar. Charlotte sat down, turned to face Robson and stabbed her finger into his chest.

"Do not, ever, speak to her like that again! Do you understand me?"

Robson smacked her hand away, telling Charlotte to lighten up. Before Charlotte could reply Jay was out of his chair and crossing the floor to meet Opal at the entrance to the dining room. He took the two wine bottles she was carrying out of her hands and quietly suggested she return to the kitchen, he'd take it from here.

When Jay reached the table he presented the bottles to Robson. Passing him a corkscrew he said, "Perhaps you'd like to do the honours?"

"I think I will," Robson said. "Given the quality of your help, a guest's got to do everything for himself around here." He grinned at his father as he jabbed the metal screw into the cork. "Hey Dad," he said with a smug smile, "consider this my gift to you."

After two fumbled attempts he prised the cork out of the bottle and was about to pour when Katie's hand shot out to cover the top of Charlie's glass. Her arm bumped the bottle out of Robson's grasp. It bounced on the table at a funny angle and splashed deep red wine across the front of Charlie's pressed blue shirt.

"For fuck's sake!" Charlie leapt to his feet, flung his napkin down on the table and stalked out of the room.

"Jesus Christ." Robson grabbed the wine bottle by the neck and glared at his mother. Parker and Charlotte were on their feet before he could say another word. Parker eased Robson away from the table while Charlotte told Elise that now would be a good time for her to put her husband to bed.

With Parker on one side and Elise on the other, they propelled Robson across the dining room into the lobby. He insisted he could find his own goddamn way upstairs, but they refused to release him, maneuvering his stumbling body up the broad staircase to the second floor landing.

Katie watched them leave in stoney silence.

"Mom," Charlotte said it loudly, as if to break a spell, "let's take the kids to the kitchen." Turning to the wide-eyed children she asked if they'd like to eat dessert with Bernard. Nodding vigorously, they slid off their chairs and raced across the lobby into the kitchen. Charlotte slipped her arm around Katie's waist and the two women followed them.

That left us alone with Jay. After a long and painful silence Louisa said, "My goodness, look how dark it is already."

We turned to stare at the windows, the night had painted the glass inky black.

Charlie yanked the gown off the hanger and flung it across the bed. I'd finally gotten Charlotte down for a nap and was trying to rest. A black spangle scratched my eye, making it water.

Get dressed, he said, stripping off his shirt and dropping it on the floor. He went back into his dressing room, yelling over his shoulder. Gord's bringing the car around in ten minutes.

My brain fizzed with exhaustion and rye.

What are you talking about? I looked at the dress. Strapless, size four. I was still nursing Charlotte. I couldn't possibly fit into it.

He hauled out his tux. Rummaged in the cufflink drawer. Raising his voice. The Chamber Dinner. I won't give them the satisfaction of showing up late. Bob Kirby, Business Leader of the Year? Give me a fucking break.

Charlie had been raging ever since the Chamber of Commerce gave Kirby the award. Tonight, it would be presented to him at a black tie dinner at the Ranchmen's Club. I was so tired I'd forgotten all about it.

He yanked open another drawer. Where did that stupid girl put my bow ties? Fix your face. You look like a hag.

I can't go. I said I'm so tired I can't see straight and it's the nanny's night off. There's no one to take care of the kids.

He glowered at me, Gord will babysit. Parker can hold the fort until he gets back.

Gord's the limo driver. Parker was nine, Robson was seven and Charlotte was a colicky two-month old. The idea was ridiculous.

Tell them I'm sick. Call someone from your office to be your plus one. That cute little accountant you've had your eye on for a while, what about her?

He lunged across the bed and grabbed me by the hair—he loved my hair once—and hauled me to my feet. Flinging the black spangled dress in my face. Get fucking dressed.

I put on a forest green gown. Everyone said I looked radiant so soon after having the baby. I smiled, green is my colour, it sets off my eyes and my hair.

When we returned home I went into the bathroom and found a pair of scissors, then returned to the bedroom and cut that black spangly dress to ribbons.

CHAPTER 14

Later that evening after everyone had returned to their rooms I was too agitated to sleep. I grabbed a sweater and parked myself on the tiny balcony to stare at the stars. Wispy clouds floated across the sliver of the moon. The Hawaiian moon has twenty-nine phases; ours has eight. I was about to google this appalling lack of imagination when soft voices floated up through the velvety darkness.

Below me and off to the left, Jay moved across the terrace carrying a hurricane lantern. The flame flickered as he set it on a small wooden table. Calling out to Charlotte, he asked her to bring him a beer. A minute later she appeared with two cans and settled in the glow of the lamp next to him. The beer cans snapped and hissed when they were opened.

"God," Charlotte said, "what a gong show."

"Nothing you can do about it, babe." Jay dragged his chair closer to his wife. "Your family is nuts."

"I know, I know, but I'm sick to death of them. Dad of all people knows how hard Mom worked to kick the booze; you'd think he'd show some consideration. Does he have to get plastered every single time he comes here? Robson isn't any better."

"Charlotte," Jay said after a long moment, "I get where—"

"And Parker, she was holed up with them all afternoon. Why didn't she stop them from getting hammered?"

Jay snorted. "Stop them? They don't pay attention to a thing she says. How the hell is she supposed to stop them?"

Charlotte took a sip of beer. "Fair point."

I really shouldn't be listening to this conversation, but if I pulled open the sliding door and went back inside, they'd hear me. I focused on my cell phone, googling the phases of the moon.

Jay reached over and rubbed Charlotte's arm. "You've got to stop blaming yourself. Katie's told you a million times her drinking had nothing to do with you. She was overwhelmed by the 'job' of being Charlie Moore's wife. She had a role to play but she wasn't up to it."

"Intellectually, I get it. But emotionally…it was horrible. Mom was in and out of treatment centres…my childhood was nothing but a string of goodbyes."

Charlotte's voice caught in her throat and she paused for another sip of beer. "When I was Amelia's age I decided we had two moms. The good Mom who took care of Parker and Robson and the bad Mom who showed up seven years later and got stuck with me. I tried to act like Parker and Robson, thinking then she'd love me, but I was too little. And by then she was a full fledged drunk…anyway…"

Charlotte ran out of words and they sat in silence for a moment.

Jay said something about Charlotte's therapist and she replied he was right. She had to focus on the here and now, to make the most of the time she had left with her mother.

There was a sound, the hollow tink of a tin can hitting the stone terrace and rolling around. "Shit." Charlotte said. Her chair creaked as she leaned over to pick it up.

"Dad wants to take Mom back to the city with him. He says he misses her."

Jay almost choked on his beer. "You're kidding. They can't stand to be in the same room with each other for more than five minutes."

Charlotte's voice grew quieter and I could barely make out her words, something about Charlie wanting Katie to sign her votes over to him. "That would shift the balance of power, three against two in Dad's favour."

"She'll never give Charlie her proxy. Not in a million years." Jay rose to his feet and moved toward the patio doors. "I'm cold, let's go to bed."

Charlotte stood up to follow him, then stopped and grabbed his elbow. "Jay, I just had a horrible thought. Dad doesn't have to convince Mom to give him her proxy, not if he has her declared legally incompetent. Oh Jesus."

The French doors creaked open and just before Charlotte stepped inside she said, "I won't allow it. He took her away from me once. He's not going to do it again."

CHAPTER 15

Sunday

The next morning a blast of *Hotel California* welcomed me into Bernard's kitchen. A bit loud, but hey, it's his kitchen, he can play whatever he wants, and truth be told, his taste in music was beginning to grow on me. We humans are so adaptable.

Louisa was already here, chatting with Bernard who was beating something into submission in a large metal mixing bowl. Behind him Opal buzzed around like a tiny hummingbird, pulling onions out of the refrigerator and glistening knives out of the knife block. They were like the professional cooks on TV, but without the histrionics.

"You're early," I said to Louisa, casting a glance around the kitchen and relaxing a little because there was no sign of Charlie Moore. The last thing I needed was a lecture about trickle-down economics—take care of the rich and they'll take care of you—or something equally laughable.

Louisa patted the stool beside her. "Come, sit. Bernard's

been telling me the most amazing stories about life in the Big Apple." Louisa has an easy way about her. People meet her and five minutes later they're spilling their life stories. I put it down to her Florence Nightingale vibe. "Bernard, tell Evie about the time you met George Clooney."

I was settling in when I spotted Keith crossing the lobby. "Hold that thought. I'll be right back," I waylaid Keith in the doorway, telling him we needed to talk.

"About what?" He looked tired. Or maybe not tired as much as guarded.

"I had the weirdest conversation with Charlie Moore before breakfast yesterday. He says BLV has to grow or die. Standing pat was not an option. When I disagreed he said I should talk it over with you. As if he had the inside track on what you're thinking. Why would he say that?"

Keith's mouth fell open, but before he could reply we heard the sound of heavy footsteps trundling down the grand staircase. We both turned around to look.

"What?" AJ said as he hustled across the lobby. "I'm hungry."

Keith's face relaxed and he told AJ to slow down before he broke his neck and said he was starved and that was it, my question was forgotten.

Bernard placed plates of bacon and scrambled eggs in front of us, asking what we were going to do on this, our last day in cowboy paradise. I glanced at my plate. It was way too much to eat but Bernard had reverted to full-on Mafia don. *This is your breakfast; you will eat it.*

"Where's the family?" I asked.

"Charlotte and Katie are down at the barn. I swear Katie spends more time with Shadow than her own husband. Parker and Robson are heading down to the conference centre, they'll be in meetings with their father all day and are not"—Bernard mimicked Robson's voice—"to be disturbed under any circumstances." He gave a dismissive shrug, "God only knows where Jay is."

Behind us came the squeal and whoop of small children. Bernard barely had time to drop his knife on the counter before Amelia leapt into his arms, Teddy pushed his way between Louisa and me, demanding to know if the eggs were any good.

Louisa looked at him, dumbfounded. They were 'free range' children, there was no place at the Ranch that was off limits to them. Not the kitchen with its hot stove and razor sharp knives, not the utility sheds crammed with rusting machinery and dodgy power tools. If our mom were here those kids would go from 'free range' to 'fricasseed' in ten seconds.

Bernard's eyes softened when he asked his 'Cupcake' if she'd like Mickey Mouse pancakes this morning.

"No fair," AJ whispered to me, "for us it was eggs or nothing."

"AJ, you're cute, not as cute as Amelia, but cute. Feel free to ask him." I smiled. "Go ahead. I dare you."

AJ shot me a wry grin but didn't take me up on it.

"Where's your mother?" Bernard asked Amelia. Teddy answered for her saying Mommy had a terrible headache and was sleeping in. I wondered how long it had taken Elise to get Robson undressed and into bed. How long did she lay there beside him in the dark, stiff as a board and afraid to move lest he wake up and start drinking and ranting again?

Now that I thought about it, the Moore women worked awfully hard trying to keep the peace.

The children dragged their stools over to the griddle and were helping Bernard put the ears on the Mickey pancakes when Charlie steamed into the kitchen, moving like an icebreaker clearing everyone and everything out of his way.

Rubbing his hands together, he told Bernard he needed a special favour. Batter dripped from Bernard's ladle, turning Mickey into a troll.

"Of course, Mr. Moore. What can I do for you?"

Charlie explained that tonight was going to be a very special night. Everything had to be perfect. "Pull out all the stops, Bernie. Go above and beyond the call of duty. You get my drift? Do that Kobe beef dish. The one you served the last time I was here with whoever the hell it was."

"Unfortunately, they finished off all the beef. We've got—"

"Nova Scotia lobster then."

Bernard made a noncommittal sound—it takes a day to fly live lobster across the country, he couldn't just snap his fingers and make it magically appear—and Charlie gave him a hard stare. "Bernie, don't let me down."

"Leave it with me, Mr. Moore."

"Good." Charlie gave Bernard a quick slap on the back. "Tonight is going to be a night to remember."

JOURNAL

Charlie took the chequebook out of my hand and shoved it back in the desk, slamming the drawer so hard it caught the leather fringes on the sleeve of my jacket and two ripped off.

There's no need to rush it, he said. By the way, did I tell you how hot you look in Western gear. He smelled of beer and his words were slurred. He ran his hands down my backside and rolled his eyes in the direction of the bedroom.

We'd just returned from a Prairie-Glam charity event— raising money to clean up a northern town's drinking water after a tailings pond leaked toxins into its water supply.

The Charlie Moore Foundation was the lead donor pledging up to $10 million in the first year and up to $100 million over the next five years.

They gave us a big cardboard cheque for the photographs. Charlie held up one side, looking like a wrangler in his black Stetson and fine leather boots, and I held up the other. We smiled nicely for the cameras. Parker and Robson looked adorable; little miniature versions of Charlie and me in their cowboy hats; grinning and stuffing footlong hotdogs into their mouths.

But Charlie, I said, the town is desperate. They've been trucking in fresh water for months. We have to get that money out to them as fast as we can.

He grabbed me by the waist and walked me backwards into the bedroom. My cowboy boots were as stiff as iron, the heel snagged on the carpet and I stumbled backwards onto the bed.

There's no rush, he said, his heavy body pressing me deeper into the duvet. Let's see how the Foundation's investments shape up before we start throwing our money around. The pledge is for up to $10 mill in year one. Up to. Anything between zero and 10 will suffice.

Six months later the Foundation posted lackluster returns. Charlie wrote a cheque for $1 million. There's not a snowball's chance in hell we'll come anywhere close to donating $100 million over the next five years.

But the photo of the family holding that $100 million cardboard cheque looks fantastic on the Foundation's webpage.

Right above the blurb that says:

The Charlie Moore Foundation was established by Charlie and Katie Moore in 2014 with one passion in mind: to brighten and improve the lives of future generations. They focus on family and community as the framework for giving. The Charlie Moore Foundation supports organizations that promote health, education, and entrepreneurship across Alberta. Their goal is to build a legacy of hope for generations to come.

A legacy of hope indeed.

CHAPTER 16

Dragon Falls. The name captivated me from the moment we checked in and Charlotte pointed it out on the little hand drawn map of the grounds. "It's not a waterfall, per se," she'd said, "more like a deep, dark gorge." She'd named it Dragon Falls— "owner's prerogative"—because it reminded her of that scene from *Avatar* where the dragons spread their mighty wings and dive straight down into the canyon. "The gorge will take your breath away. If you have time, you really should see it."

AJ and I were halfway up the north-south trail. Overhead a hawk screeched, making a sound like two screams corded together. I grabbed my phone, zooming the lens to take a photo, and slipped off the trail, twisting my ankle. AJ turned when I yelped and I waved him away, hobbling along to prove that I was fine and didn't need saving.

"This map is useless," I said through clenched teeth, my ankle throbbing. "Nothing is drawn to scale."

"We're almost there," he replied.

"How would you know?" We were weaving through a jungle of enormous fiddlehead ferns. Sunlight filtered through the canopy of pines, aspens and poplars, casting a dappled light on the dense forest floor. It felt disorienting, like being underwater.

We'd been plowing through thick underbrush for an hour, we should have been there by now, according to Charlotte's vague instructions—go past the staff quarters, turn left at the fork and follow the Trillium path to the end—but I'd been distracted by the birds, wandering off the path to photograph them. There was no sense of north and south in the dark woods. We were lost.

"We're not lost," AJ said, reading my mind. "Come on, Evie, keep up."

I stopped for a moment to rest my ankle. "Are you sure you know where you're going?" Pretty little white flowers peeking through a lush bed of hostas lifted my spirits. *Trilliums.* "AJ, we're on the Trillium path. This is good."

He took a few more steps, then noticed I wasn't moving. "You sure you're all right back there?"

"Of course I'm all right," I said, fluttering my hand at him. "Lead on, McDuff." A fallen Douglas fir, thick and covered with moss, crowded us off the path and we waded into the underbrush to go around it. The sound of our footsteps muffled by dense greenery and dark shadows.

A root as thick as my wrist appeared out of nowhere and I went down. Landing hard on my hands and knees. "That's it!" I fought back tears of pain and frustration. "I'm heading back."

"That's it!" AJ shouted, pointing to a break in the trees off to his left, then turning to see me half buried in the undergrowth. "Jesus, what happened to you?" Two seconds later he was hauling me to my feet and brushing twigs and pine needles off the knees of my pants. I felt like a right idiot.

"You found it?" I rubbed my hands together sending a sprinkle of dirt and pine needles to the forest floor.

"It's right there. A few more steps and we'd have gone right over it" His eyes sparkled, a brilliant blue gray in the dim light. "Can you make it? Do I have to carry you?"

I pulled myself up to my full height, a couple of inches above his shoulder, and said I could manage just fine, thank you.

We ignored Charlotte's map, the trail marked by a series of dots was as useless as breadcrumbs at this point, and thrashed to the edge of a small clearing. The gorge was just ten feet away. The drop off so steep I couldn't breathe.

AJ pulled out his phone and moved across the scrubby sedge to the edge of the cliff.

"Be carful," I yelled from my safe place a good three feet behind him. "The edge looks crumbly." If I was as close to the precipice as he was, I'd be crawling on my belly.

He wedged himself between two spindly poplars and started fiddling with his phone. The shutter clicked and whirred, noisy and out of place in these dark woods.

I raised my phone, intending to capture an image of the hawk circling slowly overhead, when it rang, a noise so jarring I almost dropped it.

"Jesus," AJ said as he twisted around on the thin trunk of the poplar tree.

"It's Madeline."

She talked rapidly in my ear. "Have you seen the weather? There's a storm heading your way."

"Madeline, for God's sakes, it's Sunday, have you got nothing better to do than read me the weather report?"

When my parents died, Madeline took her guardian angel responsibilities even more seriously, offering me advice on everything from my health to my love life. She wouldn't rest until she'd found me a suitable mate, not necessarily a husband, but someone with money who would take good care of me. Whatever that meant.

My snippiness rolled right off her.

"It's a weird weather front," she continued, "coming over the mountains. They've issued storm warnings for a huge swath of BC and western Alberta. They're expecting freakishly heavy rain and high winds. You don't want to be caught in it, especially not on the highway."

I reminded her that we'd come up with Keith who drives like an old lady. He'd never let anything happen to us or his ancient van.

After she hung up she sent me a couple of texts for good measure:

Bad storm coming your way. Leave now. I don't have a helicopter to come and get you.

Actually with Madeline's connections she could rustle up a Hercules if she wanted to.

I checked my weather app which was set to Calgary, Venice and Rome. Other than a wind warning for Calgary and a poor air quality warning in Venice—not a great way to start the day in that magical city—everything looked fine.

And tapped out a reply:

Just wind. Maybe rain. Nothing to worry about.

Five minutes later she shot back:

Just got upgraded. Bomb cyclone. B-O-M-B. CYCLONE. Very dangerous!

CHAPTER 17

It was just past four o'clock and the clearing was hidden by long thin shadows. I took some random shots of AJ hanging out of the poplar tree but the camera flattened the perspective and it looked like he was just goofing around, not dangling two hundred feet above the gorge.

Finally he slipped his phone into his pocket. "Evie, you've got to see this, there's a river down there. I can't describe it."

I shook my head. "Too close to the edge."

"Come on." He stretched out his hand. "I've got you."

I hesitated, telling myself this was better than the time I followed AJ up a catwalk. Then I thought he was going to kill someone, I didn't have a choice, but now he just wanted to show me the view.

"Come on," he said, "you'll be sorry if you missed it."

Reluctantly, I took a few steps forward and clutched his hand.

"Okay," he said, "You're good. Take a look."

Ashy blue-green forests rolled down the sides of the gorge. At the bottom, a silvery-white river sparkled as it rushed along the valley floor. In the distance hundreds of birds swooped and flashed their pearly wings as they skimmed the water and soared away. It was just as Charlotte had said. Magical.

"Right, it is pretty, AJ, but it's getting late. We should be heading back."

The breadcrumb line on Charlotte's map was no help as we tried to retrace our steps, searching for the Trillium path hidden in the dark shadows.

"There's a dead Douglas fir tree around here somewhere. It's huge." I thrashed through the waist high ferns. "We can't have missed it." But we did and had to double back to the edge of the clearing and start all over again. My ankle throbbed and I was moving more slowly.

"AJ, there." Finally I spotted the Trillium blooms, a swath of brilliant white blossoms, glowing like tiny, fairy hats in the gloom.

He stepped in front of me. "Stay close, Evie. I don't want you getting lost."

"Me getting lost? I'm the one who found the path, remember." Regardless, I let him take the lead and stuck close, night falls quickly in the middle of the forest.

A sharp breeze sliced through the pines fluttering the branches. Our footsteps fell softly on the twisting path. A thought occurred to me.

"AJ, are the bears out yet?" *Why did I ask that?*

"Maybe," he said over his shoulder. "Depends on the weather and their general health, and how much they fattened up before they went into hibernation. Lots of factors. But we'll be fine."

He had no grounds for saying that but I decided not to challenge him. Sometimes it's best to leave well enough alone.

Instead I focused on AJ's back as he pressed forward,

reaching out now and then to hold back a branch so it wouldn't smack me in the face. My ankle felt hot and stiff.

The path faded into the shadows, then disappeared, forcing us to retrace our steps until we found it again. Every few minutes AJ glanced over his shoulder to check if I was still alive. I would give him a jaunty smile, but didn't speak, thinking about that old adage: How do you escape a bear attack? Run faster than your companion. No chance of that, unfortunately.

"AJ, stop. Let's call Charlotte. Maybe she can get us out of here." God knows how, but it was worth a try.

He turned to me, his cell phone in his hand. "No signal."

Heads down we trudged along the darkening path for almost an hour, shining our phone flashlights into the shadows, searching for landmarks, but every tree looked like every other tree. I'd all but given up hope when we stumbled out of the woods and onto the main trail.

"Oh, thank God." I bent down and rubbed my ankle. Very swollen. "Which way, left or right?" The sky was a deep dark blue—nautical twilight, my dad used to say. There was no sun. I lost all sense of direction. Nothing looked familiar.

AJ hesitated and I realized that he too was disoriented. We'd spent so much time looping back and forth, coming off the path to photograph birds and taking forever to find our way back that the Lodge could be anywhere.

"This way." He pointed to the left. "I think."

"You don't know?"

"Well, do you?" His tone was mild, unlike mine which had taken on an edge. Grace under pressure, the prize goes to AJ.

"Sorry, no."

Chastened, I hobbled along beside him. It took me ten minutes to realize something was wrong. A sharp pain drilled through the dull throb of my ankle This was new. Something had changed. The gradient of the trail was a tiny bit steeper. We were climbing. Uphill. Away from the Lodge.

"AJ, this isn't right."

He turned to face me, then pushed up the sleeves of his hoodie. "It's okay, I can carry you." He half turned. "Hop on, piggyback."

"God no." I stepped back and my ankle told me to stop making sudden movements. "We're going the wrong way. The Lodge is at the bottom of the valley. We should be going down, not up."

He pulled out his phone, still no signal, and shone the flashlight at the thick forest thirty feet to the west of us and the dark meadow to the east. The beam was too fragile to illuminate anything we could use as a landmark. "I don't know Evie. Are you sure?"

Was I sure? My foot was swollen and my ankle was throbbing so hard I was surprised I couldn't hear it. My body was falling apart, could I still trust my instincts? "I'm telling you this doesn't feel right."

His eyes met mine. "It'll be pitch black soon. If you're wrong...I don't want to be caught out here with the wolves and ... whatever. And you're saying we should double back because it doesn't *feel* right?"

"I'm saying we should double back because the north-south trail slopes down to the Lodge and we're heading up away from it. Unless you've got a better idea. Like, maybe reading the stars?" At that we both glanced up into the sky at the few pinpricks of light glittering overhead.

"As a matter of fact, I *can* read the stars." He turned me around and pointed over my shoulder. "See that." A star low on the horizon gleamed with a steady light. "That's Venus, the evening star."

"Very nice, AJ. Got anything else? Like the North Star or a helicopter to get us out of here?" I looked up at him and smiled.

His grinned, then his smile faded a notch. "You're absolutely sure about this."

"I'm as sure as I'll ever be."

"Okay, let's do it."

We turned back. Somewhere in the forest an owl hooted. With any luck an hour from now I'd be wrapping my ankle in a cold compress and getting ready for Charlie Moore's special dinner.

With any luck.

CHAPTER 18

"And to think I doubted you, Evie Valentine." With a deep bow AJ ushered me into the warmth and the light of the Lodge.

"Oh, ye of little faith," I replied, refusing to admit that there had been a few moments during our scramble down the hill where I had doubted myself. We'd made good time despite the constant pain in my ankle because the skies opened and a cold rain began to pelt down.

Inside the Lodge, Patsy Cline sang softly in the bar. Louisa was perched on a barstool playing solitaire the old-fashioned way with real cards and Keith was slouched on the red leather sofa in front of the fireplace.

"'I'm short, fat, and proud of that,'" he said in a pouty voice. The top of Amelia's head was just visible in the crook of his arm, her eyes fixed on the book in his lap, *Winnie the Pooh*. They were doing their level best to ignore Teddy who kept popping up from behind the sofa with a tea towel over his head, yelling "Oh bother!"

An hour later when we entered the dining room, the entire Moore clan was seated at the table. Even Charlie. Who shot us a look to indicate he'd registered the fact that

AJ and I were late. I knew this would be the case and made AJ wait for me at the top of the stairs so I wouldn't have to enter the dining room alone.

This was Charlie's special dinner and everyone—except Katie who looked like she couldn't care less—was agitated, fiddling with their cutlery and shifting in their seats.

Robson looked as pale and emaciated as model in a heroin chic ad. That was to be expected, I supposed. The entire time we'd been here he hadn't set foot outside the Lodge, preferring to rise early and work out in the gym.

Parker's face was stiff. Clearly, the competition for the top job was over. Her father was a dinosaur untouched by this newfangled notion that women had brains as well as bodies. Barring some miracle, Robson would win and she would be relegated to who knows what rinky-dink job. As Madeline so succinctly put it, Robson was blessed with the chromosome Parker lacked and there was nothing she could do about it.

Despite the lack of Kobe beef and fresh Nova Scotia lobster Bernard had outdone himself by adding his own special touches to what would otherwise have been a hum-drum prime rib, served with carrots, pomegranate-green beans, and cheddar biscuits. It was too much meat for me and I picked at it. Later that night I wished I'd eaten more.

Charlie dominated the conversation, telling animated stories about his hard scrabble childhood, exaggerated for effect—everyone one knew he wasn't born in the slums—to support the narrative of the clever boy who'd pulled himself up by his bootstraps to outsmart his competitors. A winner in a world of losers.

The children's eyes glazed over and so did mine. I had tuned him out and was talking quietly to Louisa when Charlie called out Keith's name.

Charlie's face was flushed and his words were sticky as he urged us to join him in celebrating Keith's future achievements. "There was a time when a man's word was his bond; today those men are few and far between." His smug smile indicated he counted himself among those whose promise was binding. "Let's raise our glasses to Keith, the last of a dying breed of honourable men."

Puzzled, I turned to look at Keith who was sitting at the opposite end of the table. We locked eyes; the colour drained from his face and his attempt at a polite smile faltered. *What the hell, Keith?*

By then Charlie had had a skinful. He got louder and louder as he toasted his wife and each of his children, reciting their accomplishments: Katie's superb talents as a hostess, Parker's brilliant leadership in last year's take over of some multi-national company, Robson's prowess on the handball court, and Charlotte's hard work with Mirror Ranch. The only words he did not utter was the name of his successor.

Outside the rain spattered against the French doors, warping the light spilling out of the dining room onto the paving stones on the terrace. Around the table, the mood shifted from giddy anticipation to confusion with an undercurrent of panic. Elise reached across the table to touch Robson's hand but he flicked her away. Nonverbal signals shot back and forth between Parker and Charlotte. While Katie sat motionless, staring quietly into her water glass as the light from the fireplace filled it with flames.

Suddenly, Charlie snapped his fingers. "Jay, what kind of a two-bit establishment are you running here?" He made a show of cupping his hand behind his ear. "You call that music?"

Soft jazz played quietly in the background.

"Dad, I—" Charlotte was on her feet when he cut her off.

"I'm speaking to Sanjay." Charlie enunciated the words slowly. "Put on some civilized music. Debussy or Ravel."

Quickly, Jay rose from the table. "It's okay, Charlotte, I've got this." And left the room, heading in the direction of the bar. He was barely out the door when Charlotte snapped at her father. "I'm the owner of Mirror Ranch; if you have any complaints about the ambiance kindly direct them to me."

Charlie narrowed his eyes at her and said, "Charlotte, you own squat. MMG holds the mortgage and you'd be wise to remember that before you start lipping off." He glowered at her until she broke eye contact and slowly sat down in her chair.

The background music changed to light classical. When Jay reappeared he had a tentative smile on his face. "That better?"

Charlie pushed back his chair and announced he was going for a walk.

"At this hour?" Parker protested.

"Dad, it's pouring outside." Charlotte was out of her chair, heading out to the lobby.

"I'm coming with you." Robson tried to get to stand but was so drunk his feet snagged under his chair.

Charlie shook his head. "No, you're not, Robson. Stay where you are. Enjoy the evening with your lovely family."

Charlotte returned with a yellow rain slicker on her arm. She caught Charlie as he unlatched the terrace doors, a gust of cold air curled across the floor. "Dad, wait. At least put on a jacket. You'll catch your death out there."

Charlie shoved his arms into the raincoat and stepped through the door onto the slick terrace. There was a moment of stunned silence as the family watch him disappear into the night, but it didn't last long.

Robson berated Charlotte for spoiling his 'big night.' Jay leapt to Charlotte's defence, calling Robson a little shit, and Charlotte, her temper on full display, rushed back to the table to confront Robson, moving so fast she knocked over her chair.

Everyone was shouting and banging on the table when they were interrupted by a plaintive little voice.

"Mommy, I want to go to bed now." Amelia slipped off her chair and left the room.

JOURNAL

When Robson was ten I caught him gouging the eyes out of Parker's teddy bear. I insisted he apologize. He refused. Even after I threatened to tell his father. He simply locked himself into his room and built Lego towers that crashed to the floor all afternoon.

Over the last two years Parker's things were continually breaking or falling apart. Her favourite yellow wellies developed razor thin slits in the soles and the zippers in her jeans were constantly broken or jammed. I suspected Robson was to blame but couldn't prove it.

Until now. When I caught kneeling on her teddy bear stabbing the scissors into its face.

She adored her stuffed animals. They were as real to her as people and Robson knew it.

That night, when Charlie came home I told him I thought Robson should see a child psychologist. Charlie said I was overreacting. If Parker wanted to keep her toys safe all she had to do was lock her bedroom door.

Problem solved.

CHAPTER 19

Monday 1:35 a.m

Someone was thumping down the corridor outside my room. Muffled footsteps across the carpet. I glanced at my phone. 1:35 a.m. A light, urgent tapping. Not my door, but where?

Slipping into my bathrobe, I opened the door a crack. Three rooms down on the family side of the corridor, I could see Charlotte rapping on a door. Her long red hair was pulled back in a loose ponytail, her slim body rigid. "Parker!" she whispered. "Open up!"

Parker's door opened a crack and Charlotte barrelled inside. Not long after that both sisters were back in the hall. Hustling down to Robson's room. Banging on his door. Even louder.

Robson opened his door. "Jesus," he said, his voice thick with sleep, "do you know what time it is?" In the background came Elise's aggrieved cry, *What now?* Parker shoved Robson back into his room and Charlotte slammed the door shut behind them.

Five minutes later the three of them were back in the hall and trundling down the stairs to the lobby.

That's it. The night was shot. I pulled on my jeans and a heavy sweater and stepped out into the hall, running smack into Louisa who was standing outside her door, fully dressed.

"You're awake," I said, stating the obvious. Years of shift work had conditioned her to pop out of a dead sleep raring to go at the first sign of trouble.

"What's going on?" Her voice cracked and she had to repeat herself.

"Don't know. The family's in an uproar."

The lobby was ablaze with light, Robson, Parker and Charlotte were huddled in front of the reception desk arguing and didn't hear us approach.

"Parker?" I touched her shoulder. "Is something wrong? Can we help?"

Their heads snapped up, their faces marked by trepidation. Robson spoke first, flapping his hands at us. "This doesn't concern you. Go back to bed."

Outside, the rain drummed on the veranda and the wind shook the wide windows.

"For God's sake, Robson," Parker snapped. "Dad's been gone for hours"—I glanced at my watch, three hours at least— "We'll need all the help we can get."

Jay emerged from the kitchen and said, "Bernard and Opal are on their way."

Everyone was talking in loud, high pitched voices, but I'd heard enough. Charlie had disappeared into the cold, black, night.

I raced back upstairs to wake Keith and AJ.

CHAPTER 20

Monday 2:30 a.m.

By the time we regrouped in the lobby, Parker was firmly in charge of the search party.

"Charlotte," she turned to her sister, "tell them what you told me."

Charlotte took a long slow breath; a strand of hair was caught in her eyelashes and moved up and down when she blinked. "I was heading to the pantry for some Gaviscon when I noticed a light under Mom's door. It was one o'clock. Dad always checks on Mom before he goes to his room. He doesn't want her reading late into the night. It's not good for h—"

Robson interrupted. "No one cares, Charlotte, get on with it."

"Mom was fast asleep. All the lights were on and her meds were still in the plastic pill container. Obviously Dad hadn't been by to check on her." Charlotte took a moment to steady her voice. "When I checked his room, he wasn't there. Jay and I scoured every square inch of the Lodge, including the wine cellar. Jay thought Dad might have gone down there for…well…"

Parker confirmed no one had seen Charlie since he'd stalked out onto the terrace around nine o'clock. Numerous calls to Charlie's cell went straight to voice mail.

The rain was coming down in sheets and the wind howled as it battered the walls. Charlie was wearing a thin yellow slicker over a button down shirt, dress slacks and Italian leather shoes. That alone should have driven him back to the Lodge. Unless he'd been forced to shelter in one of the outbuildings. But if that was the case, why didn't he answer his phone? Had it not occurred to him his family would be frantic?

Charlotte dug out all the flashlights and waterproof clothing she could find. In silence we shrugged on ill-fitting windbreakers and oversized jackets while Parker organized us into teams of two—it was too dangerous for anyone to search alone.

Only three would stay behind: Charlotte to take care of Katie who was asleep in bed, unaware of the drama unfolding in the lobby, Elise, who'd been ordered by Robson to return to their room to keep an eye on the children, and Opal who busied herself in the kitchen brewing coffee and making sandwiches in the hope that we'd be back soon with a ravenous Charlie Moore in tow.

———

Lightning flashed overhead, transforming trees into giant spiders and bushes into bears. The woods and gardens were distorted like images in a carnival mirror, recognizable but menacing.

Parker and I were huddled in the lee of the corporate centre building, turning inward to avoid the wind ripping at our jackets and the rain running into our shoes. We could barely hear each other over the crash of thunder overhead.

The small building was packed with rooms, meeting areas, food prep stations, bathrooms, and Parker and I searched every last one of them. We found nothing.

When we left, every light in the place was blazing, transforming the conference centre into a beacon in the windswept meadow to guide Charlie in case he'd become disoriented and couldn't find his way back home.

The trail to the stables was slick with wet pine needles and my ankle twitched, telling me to tred carefully. Not easy in the fierce wind and swirling rain. The beam of my flashlight caught Parker's face. Her cheekbones were sharp and her eyes were black. From fear or anger, I couldn't tell.

"None of this makes sense," she shouted over the wind. "Why did he go out?

I shrugged, who knows.

"Why didn't he name his successor like he promised?"

Now that was a question I could answer but wouldn't. Charlie didn't make the announcement because he was a cruel man who enjoyed tormenting his family. A pleasant persona for the outside world and a bully to his family.

Parker's hair was plastered to her skull, she made a futile effort to push her bangs out of her eyes. "God, listen to me prattling on about succession when Dad is out here somewhere, cold and lost. He's got a heart condition, what if he dropped dead of a heart attack?"

"Parker, don't do that. You've been under a lot of stress. Don't torture yourself."

Her head whipped around, tiny droplets flew into the air.

"Stress? This isn't stress. I don't want that fucker to die out here before I can tell him to take his job and shove it."

She was speaking so fast, she was gulping air. "I'm done with all this. With being the good little girl working quietly at my desk. Cleaning up after Robson when he screws up. All to impress Dad. And for what? Tonight was the last straw."

She gave a bitter laugh. "What was that line in that movie? I'm mad as hell and I'm not going to take it anymore. I'm going to find the bastard and tell him to his face."

She stared at me, eyes blazing.

"Okay, then," I said, trying to ignore the rain seeping under my collar, "let's go find Charlie Moore."

<h1 style="text-align:center">CHAPTER 21</h1>

Monday 3:00 a.m.

Is it locked?" I yelled into Parker's ear as she struggled to open the sliding barn door. The metal latch slipped out of her rain slicked hands and the wind slammed into the barn, making the door rattle on the iron rail overhead. All that metal made me nervous as the lightning forked over the giant pine tree just three feet away.

"No," she shouted back. I grabbed the door latch and together we forced the door open a crack and slipped inside.

The horses stirred uneasily, their hooves crushing the straw underfoot and filling the barn with the sweet smell of hay. Shadow lifted his great head, nickering softly under his blanket as if to ask: *What are you doing here?* It was well past three a.m. The adrenaline that had flooded my bloodstream when we started the search had dissipated.

Parker was shouting, her voice vibrating with nerves. "You do the tack room and the loft." She pointed to the wooden steps leading up to the second floor. "I'll take the main level."

Thunder cracked overhead making me flinch as I poked around in the tack room. It was remarkably neat with riding gear along one wall and tables and metal cabinets along the other. The horses emanated heat and it was surprisingly warm up here. This would have been a good place for Charlie to ride out the storm.

We called out his name and searched the barn from one end to the other. He wasn't there.

Parker's cell buzzed. "It's Robson," she called up to me. I took the stairs two at a time and was by her side by the time she put the call on speaker.

"Robson, did you find him?"

"No, not yet." The wail of the wind muffled his words. He and Keith had combed through the greenhouse and the utility sheds which were packed to the rafters with decrepit equipment. "It's a bloody accident waiting to happen," Robson growled. "Jay needs to get off his ass and haul that junk away."

In the background Keith was telling Robson they had to keep moving. The chicken coops and pig house were next.

"Keith," I yelled into the phone, "have you heard from the others?" AJ and Bernard had taken the north-south trail up to the archery hut and the staff quarters; Louisa and Jay were heading farther north to the Trillium path that led to Dragon Falls. The path was treacherous in the daylight, it would be a nightmare in the dark.

"Jesus," Robson's voice sounded far away. "Elise is texting again."

Parker interrupted. "Is Dad back at the Lodge?"

"No, she's bitching we're taking too long. That bloody woman."

"Keith, have you heard from Louisa?" I said it again. AJ could handle himself, but Louisa was teamed with Jay, he was a nerdy accountant, not a wilderness man.

"Nothing yet." Keith's voice faded in the wind.

———

Parker pulled the spa door key out of her pocket. Her copper hair was dark and slicked back. She mopped her forehead with a sodden sleeve. "You bloody well better be in here," she muttered to herself as she turned the door handle.

The wind blew the door open and it slammed against the wall. Parker flipped on the light switches and called out, "Charlie? Are you in here? Dad?" The words bounced off the white glass-tiled walls and the concrete reception desk. *Charlie, Dad.*

When I entered the spa room, I half expected to find Charlie submerged in a bubbling vat of beer, his walrus mustache limp, his thick body flaccid. But when I looked, the vat was black and empty.

Parker had finished in the massage rooms by the time I caught up to her. As we searched the showers stalls she said, "Where the hell is he?" Then her knees buckled and she wobbled to one side. *She's going down.*

I eased her back out to the reception area and sat her on the wheat coloured bench while I scrabbled around in the reception desk until I found an energy bar. "Here, eat this." Then I phoned Keith.

"No luck in the chicken coop or pig house," he shouted. "They're empty. AJ just checked in. He and Bernard went through the staff quarters room by room. Right down to the laundry room in the basement. Charlie's not there."

"Okay, I guess we'll—"

"Wait, it's Louisa." He put me on hold.

Parker and I waited. The seconds crawled by. Finally Keith came back on the line.

"They found him. It's not good."

CHAPTER 22

Monday 4:05 a.m.

Later Louisa told me she and Jay all but tripped over Charlie's body where it lay, sprawled across the trail, past the staff quarters near the fork that cuts over to the Trillium path. Limbs splayed like a broken puppet, eyes wide open, rain beating down on his yellow slicker and his fine Italian leather shoes.

"It was so strange," Louisa had said, "the way he lay there, like he'd been pressed into the ground by a giant hand."

She'd put her ear close to his mouth, straining to hear the sound of his breath over the roar of the wind in the pines, then checked his pulse, knowing full well he wouldn't have one. After she confirmed he was dead, she called Keith and Jay called Charlotte who said she would wait until Parker and Robson returned to the Lodge before telling Katie.

Rain drops glittered silver in the flashlight beam as Parker and I slogged up the north-south trail. The others were already there, huddled around Charlie's body, by the time we arrived. Over the sound of the rain pelting through the trees, I could hear Robson and Keith arguing.

Keith said we could cover Charlie with our jackets and he'd stay behind and guard the body keeping it safe from animals, until the police arrived.

"Are you fucking insane?" Robson stared down at Charlie's body, watching the rain run into his eyes and fill his mouth. He dropped down into a squat and picked at Charlie's sleeve as if he were testing the weight of the dead man's arm. It lifted off the ground and dropped down again onto the path. His sleeve covered with dirt and pine needles.

"I'm not leaving my father here exposed to the elements. This isn't a crime scene."

"Jay." Robson snapped his fingers. Gesturing. *Grab his legs.* Then positioned himself at Charlie's head, grappling with his shoulders, trying to hoist Charlie's soaked body into the air. But Charlie was a big man and Robson was slight. He slipped on the wet pine needles, losing his balance.

Charlie's head flopped back. eyes wide open, mouth gaping. As his body slid out of Robson's grasp, it emitted an eerie groan.

"Jesus!" Robson dropped Charlie on the path, and lunged backward, crashing into Keith.

"It's just air," Louisa said, "escaping from his lungs because you moved him. Look, he's heavy and soaked right through. It would be easier to carry him down in a blanket. Someone could run down—"

"No," Robson was on his knees again, trying to get a grip on Charlie's sodden jacket, "there's five of us here, eight if we count the women"—why we wouldn't count the women—"we can cut down the servant's path, it's rough but much quicker than north-south. That'll get us back to the Lodge in an hour."

Keith helped Robson lift Charlie's upper body off the cold wet ground. Jay and Bernard went to his legs, taking some time to secure their grip before hoisting Charlie into the air. AJ and I positioned ourselves on either side of him and grabbed a handful of his sodden jacket to lighten the weight of his torso for the others.

Slowly we lurched after Parker, her bobbing flashlight illuminating the way to the servant's path. Louisa brought up the rear.

Charlie got heavier and heavier and after twenty minutes Robson lost his grip on Charlie's armpit and traded places with AJ. As AJ got into position behind me I thought about our hike to Dragon Falls and how we would have made it back to the Lodge in half the time had the servant's path been properly marked on Charlotte's little map.

It felt like we'd been walking for hours before we finally reached the Lodge. Charlotte flung open the kitchen door the minute Parker banged on it and led the way through to the lobby where we placed the body on the red leather sofa in front of the stone fireplace. Opal was behind us, mopping up our muddy footprints. It was an odd thing to do, but in a crisis people do strange things.

Charlotte pulled a Hudson's Bay blanket off the back of an armchair and draped it across Charlie's body before brushing her hand across his face, closing his dead eyes.

As we returned to the kitchen, Keith pulled out his cell phone, saying it was time to call the RCMP.

"Not without me, you don't," Robson said, trailing after him into the dining room. Fifteen minutes later they were back. The phones weren't working. All Keith could get was the beep, beep, beep of a dropped call.

Outside the wind raged, shaking the Lodge as if it were a child's piggybank refusing to give up its pennies.

———

A fire blazed in the massive fireplace. Charlotte must have assumed Charlie would welcome the warmth. She fussed around the sofa, tucking the blanket around his drenched, lifeless body. There was a quiet moment when she stared down at him before she turned to Parker.

"How are we going to tell Mom?"

Parker opened her arms and held Charlotte close for a long time. "I'm the eldest," she murmured, "I'll do it." Neither of them shed a tear.

Behind us came a querulous voice. Robson's wife, Elise was standing in the middle of the staircase, her terry robe flapped open revealing lacy nude lingerie. When she spotted Charlie under the blanket on the sofa, she recoiled.

"Robson...is he? Oh my God, Robson. What happened?"

"Good question." Robson shot a stony glance at Jay. "How could you let this happen?"

"Me? I didn't let anything happen," Jay shot back.

Accusations and recriminations flew around the room as the Moores argued about who was to blame for Charlie's death. Why didn't Robson stop Charlie from leaving? Why didn't Charlotte wait up for him and when he failed to return raise the alarm? I thought the whole thing was absurd. The only person responsible for Charlie's death was Charlie. When he decided to go out into the storm, nothing and no one could have stopped him.

"Come, come." A calm voice cut through the acrimony. "What's all this fuss?"

As one, we turned to face Katie who was standing at the

bottom of the staircase, in full makeup, impeccably dressed. She looked at her children one by one, as if she were getting her bearings, then her eyes fell on Charlie lying on the sofa.

"Oh for heaven's sake, Charlie." She strode over to the sofa. "How many times have we talked about this? If you're going to drink yourself into oblivion, at least have the decency to pass out in your own room."

Out of the corner of her eye she spied Bernard standing in the entrance to the kitchen. "Bernard, ignore this lout. A coffee and a muffin, if you would be so kind."

Then she reached down and ripped the blanket off Charlie's body, demanding that he go upstairs to bed.

In a flash, Charlotte was by her side. She slipped her arm around Katie's shoulders and whispered, "Mom, we need to talk." Gently leading her into the kitchen.

"Jesus Christ." Robson grabbed the Hudson's Bay blanket off the floor and flung it across his father's body. "She's really losing it." He pointed at Elise. "Upstairs." And followed her up the staircase to their room.

Louisa rearranged the blanket, tugging it up to cover Charlie's face. The green, red, yellow and blue striped throw was now a cheerful shroud. Charlie's feet poked out at the bottom, expensive leather shoes crusted with mud; one of his socks had worked its way down under his heel, exposing a pale dirt-specked ankle. I went off in search of another blanket.

Keith was pacing in the dining room, staring at his cell phone. He caught my eye and shrugged. "I still can't get a signal."

When I returned to Charlie's body with another blanket it occurred to me that leaving a dead man to stew in front of a blazing fire might not be a brilliant plan.

CHAPTER 23

Monday 5:00 a.m.

There was a dead man on the sofa at the Lodge and I was in the stables of all places with Katie and Charlotte. The barn was humid and smelled of rich earth and trampled straw. Outside the rain hammered the cedar shakes and gushed down the drainpipes, it sounded like we were in a submarine getting ready to dive. The horses shifted uneasily, their slumber disturbed yet again, for a second time.

When Katie finally understood that Charlie was dead, not just sleeping it off after a bender, she insisted on going down to the barn to check the horses. Something horrible had happened to Shadow, she was convinced of it. It was a peculiar reaction to the news her husband was dead and I put it down to shock.

Shadow whinnied softly as Charlotte ran her delicate fingers across his body, examining three deep abrasions on his flank. "Mom, look at this, you should have told me."

Katie rested her cheek against Shadow's flat jaw. "I did tell you, last night. My poor boy, what have you been up to?"

Her eyes followed Charlotte who was heading upstairs to get her vet kit. Patting his neck, Katie turned to me. "He's such a brave boy, so good natured despite his chronic pain, isn't that right Shadow?"

More loudly, she called up to Charlotte. "He needs a shot of keto, his knees are hot."

Charlotte yelled down that a shot wasn't necessary, but Katie insisted that Charlotte do as she was told. Shadow whinnied and tossed his head, agitated at the sound of their raised voices and a minute later Charlotte returned with the vet kit.

She cleaned Shadow's wounds then pulled out a syringe, preparing to fill it, but when she opened the small box labelled KETAMINE it was empty. She ran back upstairs to the tack room and returned with a fresh box of vials.

"Is everything all right?" I asked, but she was focused on administering the shot and didn't reply. The horse murmured but didn't move until it was over.

Wouldn't it be nice to be a horse, I thought. To have people who love you and who'll come out in the middle of a downpour to make sure you're all right.

When Katie was satisfied Shadow was comfortable we made our way to the wind-rattled barn door and stepped outside into the pounding rain. The wind tore at our clothes, making the slog back up the muddy trail chilling. Katie's reaction to Charlie's death unnerved me and I leaned closer to Charlotte and asked if her mother was all right.

"She's obsessed with his health. If she had her way he'd be drugged to the eyeballs."

"*Charlie?*"

"God no, Shadow. Mom thinks ketamine is a miracle

drug, she doesn't understand it's hard on him." A small frown line appeared between her eyebrows. "Wait, did I record that last shot? I swear, sometimes I think I'm losing my mind."

She spun around and raced back down to the barn to double check while Katie and I continued our trek back up to the Lodge. I'm a good thirty years younger than Katie but I had to hustle to keep up. She plowed up the trail like a woman possessed.

JOURNAL

It couldn't have been clearer if he'd put it up in neon lights: REHAB OR LOSE THE KIDS.

The first time Charlie shipped me out to Betty Ford, Parker and Robson were in their early teens and Charlotte was just a baby, not quite three. I missed them so much I couldn't eat, my stomach was a rock.

When I stepped out of the limo in front of the Centre at Rancho Mirage—Mirage, an illusion, like my perfect life with Charlie—my knees were shaking so badly I could hardly walk. They probably thought I was still drunk.

Detox was a breeze. I was nowhere near as bad as Charlie and his doctor made me out to be.

My room on the east side of the residential wing was perfect. Simple, clean, and a million miles away from HIS MASTER'S VOICE.

The staff were kind, except for Dr. Devon, the demon who decided the great Charlie Moore couldn't possibly have anything to do with my addiction. This irritated me, but I shouldn't have been surprised. Charlie is a cruel, controlling man, who shows one face to the outside world and another to me and the kids. Dr. Jekyll and Mr. Hyde had nothing on the great Charlie Moore.

Soon it became clear I wasn't getting out of there anytime soon unless I agreed with everything Dr. Devon said, so I did.

If nothing else, life with Charlie had taught me the value of acquiescence.

Dr. Devon and I drew up a recovery plan. If I promised to be a good wife, Dr. Devon would let me go home.

When I showed the plan to Charlie, he went through the roof. This is a joke, he said. No booze? Katie, you have a job to do in this enterprise. You're client relations. It's easy, be pretty, flirt with the clients, laugh at their jokes. If they drink, you drink. It makes them feel good. When they feel good they buy MMG's services. You used to be an actress, act. Is that too much to ask?

I lasted fourteen months before he shipped me back to Rancho Mirage. It became a regular cycle: Addicted, detoxed, rehabbed. Addicted, detoxed, rehabbed. Jumping on and off the jolly merry-go-round for more than a decade.

Until I decided I'd had enough.

CHAPTER 24

Louisa tapped on my door. She was holding a bag of potato chips, two cans of Pepsi and her tablet.

"That's breakfast?" I said, skeptically.

She barged in. "There's no one downstairs. I raided my minibar. Want to watch a movie?" She held up her tablet. "I downloaded the Sharknado weekend."

We were an hour into the shark movie, the hero was trapped in a flooded grocery store and everyone but the cute girl was dead, when there was a loud knock at my door. *Now what?* In the corridor stood Keith. With a worried expression on his face.

"We have a problem," he said, entering the room and sitting down at the little desk by the window.

"There's a dead guy in the lobby?" I get sarcastic when I don't get enough sleep.

"The phones are still down."

"So send the cops an email."

"We can't," Louisa piped up. "The WiFi is out. The last thing I saw on my phone was a weather warning. We're in the path of a bombogenesis and judging by that"—she waved in the direction of the rain splattered window— "we're in the thick of it now."

With a sigh I sat down at the foot of the bed. Madeline was right. I hate it when Madeline is right.

Keith looked at Louisa. "A bombo-what?"

She shimmied down to the end the bed leaving a trail of potato chip crumbs in her wake. "That's what the meteorologists are calling it. A bomb cyclone."

I shot an apprehensive glance out of my window and realized my little balcony chair was gone, probably stuck in a tree somewhere. The Lodge was a sturdy building with tall windows running along the front and east side. The kitchen was on the third wall with one small window in the back door and the bar, the snug and the massive staircase filled the fourth wall. Protection on two sides from the brutal wind howling outside. Surely two out of four isn't bad.

"Are you serious?" Keith's eyes widened with disbelief as Louisa squirmed even closer to him, trying to explain while Sharknado screamed face down into the bedspread.

"Of course I'm serious," Louisa replied. "It's a real weather phenomenon. From what I remember, it's a ferocious storm marked by a rapid drop in air pressure"—that would explain my headache— "it usually lasts about twenty-four hours, during which time it can do a lot of damage, tearing down trees, blocking roads, ripping out powerlines. It's very dangerous. People are advised to stay inside until it's over. Did I mention that it's extremely dangerous?"

I picked up Louisa's tablet and paused the movie. Turning to Keith I said, "It must have knocked out the phone lines or some cell towers, which is why you can't reach the police."

"Oh dear," Louisa bit her lip. "Charlie's been dead for at least four hours. We've got a problem."

"Yes, Keith just said—"

"No not the police. A different problem."

CHAPTER 25

You've got to be kidding me." I stared at Louisa as she walked us through it. "They've just settled down, finally." I was talking about the family.

The minute Katie and I returned from the stables, Robson laced into her about her 'precious' horse, saying Katie would be wise to enjoy her time with Shadow, because his days were numbered. Katie called him a monster and Charlotte had to give Katie something to calm her down.

"Everyone is back in their rooms waiting for the police to arrive and release them from this nightmare and you want to dump this on them?"

"I understand." Louisa frowned. "But I don't see any way around it."

When I ran out the timeline in my head I knew she was right. A bomb cyclone lasts about 24 hours. It started last night around 8 p.m. when Charlie, the idiot that he was, marched out into the driving rain. That meant it wouldn't dissipate until 8 o'clock tonight. Even if we could get through to the police there was a good chance they wouldn't be able to reach Mirror Ranch for another day, maybe two, depending on the condition of the roads and how long it took to clear away the downed trees and pow-erlines. Meanwhile Charlie was downstairs, falling to bits on the sofa in front of the fireplace.

Keith grimaced and scratched the back of his head. "You're saying we have to put the body somewhere cold, like the freezer?"

"No," Louisa said. "Not the freezer. Bernard's walk-in cooler."

———

"Absolutely not!" Jay's outburst startled me. Throughout this crisis, he'd been remarkably calm. His hair was wet and his jeans were soaked from the knees down. He'd taken Diablo out at daybreak, hoping to get a sense of the damage inflicted by the bomb cyclone, but the torrential rains and gusting wind had driven horse and rider back to the barn. Mirror Ranch was huge, 640 acres. It would take days for Jay to assess the full extent of the destruction. And it was the start of the high season.

"It's not knowing what we're up against that's killing me." He strode over to the cooler and yanked open the door. "And now you're telling me all this food has to come out? We're talking about thousands of dollars worth of beef and fish and perishables. Who's going to compensate me for that? The police? The insurance company? I doubt it. We just stocked up for the start of high season.

"Charlotte," Jay turned to his wife, "back me up here, will you?"

Parker interrupted him. "What's the alternative Sanjay? That we dump Dad outside where the wolves can tear him apart? Christ, what's the matter with you?"

Before Jay could reply Robson strode into the kitchen. "Will you keep it down. The kids are still sleeping."

Bernard stepped in—I was beginning to think he was the only sane person here (aside from Opal)—and assured Jay he'd squeeze as much food as possible into the freezer and pack the perishables into the bar fridge and the minifridges in all the guest rooms. "I'll cook what I can and freeze that too. We'll be fine."

Soon we were lugging plastic bins jammed with apples and asparagus and God knows what else out of the cooler and stacking them on the counter where Bernard and Opal sorted them into COOK, FREEZE, and MINIFRIDGE piles.

"We'll eat like kings," Bernard said, surveying the COOK pile which now occupied the entire back counter and half of the long kitchen island.

Opal looked up from her recipe folder. "More like gluttons."

Finally the cooler was empty. Parker and I stacked thin mats, like the kind furniture movers use, on the cement floor. It was as if we were trying to make Charlie more comfortable in his undignified final resting place, then stood back to allow the men to haul Charlie's stiffening body, still wrapped in the gaily striped blanket, into the cooler and deposit it by the back wall under the whirring fans.

When the cooler door hissed shut for the last time, Robson went to the kitchen sink and washed his hands for a very long time.

CHAPTER 26

E vie, can I interest you in a refreshing lukewarm beer?"
Hands on hips, AJ was standing behind the bar staring at the flats of beer stacked on the floor. We'd emptied the bar fridge two hours ago to make room for Bernard's perishables—open any minifridge in the Lodge and you'd come face to face with a pound of raw hamburger or a dead eyed fish. I never drink this early in the day, but after the trainwreck of last night and this morning I was prepared to make an exception.

"If you're offering a lukewarm G and T, I'll take it. With ice—"

"Too late, it's already melted."

AJ handed me my drink and we were ambling across the lobby, steering clear of the red leather sofa, Charlie's not quite final resting place, when I spotted the phone sitting quietly in the corner on the reception desk. A black Bakelite rotary phone. A land line.

"AJ, look." I tugged him over to the reception desk. "Do you think it works?" Our mobile phones had been offline since last night. The storm must have taken down a cell tower.

I picked up the clunky plastic receiver and put it to my ear. "Listen! It's humming." AJ leaned closer and the encouraging sound of an old fashioned dial tone buzzed in our ears. "This sounds promising."

"What's the number for the RCMP?" he asked, rifling through the papers on the reception desk as if he expected to find it written down on a Post-It note.

I dropped the receiver back into the cradle and pulled open a drawer, searching for a phone book. To my surprise I found one, a very thin book, the yellow pages, and was flipping through the Ps—*Poles, Political Organizations*—when I remembered all we had to do was dial 9-1-1.

The rotary dial clicked as the numbers rolled by. We waited. The dial tone hummed in my ear, but nothing happened.

"Damn it." AJ pulled his phone out of his pocket and swiped at it. "There's got to be a way to do this." Then he remembered we had no Wi-Fi and shoved his cell back into his pocket. "I know this," he muttered tapping his fingers against his forehead. "Think, think."

Outside the torrential downpour beat against the windows which were firmly shut, making the lobby feel hot and muggy.

I said I'd go find Charlotte. "Maybe it needs an adaptor or something."

"It's a star code," AJ said, "*72 or *73."

I took a closer look at the rotary dial. "It's got numbers and letters and even the word *operator*, but it doesn't have a star. AJ, I'm going to find Charlotte."

"No wait." He pulled the phone closer to him, its rubbery feet squeaked across the desktop. "I remember, you have to dial 1-1."

I tried not to let my impatience get the better of me

as I watched him run through the sequence of numbers again and again. Finally he smiled and in the watery light flooding the lobby his eyes changed from deep blue to gray. "It's ringing."

I raced into the kitchen, returning with Charlotte and Jay. Robson trotted along behind them. By then AJ was having an animated conversation with someone at the RCMP office, telling them how we'd found Charlie dead on the path. After a long pause he recited his cell number and passed the receiver to Charlotte who repeated what AJ had said, then confirmed the phone number for the rotary phone and her cell and hung up.

"Well?" Robson was so agitated I thought he was going to jump over the reception desk. "When will they be here?"

"They couldn't give me a definitive ETA," Charlotte said. "The road crews are working day and night. They follow a strict protocol, major thoroughfares first, the main highways are blocked with fallen trees and powerlines, then they'll move to the arterials and collector roads like ours, but constable whatever-his-name-was assured me that given our unique situation they'd make getting to us a priority."

"*Our unique situation*? Is that police-speak for a dead man rotting in the cooler?" Robson made it sound as if someone had forgotten to take out the trash.

"Really Robson, there's no need to be crass. They said they'd get here as soon as they could and we did the right thing by putting Daddy's body in the cooler." Charlotte paused for a moment. "We have to stay put until they get here. They want to interview everyone who was at the Lodge when Daddy died."

"What the hell for?" Robson barked. "In case you've forgotten, I've got a business to run."

"Get over yourself, will you," Jay said, pointing to the

rain sheeting the windows. "You're not going anywhere in this weather."

Jay was right. No one was getting out of here for at least a day or two.

I picked up my G and T and wandered over to the small plaid couch just outside the dining room. When AJ sat down beside me I said, "You didn't tell me you were handy with rotary phones."

He laughed, saying they were engineering marvels. "Did you know that Winnipeg was the first city in North America to adopt the 9-1-1 emergency system?"

Enthusiastically he took me through the history of the three digit number and I didn't have the heart to tell him that you could dial 9-1-1 all day long but it would do you no good if your rescuers couldn't reach you before the unthinkable happens.

CHAPTER 27

Just before dinner Teddy came downstairs, stood by my chair and stared at me until I invited him to sit down. I'd meant in the chair opposite, but he crawled over me and squashed his small body next to mine in the oversized armchair. He was a strange little boy, with a pointy face and a sharp thin nose, a miniature version of his dad. For Teddy's sake I hoped his features would soften as he matured.

I smiled at him. "How are you doing, Teddy?"

He shrugged. "Okay, I guess." He stared across the long room in the direction of the kitchen. "Grandpa's in the freezer." Actually, it was a cooler, but there was no need to correct him.

I ruffled his hair which was dirty blonde and resisted my fingers, preferring to follow the whorl of a cowlick on his crown. "Yes, I know."

Who would give him fist bumps now? In an effort to divert his attention from the cooler I asked what he wanted to be when he grew up.

He sat up straighter and declared he was going to be an astronaut and fly to Mars. "Grandpa said I couldn't, but he's dead now so I can." Every cloud has a silver lining, I guess.

Pulling his cell phone out of his pocket he scrolled through his photos until he found *Sojourner*. He said it was launched a long time ago, but it would always be his favourite because it was the first rover to land on Mars. Teddy was telling me about a multi-billionaire's Mars project when Louisa came up and touched my shoulder.

"Evie, can I talk to you for a second. Upstairs, please."

I felt like I'd been summoned to the principal's office.

She unlocked the door to her room, which looked exactly like my room, but a whole lot messier, pushed her inside out jeans to the side of her bed and sat down.

"What's up?" I asked, tossing her PJ bottoms on top of her jeans. The pile teetered and the clothes slipped off the bed.

"I'm worried."

"I'm not surprised. You're supposed to be working tonight, right?"

"No, not about work." She leaned forward, her arms resting on her thighs and said, "It's Katie. there's something off with her…and how she's reacting to the death of her husband."

"Well, I don't think she liked him very much."

"The man is dead and mouldering in the cooler for God's sake. It's as if she's forgotten he's in there"—Louisa glanced at her own little minibar fridge— "which is impossible given that every fridge in this place is jampacked with raw beef or eggs."

"*Mouldering*? Really, Louisa, is that any way for a nurse to talk?"

She shot me a look, she was not in a joking mood. "I don't know Katie well—"

"You don't know her at all."

"—but she's not right."

"Can you blame her? The poor woman goes to bed one night and wakes up the next morning to find her dead husband stretched out on the sofa in front of a blazing fire. That would unnerve anyone."

"Exactly," Louisa picked her *Savage Kitty* T-shirt off the floor, rolled it into a ball and shoved it under her pillow. "That's my point. Shock can make a person act spacey, but she's been acting strange ever since we got here. Remember the fuss when she got lost—"

"She wasn't lost; she was out riding Shadow."

"—and at dinner, she never engaged with Charlie, not unless he engaged with her first, and even then she did so under duress."

"She doesn't have to be congenial just to make him feel good. She played that role for decades. Mirror Ranch is Charlotte's home. Here, Katie can relax, be herself."

Louisa nodded. "Yes, I see that, but still. The other night I found her trying to get into my room. She said her key wasn't working,"

"That could happen to anyone. Every door in the hallway looks the same."

"I don't buy it. Her room is at the other end of the hall with the rest of the family. Why was she trying to get into my room?"

The mirror on the dresser caught Louisa's reflection. Her dark wavy hair bounced on her shoulders as she moved her hands about, emphasizing her point that Katie had been cold to Charlie from the day we'd arrived. "She talks to Bernard more than she talked to Charlie."

Tears glistened in her eyes and I wondered whether Charlie's death had brought back memories of our own grief when our folks died. Mom went first, she had a stroke and was gone in a day, Dad went a few months later. We always thought he'd died of a broken heart. Louisa said broken heart syndrome was a real thing, tako cardio something.

"Everyone grieves differently, I know that." Louisa turned to me and touched my hand. "But I don't think Katie is grieving at all. Neither is the rest of the family, come to think of it."

Louisa had a point. The last twenty-four hours had turned our lives upside down. But the Moore family was acting weird. Death has a way of turning villains into heroes in the eyes of their loved ones. The horrible things they did while they were alive turn into charming *remember when* stories after they're dead. Was there nothing about Charlie Moore that they could remember with fondness?

I bounced up higher on the bed so I could lean against the headboard. "They're not like us, Louisa. We're just ordinary people living ordinary lives. Charlie started out ordinary but shot up into the stratosphere and took his family with him. We're in awe of their jets and yachts and mansions, but to them, its just another day. That kind of money changes people in ways we'll never understand."

"Damn it," Louisa said as she slid off her bed and got tangled up in the clothing lying on the floor. She picked up her jeans, then turned them right side in and lay them on her bed. "The Moore's may be billionaires but even billionaires have feelings, and I'm telling you there's something going on with Katie and it's got me spooked."

Charlotte asked me the strangest question a week before she married Jay.

She was standing on a podium in the middle of Francine Martin's bridal shop. Francine was irritated that Charlotte had lost weight and the bodice of her strapless gown sagged. It would have to be completely reworked. Repositioning those tiny seed pearls would take forever.

I'd put it down to nerves until Charlotte said, Mom, does Dad like Jay?

Of course he likes Jay, why would you ask me such a silly question.

She said she'd asked Charlie whether it was possible, given that Jay's parents were coming all the way from New Delhi, to include some traditional Indian elements in the wedding, nothing over the top, no grand entrances on elephants or anything, perhaps something simple, a few Indian side dishes and marigolds to symbolize happiness.

Charlie's response: Absolutely not. There would be no squawking sitars or tatty orange flowers littering the marble floors of the Banff Springs Hotel. He was paying a fortune for *a traditional wedding. Elegant and refined. Need he remind her who was on the guest list?*

She said indeed he should because her guest list had been whittled down to twenty people, the remaining two hundred and eight were people she wouldn't recognize in a police line up.

(That was a clever jab on her part—one of Charlie's friends had just been convicted of securities fraud).

Charlotte said she thought Charlie was racist.

What nonsense, Charlotte, I'd said.

Later when I told Charlie about our conversation he became very angry, saying he would not apologise for wanting his baby girl to marry someone more to his liking.

When I asked him to describe who this ideal someone would be, he replied: the male equivalent of Elise, Robson's wife.

Pretty little pale blond Elise.

CHAPTER 28

I tugged on the blanket. Reluctantly, Louisa let me have another two inches. It was the middle of the day and somehow I'd managed to doze off in the middle of yet another shark movie despite the scary music and screaming sunbathers. Now the shark mayhem was taking place at a ski resort. Very odd.

"Did the heartthrob guy get away?" I asked.

Louisa looked at me, bleary-eyed. "I have no idea." She yawned. "As spa weekends go, this one's a bust. Not as bad as that shark infested ski resort, but a bust nevertheless."

"That's what happens when they give you a deep discount. We couldn't possibly afford this place otherwise."

I tallied up the amenities and Louisa agreed Mirror Ranch would cost a fortune to run. "Guests who pay top dollar expect the very best, even from a place that bills itself as rustic. Gourmet food and expensive wine, to say nothing of Jay's grandiose expansion plans—Charlotte says he's thinking about putting on a mini-rodeo—all that costs money."

"True," Louisa picked up her tablet and turned down

the screaming. "It's a good thing Charlotte is rich. She can bankroll Jay's dreams."

I shook my head. People think the children of billionaires are also billionaires in their own right, when in fact they're living on Daddy's credit.

"Charlie's the one with the fortune, his estate would be complicated, it could take years to sort it out before probate is granted. In the meantime Charlotte has to pay the bills. The vet bills alone would choke a horse." Louisa rolled her eyes at my inadvertent pun.

Last night when Parker and I were searching the barn for Charlie, I'd combed through the tack room. The horse meds, the food, saddles, bridles and other riding paraphernalia. The cost of keeping one horse would be high, six would be astronomical. I thought of Quincy, he has joint problems, his vet bills would bankrupt most people.

"We should call Quincy tonight." That's one of Louisa's superpowers; she can read my mind.

"Okay we can try." Cell service was still spotty. I glanced out of the window, slashes of light flickered behind gray clouds. Lightening? "It's not like we've got anything better to do before dinner."

She paused the shark movie while I dialled Madeline on Facetime. "Louisa," I whispered, "whatever you do, don't say any word about Charlie being dead."

"Charlie Moore is *dead*?" Madeline's face filled the screen. Behind her on his tall perch Rupert the cockatiel flapped his wings and mimicked her voice: *more dead, more dead.*

"Jesus, Madeline, be quiet!"

She lifted her chin and fixed those icy green eyes on me. No one tells Madeline to be quiet. I flashed an apologetic smile and said we wanted to talk to Quincy.

She said she wouldn't produce the dog until we told her what was going on with Charlie Moore.

"You're holding the dog hostage? Really, Madeline, how could you stoop so low?" My feeble attempts to shame her had never worked in the past and it didn't work now.

"Damn right," she replied. "Unless you tell me what's going on, the dog gets it."

Dog gets it, dog gets it. Rupert squawked, sounding more like a Mafia thug than Madeline did.

Louisa tipped her head, *for God's sake, tell her.*

With a resigned sigh, I explained the horrific events of the last twenty-four hours and stressed that Madeline could not say a word, not one word, about Charlie's demise to anyone. The family had not yet issued a statement, they wanted to hold off until the police arrived, but the delay could put them in a difficult legal position if the news got out and the rumour mill messed with the share price.

With a *pfft* sound, Madeline dismissed my concern. Of course she wouldn't say anything, what did I take her for.

"Other than a dog napper, you mean?"

She ignored the comment and pelted us with questions. What happened? Was it an accident? Had he been drinking?

"Drinking?" I interrupted. "Why would you say that?"

Madeline explained that everyone knew Charlie was a drunk. I reminded her that her 'everyone' was not the same as our 'everyone.' For one thing, our 'everyone' were significantly poorer. That being said, I had to agree, Charlie Moore liked his booze.

"Liked his booze is putting it mildly," Madeline replied. "Did he show you his silver flask, the one that some billionaire sheik gave him? He's ridiculously proud of that flask and whips it out every chance he gets. I've never met such a gauche and uncouth billionaire. Tacky doesn't begin to describe it."

As Madeline talked, my mind went back to my conversation with Parker. She'd mentioned Charlie's health issues and I'd assumed he'd died of a heart attack or stroke brought on by exertion and exposure to the elements. The wind and the rain last night were like nothing I'd ever seen before. It wasn't called a bomb cyclone for nothing. Now I wondered if, in a drunken haze, he'd tripped over a rock and fractured his skull.

If it was common knowledge he packed a flask of booze everywhere he went, why did the family allow him to go out into that miserable storm? Didn't they see the risk? A little voice in my brain said: *Of course they saw the risk, but they couldn't stop him. What Charlie wants, Charlie gets.*

I passed the phone to Louisa. "He's your dog, you talk to him." Behind Madeline there came a frantic yipping and scrabbling of feet. Quincy was desperate to get to Louisa and I was itching to get off this phone call. Something had occurred to me.

CHAPTER 29

Aw, do we have to?" Louisa moaned after she hung up the phone and I informed her we were going for a nice walk before dinner. "The sharks just invaded the ski chalet. Don't you want to see what happens?"

"Everyone dies. Now let's go."

She pulled the blanket over her head and refused to move. I pushed her to the edge of the bed.

"You coming?" I flexed my fingers into her back.

"Nope." Her muffled reply.

One tiny little push and she went over the side and landed, squealing, on the floor. "All right, all right! If you're going to be beastly about it."

"The fresh air will do you good." I stepped out onto the balcony to feel the temperature. The wind was making a shushing sound, like waves rolling onto a sandy beach, and it was still raining. "Wear something warm." I pulled a jacket over my heavy hoodie.

Soon we were outside, marching down the north-south trail toward the stables, I was trying to ignore the muscle pinging in my ankle. If I said anything Louisa would bundle me back up to the Lodge and slap an ice pack on it.

I edged closer to Louisa, hooking my arm through hers and asked her to describe how Charlie looked when she and Jay found him.

"Why? You saw him."

"Humour me."

Louisa said she and Jay were drenched when they stumbled upon the body. Soaked to the skin from crawling through sagging pine boughs and tangled bracken fern.

"Jay was just ahead of me. His flashlight was bouncing around. When suddenly he yelled: *He's here, I've got him.*" Louisa's face became still. In her line of work she's seen many dead people, but somehow this was different.

"How was Charlie positioned? Did you touch him?"

"Well, of course I touched him. How else was I going to check his vital signs? You saw how he was positioned. On his back, splayed across the path like he'd been poleaxed. No one else touched him until you guys arrived and carried him down to the Lodge."

No, I thought, that wasn't necessarily true. Jay reached the body first; Louisa couldn't be certain that Jay hadn't touched him in the ten or twenty seconds it took her to catch up to him.

"Did you check his pockets?"

"For what? His ID? Really Evie, why on earth would I check his pockets?" Her tone was sharp and impatient. We were almost at the stables. Then she paused, a small smile on her face. "Oh, wait, I get it now. You're wondering if Charlie had the flask on him, if he'd been drinking and was too drunk to find his way back to the Lodge."

"Something like that."

By the time we reached the barn we were both reeling from the exertion of fighting the wind all the way down here. It blew in spurts, making it difficult to stay upright.

Louisa leaned against the stable wall while I hauled the barn door open. The comforting smell of horses and hay greeted us as we stepped inside.

Louisa's little horse bobbed its head when she said hello. I clucked at Shadow who flicked his ears to acknowledge me: I was okay but no match for Katie.

"Come on," I said, "let's check the tack room."

Upstairs I glanced around. Something about this room bothered me, but I couldn't put my finger on it. "Louisa, what do you see?"

She narrowed her eyes at me. "You dragged me all the way down here to look at the tack room?"

"Humour me," I said, making myself comfortable on a small wooden chair next to a beat-up desk in the corner of the room. "Pretend you're a tour guide, tell me what you see."

She shook her head in disbelief then turned to stare at the far wall. "Blankets folded on open shelves, saddles, reins and whatever that leather thing is, hanging from a hook on the wall, a small table…do you really want me to go on"— I waved my hand, indicating yes I did— "a small table piled with riding paraphernalia."

She turned to look at the end wall. "A big metal cabinet, waist high. Over that what looks like a large medicine cabinet with a clip board hanging from a nail in the wall next to it." She turned again, "On the other wall…hold on." She turned back to face the medicine cabinet. "That's odd."

"What's odd?"

She went over to the medicine cabinet. The metal door didn't sit properly in its frame and resisted her effort to open it. She tugged harder on the round metal knob until it popped open with a loud screech. Below us, one of the horses whinnied softly. The door screeched again when she forced it shut.

She stepped back and directed my attention to the blue and white sticker plastered in the centre of the metal door.

"The cabinet is full of all sorts of controlled substances. It should be locked. Why isn't it locked?" She went around me and pulled the clipboard off its nail. The pencil tied to the clipboard's metal bracket swung around in tiny circles.

"Look." She showed me the top page. "This is a list of all the pertinent medical information any vet would require: the name of the horse, the date, dosage and type of medication administered. It's all recorded here as part of the horse's health record. These are powerful drugs. You wouldn't want to overdose the animal." She scanned the list and shook her head slowly. "It's like at the hospital. The meds cupboard should be locked at all times."

That's what had been bothering me about the tack room. I hadn't twigged to it last night when Parker and I searched the barn for Charlie, but later when Katie dragged Charlotte and me back to check on Shadow, Charlotte seemed surprised to discover one ketamine vial was missing.

"I think this is important," I said to Louisa.

She shot me a skeptical glance as she hung the clipboard on its wobbly nail. "Why?"

Of course I hadn't the slightest idea.

CHAPTER 30

Katie entered the dining room and went straight to Charlie's chair. She raised her chin and gave us a calm smile after she sat down. The message was clear, this was her rightful place. It always had been.

The rest of the family had not yet arrived. I glanced at AJ and smiled. We'd have a ringside view of their reactions as they entered the dining room and discovered it didn't matter who Charlie's successor was. Katie was the head of the family now.

Parker and Charlotte entered and kissed their mother on the cheek before sitting down, apparently comfortable with the new normal in Mooreland. Elise hesitated on the threshold, then settled herself and the children in their usual places, leaving Robson standing in the doorway, looking irritated and confused.

"Do come in, Robson," Katie said, pointing to her old chair next to Elise, "we've been waiting for you."

When he passed behind Teddy, the little boy raised his hand for a fist bump, but Robson was too flummoxed to notice.

Bernard and Opal talked quietly as they served the

meal and the room filled with the clink of cutlery and the sound of small voices as the children prattled on about any random thing that popped into their heads.

Solemnly, Teddy declared, "Grandad wasn't a lucky pig."

His mother gagged on a bite of chicken. "I beg your pardon?"

Charlotte reached across the table, patting Elise's hand. "It's okay, I think Teddy's referring to Lucky the Pig."

Mirror Ranch was an organic enterprise, Charlotte explained, almost everything they prepared for their guests came from their own gardens and greenhouses, or local organic suppliers. The chickens were free range and the pigs didn't eat slop; they were fed nutritious food free from unnecessary antibiotics and growth hormones. It sounded like an idyllic existence until you remembered that the whole point of this exercise was to ensure the pigs were nice and plump when we feasted on them.

Last year a pack of wolves broke into the pigpen and slaughtered the entire herd, but one. In the melee a tiny piglet managed to get stuck under a box at the back of the pen. "We named him Lucky and decided to keep him as a pet. How could we butcher him after what he'd gone through. Now he's one of our star attractions."

Amelia added that Lucky was just a year old and already he weighed two hundred pounds. "He's going to be as big as this house when he's an old man pig."

From the time Lucky was little Charlotte let the children walk him in the meadow. He was very docile and loved the attention.

For me this entire conversation was jarring, like a piano key out of tune. We were chuckling about Lucky's near-death experience when Charlie Moore's very dead body was wrapped in a blanket in the cooler in the kitchen.

After dinner AJ corralled me in the dining room and said Keith wanted to talk to us in the snug, the cozy, semi-private area behind the bar.

Glancing across the room I caught a glimpse of Keith tucked into a dark corner of the small mahogany enclosed space. He was sitting on a padded leather bench, his elbows up on the tall wooden table in front of him. The room was crowded with clunky wooden furniture, more like a miniature Irish pub than a western saloon, but nevertheless, it looked welcoming.

As we approached the snug, AJ spoke softly in my ear. "Keith thinks we should take advantage of our downtime to revisit the future of the firm."

"Does he now. Only Keith would consider being stuck at a resort with a dead body as downtime."

Keith smiled as AJ and I entered the small room and pulled two padded stools out from under the other side of the table. He waited until we were settled, then embarked on what sounded to me like a scripted speech.

I tried. I really did. But when he started repeating the spiel our facilitators threw at us for two solid days my mind drifted to something Charlie had said. *Some are born to be horses, others are born to ride.* It was part of his ridiculous argument that all growth was good. When I objected, he told me to discuss the 'opportunity' with my partners. At the time I thought Charlie was trying to undermine my confidence by implying my partners knew more about our business than I did. Now…

"Wait." My fingers drummed the tabletop. "Did Charlie Moore make you an offer of some kind? An opportunity too good to refuse?"

AJ's eyes bounced from me to Keith. He's quick. He put it together right then and there. "What was all that business at dinner last night? When Charlie talked about a man's word being his bond and toasted you for being an honourable man who keeps his word?"

"I, ah, I…" Keith stammered.

"Oh Keith," I reached across the table to grab his hands but he pulled them away, hiding them in his lap. "What did you do?"

CHAPTER 31

Keith turned an awful shade of gray, like a bottle of Elmer's paste that's been stuck in a child's desk too long.

"For Christ's sake, Keith, answer her." AJ leaned across the scruffy wooden table. "What did you do? Did you make a deal with Charlie without having the decency to talk to us first?"

Keith brought his hands to his face and rubbed his cheeks hard. "I'm sorry, this is coming out all wrong."

"Fine," I crossed my arms. "Any time you're ready, we're all ears."

Keith slumped back on the hard bench. "All I ask is that you hear me out before you hang me from the rafters."

"Um, excuse me." Charlotte popped her head around the mahogany screen separating the snug from the bar and asked if we were all right. *Were we arguing so loud that everyone could hear us?* She gave us a polite smile—even in this appalling situation she was the gracious host—and asked if we'd like something more to eat, perhaps something to drink? I shook my head, AJ mumbled there was no need and Keith just stared at her, pale and glassy eyed. Charlotte ducked her head and disappeared behind the mahogany screen without another word.

In that tiny interval of less than five minutes, the switch that controls my temper flipped. My last shred of patience snapped. The words came out like bullets, hard and fast.

"Keith, admit it. Charlie made you a very generous offer and you accepted it. Hello Charlie-Moneybags-Moore, goodbye Evie and AJ. Been nice knowing you. Don't let the door hit you on the way out."

Keith stared at me in horror, then unleashed a torrent of words I'd never heard him use before. In the course of his diatribe, he confirmed that yes, Charlie *did* suggest an opportunity, we could sell BLV to MMG. It would become MMG's legal-regulatory flagship on the clean energy side of the business.

But no, he was not abandoning AJ and me. He was stunned we'd suggest such a thing— "It's quite the opposite, in fact." We'd *all* join MMG as consultants.

"Cogs in their corporate wheel, subjected to their up-or-out annual review process, how nice." I couldn't keep the sarcasm out of my voice.

Keith motored on without acknowledging my snarky interjection. He'd told Charlie he wouldn't agree to anything without discussing it with us first. We were equal partners after all. "We all go or nobody goes." He flicked his eyes from me to AJ. "But before I brought Charlie's offer to you two, I had to process it first."

Well, of course he did. Glaciers move faster than Keith does.

AJ cleared his throat. "Have you processed it now?"

"No," Keith said with a sheepish look on his face.

AJ groaned and leaned back to peer around the

mahogany screen. "Where's Charlotte. I think I need that drink after all."

Keith grinned. But his eyes didn't. This puzzled me. He'd kept Charlie's offer a secret for days. He should be relieved to have it out in the open and yet his eyes were troubled. Something else going on.

I reached across the small table and this time he let me take his hand. "Keith, are you okay? Is everything all right?"

Another artificially bright smile. "I'm fine. Of course I'm fine. We're all fine."

AJ stood up. "Buddy, if there's anything you need, anything at all, all you have to do is ask. You want to go home, I'll get us home." I had a fleeting image of AJ grabbing an axe and hacking his way through the downed trees carrying Keith on his back.

Keith laughed. "Sit down, AJ. Everything is under control." His face was still pale, he took a deep breath and said, "But you know, that conversation with Charlie got me thinking. About the future."

And that's when I realized this entire conversation had not never been about BLV's future. It was about Keith's future and whether it would be with or without BLV.

I came around the small table, drew Keith up off the leather bench and gave him a long hug. Unlike AJ, Keith is not a huggy kind of guy, but he hugged me back.

"Guys, I'm exhausted." I nudged Keith out of the snug. AJ followed us. "Let's put Charlie's so-called opportunity out of our minds. We can sort it all out when we get back to the city. For all we know Charlie's offered died with him. Okay?"

Keith nodded and loped up the stairs, AJ hung back and caught my arm. "You're not seriously considering Charlie's proposal, are you?"

I put a reassuring smile on my face. "It's okay AJ. Trust me."

Of course I had no idea what I was talking about, but I would once I figured out what Keith was hiding.

————

Halfway up to my room I noticed Parker standing in the shadows at the top of the staircase. Her arms were resting on top of the rail and she was staring down into the lobby, so lost in thought that she didn't notice me until I was almost on top of her. When I asked her how she was doing, she replied she was okay. *Everyone says they're okay and they're all lying.*

Her eyes drifted from my face, back down to Amelia who was skipping around the red leather sofa where Charlie had lain just a few hours ago. She was humming *Ring around the rosy.* A nursery rhyme about the Great Plague. If she wasn't five I'd think she was being clever.

"Parker, earlier on you mentioned Charlie had health issues…?"

"Yes," she replied, "Dad had two heart attacks, the doctors put in stents after the last one and he said he felt like a new man. The doctors said if he took care of himself, drank less, exercised more, he'd live a long and healthy life."

Her lips twitched. "Drink less. Good luck telling Charlie Moore to drink less. Dad fancied himself a modern-day Ernest Hemingway. Work hard and play hard, that was his motto. Look where that got him, dead before he could pass on the company."

Parker made it sound as if Charlie chose to die simply to spite her.

"Was he drinking more than usual yesterday?" He'd

looked pretty glassy eyed to me when he entered the dining room.

Parker tipped her head. "A bit maybe, but not much. Yesterday was like any other day. Here's what you need to understand about Charlie Moore. He was a functioning alcoholic. Plain and simple. Or as Mom puts it, 'a nasty, slobbering drunk.' She got herself sober and it infuriated her that Dad couldn't do the same. He tried to hide his addiction by stashing booze everywhere, in the office, around the house.

"He packed around a little silver flask in case he needed a top up. People whispered about it behind his back, they thought he was showing off—it was a gift from MBS or whatever that guy's name is—but it was his life preserver, right there in his pocket, in case he needed it to get through the day."

As Parker talked, an idea took root in my brain. I needed Louisa again and she wasn't going to like it.

JOURNAL

I used to think I was going mad.
My meds kept getting screwed up. Pink, white, and blue
tablets nestled in their little plastic compartments. Three
at breakfast, four at bedtime. How hard is that. And yet,
Charlie says he's worried I'm having so much trouble keeping
them straight.

Charlie said it was neurological and hustled me off to see
Dr. Gibson. Dear old Dr. G. He's the reason I'm popping so
many pills in the first place. Pills to sleep, pills to wake up.
Pills to flatten my mood, pills to control my blood pressure
and to deal with ailments I didn't even know I had.

Dr. G. suggested a dementia test. Nothing to worry about,
he said, purely routine. To get a baseline reading.

I passed with flying colours, but he made me take the test
again and again over the next few months. I took so many
MOCA tests I could name twenty animals in alphabetical
order in under thirty seconds. Hell, I could probably do it
backwards if I had to.

It took me a while to understand what Charlie was up to.
Then I figured out the pattern. The MMG board meets once a

quarter. A week or so after the board meeting Charlie takes me to see Dr. G.

Charlie isn't worried about my mental state. He's giving me a warning. If I don't stop asking awkward questions about MMG's *business, he'll get me out of the way…to a lovely sanitorium in the Swiss Alps.*

Dr. G. was Charlie's physician long before he became mine. If Charlie told him to prepare the paperwork, Dr. G would do it in a heartbeat.

CHAPTER 32

When I returned to my room, I found Louisa asleep on my bed. She was slumped against a pile of pillows, clutching a half-empty bag of potato chips. Oblivious to the shark soundtrack—*da dah, da dah, da dah*—blasting from the iPad lying face up on her lap. Someone was about to die, again, but she was too far gone to care. Her wavy hair fanned across the pillow, her mouth was slightly open and she was making that strange bleating noise she makes when she's almost but not quite snoring.

People say we look alike and while it's true that we have the same dark hair, fair complexion and runner's build, I don't see the resemblance. Probably because I'm fourteen months older than her and have spent my entire life telling her I'm the original and she's the copy. It drives her crazy.

I slid onto the bed next to her and settled in to watch the next movie in the *Sharknado* extravaganza. We wouldn't be going anywhere for a couple of hours.

By eleven o'clock the Lodge was quiet. No one had walked down the corridor for at least an hour. Time to move. I leaned over and eased Louisa's iPad off her lap.

"I was watching that," she mumbled.

"Your eyes were closed."

"It's *Sharknado*, I always watch it with my eyes closed."

The bed creaked as she fluffed the pillows behind her back and sat up taller. "I've been thinking about your question of earlier today."

"Which question was that?"

"On our walk to the barn. You asked about Charlie's body, what it looked like when Jay and I found him on the trail." She picked up the bag of potato chips, peeked inside, then set it on the bedside table. "I did notice something, but forgot about it until now."

She gazed at me with calm brown eyes. "If I tell you, you have to promise not to go all weird on me again."

"What on earth are you talking about?"

"You know exactly what I'm talking about. In situations like this if something is off, even a tiny bit, you blow it all out of proportion into something nefarious—"

"For God's sake, Louisa, tell me or I'll send you back to your room and you can have Sharknado nightmares all night long."

The look she gave me took me right back to when we were kids. How could I suggest such a thing? A big sister is supposed to protect her little sister. We both knew I didn't mean it, but still I felt a twinge of guilt.

Slowly, she explained that when she'd examined Charlie's body on the rain-soaked path, she'd noticed his belly was distended. "I hadn't spotted it before, he was such a big, broad shouldered guy."

"Doesn't everyone get a pot belly when they get older?"

"Well, sure, but this was different. His belly was hard and veined. The kind of thing you'd expect with someone who is a hardcore alcoholic."

"He *was* a hardcore alcoholic. He carried a silver flask

with him everywhere he went. Just in case he needed a drink. I wonder what happened to it."

She gave me a blank look.

"Louisa my dear, we've got work to do."

———

At eleven-thirty, after I was positive everyone was safely tucked up in bed, Louisa and I were standing in the middle of Bernard's kitchen, facing the walk-in cooler. Outside, the wind and the rain tapped against the black windows. The room was dark except for a feeble pool of light cast by a small gooseneck lamp on Bernard's desk.

"Are you sure we should be doing this?" Louisa whispered as I adjusted my grip on the stainless-steel latch and gave it a yank. The handle clicked, but the door stayed firmly shut.

"Damn, it's locked."

"There." She shone her phone light on the door handle and pointed to a sliding button.

This time I pressed the button with my thumb as I pulled the heavy door toward me and it swung open with ease. Florescent lights flickered inside, making a tinking sound as they came on. I turned to Louisa. *We're in*. She looked haggard, dark lines were etched under her eyes. I'm sure I looked no better.

Quickly we got our bearings. Stainless steel shelves holding a few empty white plastic trays ran along the side walls. High on the back wall, a line of fans whirred steadily. And there, at the base of the wall, was Charlie, lying on his back on a thin padded quilt, covered by a couple of Hudson's Bay blankets. I shuddered. From this day forward whenever I see a gayly striped blanket I'll associate it with a corpse.

"Come on, let's get this over with." I nudged Louisa in front of me as we approached the body. She knelt beside him and I folded the top of the blanket down so I could see Charlie's face. God knows why. It's not as if we'd stuffed someone else into the cooler.

Charlie's face looked waxy and his eyes were closed. As I eased the blanket back over his face my hand touched his cheek and his mouth fell open. "Christ!" I leapt up, stumbling over Louisa. "Hurry up,' I whispered loudly. "Do it." And edged back away from her.

She glanced up at me and said, "Do what, exactly?"

"I don't know. Look at his belly. Find out what killed him."

"Don't be silly Evie, I'm a nurse, not a pathologist. I can't tell you anything other than he's dead."

"You've been trained in these things."

"What, poking dead people?"

"Yes, poking dead people! Take a closer look. You thought his belly was strange. Is there anything else out of the ordinary?"

She pointed to the matted blood in his hair, saying he may have stumbled and hit his head, then she lifted his shirt which was stiff with dried mud and said his beer belly, for want of a better word, confirmed that Charlie was a heavy drinker.

"See how the stomach is distended and squishy. The veins are enlarged and close to the surface. It's symptomatic of long-term alcohol abuse which leads to all sorts of diseases, cancer, liver damage, stomach ulcers."

Her hand hesitated over his stomach, as if she wanted to touch him, but knew she shouldn't. "I wonder..."

"What?" I tore my eyes away from the fans spinning

slowly on the wall and forced myself to glance down at the body. "What do you wonder?"

"We found him on his back. See these large purple splotches on his front. They could indicate internal bleeding." Gently she released the edge of Charlie's shirt and it settled back down onto his belly. Then she stood up.

"Internal bleeding, meaning what?"

"Well," she said looking down at him with sympathy. "If he had internal bleeding that could mean a ruptured ulcer, a ruptured spleen, a lacerated liver. Any number of things. The poor man, the pain would have been excruciating."

The memory of his face when we found him on the path came to me, blank and slick with rain, sightless eyes staring up at the drooping pine boughs. Did he know he was dying? What were his final thoughts? Family or business?

"What would have triggered the bleed?"

"Any number of things. If he tripped, the impact of the fall. Or maybe it was just his time. Like I said, I'm not a pathologist." She rubbed her arms as if she were cold. "Let's get out of here." And took two steps toward the door.

"No wait," I caught her elbow and turned her to face Charlie's body. "Does he have the flask on him?"

"What does it matter? We already know he's an alcoholic."

"If he was drinking on the trail that might explain something." What, I didn't know. It just felt like it mattered.

"You want to rifle through his pockets? Be my guest." She gestured toward the body.

I shuddered again. "Aw, come on. I'm a lawyer, you're a nurse, you're used to touching dead people."

She took a long slow breath and released it before grudgingly returning to the body. Louisa has the worst luck. Charlie was wearing chinos, the old fashioned kind with pockets everywhere. One by one she felt them, occasionally dipping a finger into a side pocket that felt promising but yielded nothing but crumpled tissues and gum wrappers.

"No flask. There, are you satisfied?"

We were almost at the door when we hear a loud click. The stainless-steel door, which we'd left slightly ajar clicked shut. On the inside, the door was smooth metal, flat and shiny. There was no doorknob or handle. To get out, you had to push.

Louisa pushed. The door didn't budge. She pushed again. It was locked.

CHAPTER 33

O h dear God!" I slammed my shoulder into the door. Once, twice, three times. We were trapped in what suddenly felt like a very small space. With a dead man. "Oh God." Terror was rising up into my throat.

"Evie, stop," Gently, Louisa shifted me out of her way. "Take a deep breath. We're fine. There's got to be a release switch around here somewhere." I stepped back while she turned on her phone light to augment the miserable fluorescents.

"There." She pointed to a large red plastic button on the wall next to the door.

"Hit it, hit it!" I tried to stay calm but my voice was shaking. Too many memories.

She hit the button. But the door didn't open.

"Try the lever." I pointed a trembling finger at the white plastic lever under the red button. It was pointing straight up. "Rotate it."

Louisa turned the lever clockwise, smiled at me, and pushed. It still didn't open.

"Shit," she said.

"Turn it the other way." My chest was thrumming. I had to get out.

She pivoted the lever counterclockwise and I barreled into the door. It flew open, hit something and bounced back, hammering into my shoulder as I charged out.

"Shit!" A loud howl of pain from the other side of the door.

Louisa scrambled out behind me almost bowling over the shadowy figure stumbling into the weak glow of Bernard's gooseneck lamp.

"What the hell do you think you're doing?" Jay's voice. He groaned and pinched the bridge of his nose. "I think you broke it."

If law has taught me anything it's this: When cornered, the best defence is a good offence. I squared my shoulders and glared at him. "I could ask you the same thing,"

"I'm getting a snack for Charlotte"—I glanced at his hands, they were empty— "wait, I don't owe you an explanation. I have the right to be here. This is my place. What are you doing here?" He stood a little taller and that's when I noticed he was wearing jeans and a heavy sweater. Not the outfit of someone popping out of bed to get his wife a glass of warm milk.

"Sorry about your face," I said, casting about for a plausible explanation of why Louisa and I were in the cooler. There wasn't one. So I went with the truth.

"Listen Jay, I understand Charlie was a big drinker. I thought he might be carrying a flask."

"So?"

"So, it might have a bearing on how he died." Then again it might not. And it certainly didn't explain why we were creeping around in the cooler looking for it.

Gingerly, Jay raised both hands and touched the sides

of his nose, this brought tears to his eyes and he blinked rapidly for a few seconds. Behind us the cooler fans buzzed and the radiator on the far wall woke up with a loud clunk, making all of us jump. I stepped out of the entrance to the cooler and gently closed the door. The metallic click was less frightening on this side of the door.

"Did you find it?" Jay's anger had dissipated.

I shook my head, and his eyes travelled up and down my body and then Louisa's as if he thought we were trying to smuggle it out of the kitchen in our underwear.

"That's too bad." He leaned against Bernard's desk and admitted that he too was searching for it. He knew the flask wasn't on Charlie's body, he'd checked right after he and Robson put the body into the cooler. He thought someone may have found it on the path and brought it back to the kitchen.

"Why are you looking for it?" Louisa asked.

With a long sigh he explained that it was a matter of family pride.

"I'm not following you," I said, thinking how strange it was that we were having this conversation. It was almost as if we were getting used to the idea of a dead guy lying on the other side of the cooler door.

"Charlie was a legend," Jay said. "You've seen the stories. Local boy makes good. A shrewd businessman and mega-philanthropist, a pillar of society. There's nothing the world likes better than to see a great man fall. Can you imagine the gossip if it came out that Charlie Moore, outdoorsman extraordinaire, was so pissed he got lost in the woods and died of exposure? What a pathetic end to the Charlie Moore saga. The family has to protect his reputation."

"You're worried about Charlie's reputation?" Madeline's

words rang in my ears—everyone knew Charlie Moore was a drunk—there was no reputation to protect.

Jay gave a small shrug. "His standing in the community may not matter to you, but it matters to the family." *Really?* As far as I could tell the only thing that mattered to the family was who was going to run the company now that Charlie was dead.

"Evie, let's go." Louisa tugged at my sleeve.

As we left the kitchen, she called over her shoulder to Jay. "Put some ice on your nose to keep it from swelling. You don't want people thinking you've been in a bar fight." Then she turned to me and lowered her voice. "Seems like an awful lot of fuss about a flask and Charlie Moore's legacy."

CHAPTER 34

Tuesday

Early the following morning I was pounding down the north-south trail. It was a perfect day for a run. The bomb cyclone had passed, right on schedule just like the meteorologists had predicted. The violent wind and pounding rain left the earth smelling fresh. The morning sun shimmered in the pale blue sky, looking almost iridescent.

Whether it was lack of sleep or the body in the cooler, I needed this run to settle my nerves. Instead it woke up my ankle. Unlike AJ who (like every other man I know) believes the best way to deal with an injury is to "push through it" I'd coddled my ankle for a day. It wasn't enough and soon I was half limping, half jogging down the path.

When I reached the gate I took a moment to catch my breath. Overhead, something creaked like an old door on rusty hinges. The silvery N in the MIRROR RANCH sign was hanging by one nail. A sudden blast of wind would knock it off into the cattails growing in the gully beside the road. Another job for Jay. Was he really happy here mending fences and repairing roofs after the glamour and excitement of MMG?

Bernard and Opal were preparing breakfast when I came through the front door ninety minutes later. From the dimly lit dining room came the sound of a conversation. Amelia was sitting at the mahogany table talking to herself.

"Hey kiddo, whatcha doing up so early?" I stopped and watched her from the doorway.

Startled, she snatched a piece of paper off the tabletop and shoved it in her lap, where it rested for a moment before sliding off onto the floor.

"Nothing," she said, her eyes fixed on the stubby, chewed up pencil sitting on the table in front of her. What was left of its eraser was scattered across the table in crumbs.

Everyone knows that when a kid says they're doing nothing, they're up to something. It had been distressing couple of days and I didn't want Amelia to think I was going to scold her for a silly little misdemeanor so I joined her at the dining room table.

Gently, I said, "Were you writing a letter? You're only five, I didn't know five-year-olds could write." Frankly, I was surprised they could even read.

She hopped off her chair and raced past me up the stairs to her room without another word. *What was that all about?*

Slowly, her stubby pencil rolled off the edge of the table, bounced on the seat of the chair and clattered onto the wooden floor. I crawled under the table to retrieve it and found the piece of paper she'd been scribbling on.

It looked like Charlotte's cartoon map of Mirror Ranch with some additions. Amelia had drawn a big black X in the middle of the meadow across from the conference centre, a dotted pencil line ran along three sides of the property forming a perimeter fence that did not actually exist. The gorge on the fourth side was carpeted with tiny stars. Amelia's drawing looked pretty accurate. She couldn't have drawn this herself.

Holding the map up to the light from the deer horn chandelier, I could see she'd traced the faint lines super-imposed on Charlotte's map: the perimeter fence, the stars in the gorge and a small box in the middle of the meadow. Using the gnarly eraser on the end of the chewed up pencil I rubbed away the graphite revealing what was underneath.

The word *mines* appeared in the star-filled gorge, small circles labelled *tower* appeared at regular intervals along the dotted-line perimeter fence and Amelia's big fat X covered a square in the meadow labelled *chute*. Coal chute? No, Charlotte would never resort to coal at Mirror Ranch. Root cellar? Too far from the garden and the greenhouse. What was that thing?

I went off in search of Charlotte.

———

The delicious scent of maple-cured bacon sizzling in an enormous skillet made my stomach growl as I entered the kitchen. Bernard said Charlotte was in the greenhouse checking the baby tomatoes, but Parker would be along any minute now.

He poured me a cup of coffee and I settled at a small round table close to the back door.

Parker didn't break stride when she sailed into the kitchen, bee-lining straight to the coffee station before joining me at my table.

I placed Amelia's map on the table between us and asked

if Charlotte was planning on beefing up security at Mirror Ranch. "It looks like a fortress."

Parker stared at Amelia's drawing, then frowned. "I don't understand." Behind us Bernard cracked more eggs into a skillet and took the bacon off the heat.

"Check out the chutes, turrets and those star shaped things in the gorge. Any of that look familiar to you?"

Bernard appeared with our breakfast plates. His eye catching on Amelia's map. "Well, I'll be damned. He's really going to do it."

Parker reached for a slice of toast. "Who's really going to do what?"

Bernard pulled up a chair and explained that Charlie and Robson had been exploring the idea of turning Mirror Ranch into a doomsday bunker for billionaires.

Parker coughed, grabbed her coffee cup, gulping and swallowing until she could speak again. "Are you kidding me? Where did you hear that? It's crazy."

Bernard explained that a few days ago, Robson was pitching the idea to Charlie when Opal walked in on their meeting with fresh juice and coffee. They'd barely acknowledged her presence.

"No one sees the servants, we're invisible. According to Robson, doomsday bunkers present a lucrative business opportunity in these unsettled times. With a few tweaks here and there," he waved at the map, "Mirror Ranch would be perfect, it's huge, relatively isolated, and practically self sufficient. MMG would make a killing."

At the other end of the kitchen Opal was maneuvering a large greasy frying pan into the sink. Her back was to us but it was obvious from her stiff posture that she was listening.

Madeline once told me that one of her super rich friends had bought a private island in the Caribbean where they were building a luxury bunker, a bolt hole where they could ride out the fall of civilization. "The poor dear, he's so deluded," Madeline had said. "In the apocalypse who's going to risk their lives bringing the one-percent food and water and medicines, let alone give them facials and massage their pampered little feet?" She had a point.

Bernard tapped the map. "The super rich are bracing for Armageddon. Climate change, the breakdown of society. Fortress Mirror Ranch beats being holed up in an abandoned missile silo in Colorado. At least that's what Robson said."

"Or taking a one-way trip to Mars," I said.

Bernard snorted. "That was one of Robson's selling points. If the end is nigh, there's no time to wait around for Musk to finish building his rocket ship."

Parker shook her head. "Does Charlotte know about this? Is Jay in on it?"

The scent of wet pine wafted into the kitchen on a cool breeze as Charlotte came through the back door. Her copper hair was pulled back in a long ponytail and her cheeks were pink. She looked like an ad for outdoor living. Bernard waved her over, saying Parker had something to show her.

Charlotte deposited a basket of greens with Opal and joined us. "What's up?"

Parker handed her Amelia's map while I explained Amelia had left it behind in the dining room when she darted out.

Charlotte stared at it for a moment. "I don't understand."

Bernard explained the billionaires' bunker business opportunity and I could almost here the wheels whirring in her head as Charlotte's face changed from what-the-hell to I'll-kill-him.

Robson couldn't have time his entry better if he tried.

He sailed into the kitchen looking calm and rested in his brand new khaki slacks and pristine hiking boots. The children tumbled along behind him. As usual, there was no sign of Elise.

"Parker," Robson said as he approached our small table in the corner. "Here's Dad's death notice." He passed her a sheet of paper covered in his handwriting. "The minute the WiFi's is back, it's going out."

Parker ripped it up after reading the first sentence. "Over my dead body."

Charlotte grabbed Amelia's map and shoved it in Robson's face. "What the hell is this?"

CHAPTER 35

Bernard's expression was one of studied neutrality as he drifted back to the island to tend to the raucous children while Charlotte and Parker yelled at their brother.

"Ladies, ladies," Robson said in a patronizing tone, "one at a time, please."

Parker nodded to Charlotte. "You first." Her mouth tightened as she marched out into the lobby.

"Robson, I asked you a question." Charlotte waved Amelia's map in his face. He gave it a cursory glance, then gazed at his children who were shrieking and tugging at Bernard's apron. Robson appeared to be weighing his options: could he BS his way out of this or would he be forced to fess up?

He snatched the drawing out of Charlotte's hand, folded it in half and tucked it into his shirt pocket. "Charlotte, it's exactly what it looks like. A haven for those who can afford sanctuary should the need arise, God forbid."

"Perimeter fencing, turrets, and land mines at the bottom of the gorge? Are you insane?" Charlotte's voice was rising.

Robson shook his head, his fingernails tapping the tabletop. "Not insane, quite the opposite in fact. This is a creative, innovative, and profitable business opportunity." He glanced around the kitchen again, Bernard had settled the children and Opal was carefully drying a heavy skillet. Both of them had their ears cocked, eavesdropping on this conversation.

"Mirror Ranch is not your plaything," Charlotte said. "It belongs to me. So you can take your precious bunker and shove it up your—"

"And Jay." A thin smile crossed Robson's lips. "Jay is also on the title."

Doubt flickered in Charlotte's eyes as she considered the possibility that Jay might be on board with Robson's plan to convert Mirror Ranch into a fortress.

"I don't care. It doesn't matter if Jay's on title or not, he has no authority to proceed with this, this, abomination. Not without my express approval. Which I will never give. Do you understand me?"

Robson sat down, crossing one leg over the other, his thin body looking smaller, more fragile than the harsh words pouring out of his mouth.

"Read your loan agreement, Charlotte. You bought Mirror Ranch with a loan from MMG. I can call that loan on a month's notice any time I want to, but leaving that aside for a moment surely even you realize that the world has become a nasty place. A lot of extremely successful people are nervous about their personal security. The mob is getting restive, crying the blues about the one percent. You've heard them, they always want more. When everything goes to hell in a handbasket you can bet on it, they'll be coming for us."

Some men are horses, so others can ride. Charlie's words. What happens when the horses refuse to be ridden any longer?

"Stable communities"—Robson was in full bore, sales pitch mode now— "are popping up here and there. There's a very nice prototype thirty miles outside of New York City. A high end, self sufficient farm, like Mirror Ranch only smaller. It's a niche market, Charlotte, just waiting to take off. You should be thanking me. Whoever gets in on the ground floor will make a killing."

"Really?" The word popped out of my mouth before I could stop myself. "The uber rich could use their money to help save civilization but they'd rather capitalize on its demise and then hide away until Armageddon blows over? And just how are these rich doomsday preppers going to keep the starving mobs at bay?" Visions of vigilante bands roaming the countryside Mad Max style came to mind.

Robson looked at me as if I were an imbecile. "The cost of armed security is factored into the price. Ex-Navy Seals, SAS. Guarding Mirror Ranch will be a cake walk compared to a tour of duty in Afghanistan."

Surely he wasn't serious. "Mercenaries have families, husbands, wives, kids, parents, siblings. Are you going to shelter their families too? Because if you don't your guards will slaughter you in your beds before they'll abandon their families on the wrong side of the fence."

I wondered why I was bothering to have this ridiculous conversation. Robson and his cronies lived on a different planet where everything has a price, even love.

He flicked a hand at me as if I were a mosquito buzzing around his head and returned to his sales pitch: unique growth opportunity, billionaires running scared with money to burn. "MMG will give them peace of mind…for a price. Mirror Ranch will be our prototype, the first of many sanctuaries."

Charlotte leaned closer and tapped the map which was

still in Robson's shirt pocket. "I'm only going to say this once, Robson. No one, least of all you, is going to take Mirror Ranch away from me." Then she turned and stalked out the back door.

Robson shrugged then caught sight of Parker in the lobby. He called out to her. "I showed you the press release as a courtesy, I'm not accepting any changes. It's going out the way it is."

Parker returned to the kitchen and sat down at the little table across from him. "Robson, Robson, Robson." She sounded almost sad. "Will you never learn." She slid a piece of Mirror Ranch note paper across the table. "I just got off the phone with my lawyer—"

"You've got cell service?" Robson pulled out his phone, staring at the dead screen."

"No, you nit. I know how to use a rotary phone. Now, eyes down. Read the words on the page." She tapped the note paper lying on the table between them. "The release will say: *Charlie Moore, founder of MMG, is dead at the age of sixty-six. The family will issue a formal statement in the coming days.* If you change so much as one word, I will sue you to hell and back. Got it?"

Robson's eyes narrowed. "Don't you try to threaten—"

Parker was on her feet and halfway to the lobby before he could finish his sentence.

The kitchen was silent but for the soft *snick* of Bernard's knife. A fish lay on the cutting board in front of him. He inserted the sharp thin blade behind its gills, sliding it down along the backbone. With a quick smooth motion, he lifted the fillet off the ribcage and set it on the cutting board. Then flipped the fish over and began the process all over again.

He was focused on the task at hand and didn't hear me leave.

JOURNAL

What's happening to my girls?

MMG is taking over a multibillion dollar AI company and Parker is leading the transaction. Charlie says I'm not to bother her with silly phone calls and petty complaints. He says Parker needs to keep her head in the game and doesn't have time to listen to her mother whining about getting old and feeling lonely. I thought she enjoyed our phone calls. We used to laugh all the time. But Charlie said she's just being diplomatic. She doesn't want to hurt my feelings. I said, I understand. And stopped calling.

Charlotte's been cool to me ever since Charlie fired Jay. She thinks I should have done something to stop it. Poor Jay. Charlie treated him so badly. Berating him in front of the executive team, then ten minutes later sending out a company-wide email saying Jay was no longer with the company. Charlotte found out about it in the ladies washroom from her personal assistant, she was so angry when she called me she could barely get the words out. She said Charlie's behavior was humiliating and abusive, and at the very least I could have given her a heads up. I had no idea it was coming.

I'm losing my girls.

CHAPTER 36

AJ and I were in the middle of a meadow ringed with tall pines under a misty sky. The cool air and wet grass reminded me of the Scottish moors. The closest I've been to the Scottish moors was on a vacation with Louisa. We took a bus trip to Loch Ness—sadly Nessie refused to show herself—and on the way home our driver let us off for ten minutes to stretch our legs, warning us not to wander away. Sure enough three German tourists got lost. The driver honked his horn until they found their way back, shivering and soaked to the skin, complaining that the mist played havoc with their sense of direction.

"AJ, I don't think I've ever seen you in such a charming outfit." He was wearing a goofy white hat with a floppy brim, it was a little wilted after an hour outdoors, and a sturdy blue windbreaker borrowed from Jay. He looked like he was about to go twitching with some geriatric Brits.

"Didn't I tell you this would be fun?" He shot me a lopsided grin.

After breakfast he'd suggested we go for a walk. I'd moaned and fussed, I don't like wandering around without a purpose, and he'd replied, "If it's purpose you want, we can go to the fishing hole, drop a line, and bring back dinner for Bernard." He'd stuck his head into the kitchen. "You'd like that wouldn't you, Bernard."

Bernard had replied by cranking up the volume on his rock radio channel.

"Where's this mysterious fishing hole?" I pulled Charlotte's map out of my pocket. "There's nothing on the map." At least not yet. Jay wanted to dig out a man-made lake and stock it with trout. Jay was the kind of guy who threw everything at the wall until something stuck.

"Trust me, Evie, there's a fishing hole."

As we wandered through the sedge and beebalm AJ entertained me with stories of his misspent youth on the family farm.

When his grandfather became rich mining potash in Saskatchewan he gave AJ's dad a farm in central Alberta, hoping the task of raising cattle, sheep and chickens would cure him of his feckless, playboy ways. But AJ's dad couldn't bring himself to slaughter the animals and the farm was a colossal failure.

Everything was sold when AJ went off to university and the family scattered. His father moved to a tiny island off the West Coast and his mother relocated to Boston. AJ didn't keep in touch with anyone but his grandfather. Old man Braxton was convinced that one day AJ would see the error of his ways and ditch BLV to take the helm of the world's biggest potash company. Granddad offered a multimillion dollar compensation package as inducement but luckily for us, AJ was not motivated by money.

AJ snapped his fingers. "Hey, want to learn how to make a grass rope?" He pulled a knife that looked like a miniature machete out of a leather sheath on his belt, and snicked through the tall grass, leaving a swath of slender stalks in his wake. These he separated into two bundles, one for him and one for me. Grabbing one bundle in the middle, he turned it into a U and twisted the legs of the U together, tighter and tighter, feeding in more grass as he went along. It was like braiding hair—something I've never been good at—but using two strands instead of three.

We twisted our ropes in silence, listening to the creak of baby grasshoppers popping around in the meadow.

"Okay, show me what you've got." He held out his rope. It was an inch thick and at least six feet long. Mine was twice as thick and half as long and looked like a floppy club.

"Not bad, Evie. For a beginner."

I felt like a Brownie who'd just won a special merit badge.

As we waded through the grass in the direction of the pond I told him about Robson's argument that morning with Charlotte. "It sounds bizarre, but I think he's serious."

AJ looped his grass rope around his neck like a lei. Mine wasn't as sleek as his and the grassy bristles poked me in the throat.

"Not to side with Robson," AJ said, "he's a miserable prick, but he may be on to something." His grass rope sailed through the air like a whip.

"Careful with that. You're going to put someone's eye out. Mine."

He smiled and twirled his grass rope in small circles. "Did you know an underground condo in an abandoned missile silo in Colorado will set you back three million dollars a year?"

His grass whip caught me on the leg and I narrowed my eyes at him. "What did I tell you?"

He grinned and in that moment I saw the boy he used to be, impish blue eyes, spikey sandy hair, charming and reckless.

"Living in a silo? Sounds horrible." I swung my grass rope at some dead reeds. "Off with their heads!"

"What? Like in the French Revolution?"

"I'm the Queen of Hearts, silly. From Alice in Wonderland. Off with their heads." I swacked at the reeds, old seed heads and bits of grass flew everywhere.

Satisfied I wasn't planning to kill the rich, AJ explained that three million a year would get you amenities like the holographic view of your choice outside your fake windows, a gym and swimming pool. And a 'time out room' for residents who break the rules.

I laughed. "Can you imagine Jeff Bezos ordering Elon Musk to take a time-out. What happens if someone gets sick?" My rope started to fray and I passed it to AJ so he could tighten it. "It's not as if you can press gang a bunch of doctors and nurses into a silo in case you need open heart surgery one day." Louisa had horror stories about luxury cruise ships where the limited medical care left a lot to be desired.

We crested a small hill and finally I saw it. A round, blue-black fishing hole about the size of my living room. AJ sprinted down the hill, arms windmilling as he struggled to stay upright on the slippery grass.

When I caught up to him he was standing at the edge of the pond, his arms crossed and a small frown on his face. "It looked a lot bigger on Google Earth."

"It's a lovely pond, AJ." I spread my jacket on the damp grass and sat down to contemplate the view. A gentle breeze rippled across the surface blowing the water striders off course and a fat frog edged up a long stalk which bent lower and lower until he slipped into the water with a wet plop.

AJ flapped his jacket a couple of times, then spread it on the grass beside me. He stared across the misty meadow for a minute before asking what I thought was going on with Keith. "I still can't understand why he'd consider accepting Charlie's offer."

I was about to say I had no idea when my phone rang, the noise jarring the birds out of the bushes and chasing the frog back into the reeds.

"Speak of the devil." I put Keith on speaker and he said Charlotte had received another call from the RCMP.

"The highways are worse than they anticipated. They won't be here until tomorrow at the earliest."

"Wednesday?" I rolled my eyes at AJ. "They do understand that Charlie's been in the cooler for more than forty-eight hours, right?"

"How did the family take the news?" AJ asked.

"As you'd expect. Robson is freaking out. Parker and Charlotte are stoic and Katie doesn't seem to care."

I stared past the pond and the meadow to the ridge of blue mountains in the distance. It was hard to imagine a place this beautiful could be a prison.

Beautiful prisons. Like Gates, Case and White. Keith and I had been seduced by its marble floors and expensive artwork, slaves to its high salaries and stellar reputation. It took a vicious attack by a lunatic lawyer to drive me out. Keith came with me. And now he was prepared to give up our freedom to become a cog in the MMG empire. Why?

"Keith?" I asked, "you doing okay?" A dragonfly hovered over the cattails like an iridescent helicopter as I waited for his reply.

"I'm fine. One more day won't kill me." And he hung up.

CHAPTER 37

G ood book?" AJ asked, a couple of hours later.

I was curled up in a poofy armchair in front of the fire, my book face down in my lap and my head drooping like wilted daisy. I couldn't keep my eyes open despite the children pawing through the games shelves and shouting over me to their mother who was sitting across from me in a quiet haze. Elise was finally awake and downing coffee so fast Bernard could hardly keep up.

The gray morning mist morphed into towering rain clouds and AJ and I barely made it back to the Lodge before we heard the rumble of thunder echo through the valley. Every lamp in the lobby was lit, but even the crackling fire could not dispel the gloom.

It was three o'clock and I needed a nap. How pathetic.

"Well?" AJ repeated his question. "Is it a good book?"

"As a matter of fact, it's a brilliant book." I hoped he wouldn't ask what it was about because I was so brain dead I couldn't remember.

"Daddy!" Amelia shouted when her father appeared at the top of the staircase. "Play cards with me."

Her brother picked up the refrain. "AJ taught us a game. I want to blow you up!"

Robson shook his head. "Not now. Where's Charlotte?"

Teddy frowned and threw himself into an armchair. If pouting were an Olympic event, this kid would take gold.

I turned to AJ. "You taught the kids how to blow up their dad?" Then lowered my voice. "Can you teach me?"

He laughed and challenged me to a game of *Exploding Kittens* "It's really quite ingenious; if Amelia can get the hang of it, I'm sure you can too. Although you're much older than she is and your brain isn't as flexible so it might take you a while to catch on."

I told him I'd pass. I was going to go to the kitchen and make myself a fried egg sandwich. This was *Tizórai*—the Hungarian version of elevenses. "Want one?"

"I don't know," he said, "would it be safe to eat?"

"Bernard says the eggs are fine."

"I was talking about your cooking."

"Ha ha."

He bent down and pulled me out of the squishy armchair, whispering in my ear. "Whatever you do, don't mention the Wi-Fi."

"Why not?"

"It's still down and Robson is having a meltdown."

"That explains it," I glanced into the kitchen where Robson and Charlotte were standing nose to nose, stiff as a couple of planks. Robson was so angry his voice carried clear across the room.

"This is intolerable," he bellowed. "In case you missed the memo, Dad is dead and I have a business to run. Which is damn near impossible without the fucking Wi-Fi!"

In an equally antagonistic voice, Charlotte said Jay was working on it. A second later Jay appeared, lugging a large red toolbox. Robson and Charlotte stopped shouting long enough to watch Jay pull a rain slicker off the coat rack by the front door and stride out into the driving rain.

The door slammed and Charlotte turned to Robson saying Mirror Ranch was so bloody remote it was a miracle the WiFi worked at all. The nearest cell tower was miles away and the signal had to be boosted by a jerry-rigged combination of satellite dishes and "soup cans on string!" Jay had been working on it for days.

"And if he can't fix it?" Robson asked.

"Then we call in the experts. Who can't get here until the roads are clear. By which time you will be long gone. Thank God for small mercies."

A harsh, insistent ringing pierced the air. It was the ancient Bakelite phone sitting on the registration desk. Charlotte rushed out of the kitchen and picked up the receiver, she nodded twice as she glanced around the lobby, then beckoned to me.

When she handed me the receiver I said hello to Madeline. The ancient phone had no caller ID but who else would it be?

"When are you coming home?" she demanded, with no preamble whatsoever.

"Is there something wrong with the dog?"

"God no, your demented mutt is eating me out of house and home."

I pulled a tall pine stool out from under the desk and made myself comfortable, I could be here a while.

I explained that the roads were still blocked and we were trapped at the Lodge…and yes, Charlie was still in the cooler. Lowering my voice to a whisper I added that when Louisa and I examined the body, there was no sign of the silver flask.

After Madeline finished making gagging noises she explained she'd called to pass on some important information. "By the way, what's wrong with your cell, I've been calling you guys all day but no one picked up."

"WiFi and cell service are out. What's going on?"

There was a pause. In my mind's eye I could see her sitting behind her desk, smiling to herself. Madeline has a Cheshire Cat smile when she's got a secret. If she held that smile long enough I'm sure she'd disappear.

"Rumour has it that Robson and Parker are gearing up for the legal battle of the century. This is going to be even juicier than *Rogers v Rogers*."

"That's hardly surprising," I said. "It could drag on for years."

"Maybe not. Probate will be delayed until Charlie's successor is named, that will speed up the litigation, if nothing else."

A small hand tapped my bare ankle and I almost fell off the stool. Amelia had crawled behind the registration desk and was whispering up at me. Could she hide under the desk at my feet? I nodded. Giggling she squashed herself into the tiny cubby space under the desk.

I held the phone closer to my lips and said, "I don't understand. There's no connection between probate and succession…is there?"

"Hold on," Madeline set her phone down on her desk. I heard her door close. She and Bridget were at the office, proving once again that they could manage the office just fine without us. A moment later she came back on the line. "There's no reason why the will can't be probated before Charlie's successor is appointed…except that Charlie made it a condition of his will. It's like Giorgio Armani's will where he instructed his heirs to sell 15 percent of his empire."

"Is it binding?" I asked.

"It is in Italy," Madeline replied.

"I meant here in Canada. No, never mind, I don't need to know."

In death as in life, Charlie was the master puppeteer, jerking his family around like marionettes on a string. No one was going to collect their fortunes until his successor had been named. Effectively making the Parker-and-Robson succession problem an issue for Katie and Charlotte as well. *Charlie, aren't you a clever bastard.*

Amelia tapped my ankle again. Making me shiver, her tiny fingers were very cold. "Shhh, Evie, be quiet or he'll find us."

"He's looking for you, not me," I whispered.

"Who's looking for me?" Madeline asked.

Teddy was marching across the lobby, arms sticking straight out, fingers wiggling. He'd scoured the kitchen, the dining room, and the bar and was now heading our way, chanting "I'm going to get you," like a miniature Freddy Krueger. Then he stopped directly in front of the registration desk and pounded on the call bell.

"Jesus," Madeline yelled in my ear, "what was that?

I grabbed the bell with my free hand while Teddy stood in front of me, lips pursed, eyes hooded, looking very much like one of the demented children of the corn.

"Madeline, I've got to go."

Suddenly Amelia charged out of the cubby hole, almost tipping my stool as she screamed off in the direction of the dining room. Teddy tore after her. And the only thought in my head was: *I have got to get out of here.*

CHAPTER 38

When I'd asked Opal about the laundry facilities she almost bit my head off. "I cook, I clean, I look after those horrid children," she snapped. "No, I didn't mean that. The children aren't horrid, just…rambunctious." She gave me a weak smile before continuing. "But you must understand, I am *not* your servant and I will *not* do your laundry."

Pointing to my laundry bag, I assured her I was more than capable of doing my own laundry and Louisa's too for that matter. All I needed was a washer and dryer.

Opal's fit of temper faded as she led me across the lobby and into the kitchen where AJ joined us just as we reached the door leading down to the basement. Being the intrepid soul that he is, he suggested that I could do his laundry as well.

The look I gave him suggested otherwise and he scrambled upstairs, threw his dirty clothes into a pillowcase, and was back in time to hear Opal explain the intricacies of the commercial washer and dryer.

Despite its low ceiling, the laundry room was a pleasant place with bright white walls and small narrow windows through which I could see the rain pattering down on the beargrass. Next to the stacked washer and dryer was a multi level drying rack and what looked like a not-to-be-trifled-with ironing machine.

AJ and I stuffed our clothes—mixed up in one giant ball—into the massive washer drum and were now sitting on a bench, mesmerized by the sight of our clothes sloshing around in the bubbly water.

I started to tell AJ about my conversation with Madeline but he was more interested in how she'd managed to track down the Ranch's rotary phone number.

"Hey, this is Madeline we're talking about," I said, "there's nothing she can't do. Now focus." I snapped my fingers. The rhythmic hum of the washer was incredibly soothing. "Madeline says probate of Charlie's estate is going to be tied up until the question of succession is settled."

"Whoa, that'll crank up the tension around here," AJ replied. "Did you hear Charlotte and Jay going at it after lunch? No, I don't suppose you did. You were sleeping—"

"Reading."

"*Reading.* They had a rip roaring whisper-argument in the kitchen."

"Whisper-arguments. They're the worst kind. What about? Robson's billionaire bunker idea? Let me guess. Jay likes the idea."

"No, Jay swears he knows nothing about it and he's adamant it will never happen. What set Charlotte off was the fact the WiFi still wasn't working."

The wash machine started to vibrate. I shot AJ a worried look. We should have separated our clothes instead of tossing them into the machine in one gigantic ball. AJ said it would sort itself out and after three loud clunks the machine settled down.

"It's hardly Jay's fault," I said, turning my attention back to AJ. "That bomb cyclone came up out of nowhere."

"True, but what rankled Charlotte was the Wi-Fi went down *after* Jay spent a small fortune on upgrades. She wanted everything to be in tip top working order when Charlie arrived and reminded him of the division of labour around here. She oversees the staff and takes care of the guests and the animals and he's responsible for the property, the buildings, and the infrastructure, including the Wi-Fi, the CCTV, and all the electronics."

"What? They have CCTV cameras? AJ, that's fantastic." I didn't recall seeing any cameras, but knowing Jay he'd have installed the best state-of-the-art mini cameras money could buy.

"We have to view the tapes." I hopped off the bench and hurried over to the washer which was spinning our clothes at supersonic speed and started pressing buttons. "God, how do you stop this thing?" The washer sounded like a jet engine preparing for take off. "If Jay has footage from the night Charlie died we might be able to piece together what happened between the time he left and the time we found him. He was an awful man, but he wasn't a complete idiot. Something must have stopped him from taking shelter when the bomb cyclone hit."

"Whoa." AJ came up behind me and gently peeled my hands off the buttons. "Opal will kill you if you break her machine. Besides, if it destroys my clothes I've got nothing left but the clothes on my back."

I smiled. "Then, you'll have to wear a bathrobe like Hugh Hefner."

We returned to the bench and sat down. According to the timer, the spin cycle was almost finished.

"That's a great idea, viewing the CCTV tapes," AJ said.

"Jay and his little toolbox are outside in the pouring rain right now, let's give the poor guy a minute to come in and dry off before we demand to see them."

We sat in silence staring at the blob at the washer until it buzzed. AJ hauled the heavy wet clothes out of the washer, stuffed them in the dryer and set the dial on high.

"You can't dry everything at Chernobyl degrees centigrade," I said. "Your jeans will come out so small they won't even fit Amelia."

He laughed, waving away my concerns. An hour later, I was chagrined to discover that AJ's jeans survived but my T-shirts would never be the same again.

CHAPTER 39

That evening after dinner Jay made a truly brilliant suggestion that sounded utterly ridiculous at the time. Nightfall had forced him back into the Lodge before he could finish repairing the Wi-Fi and the reception was dodgy. Everyone was grumpy because as we all know intermittent Wi-Fi is worse than no Wi-Fi, because you keep testing it to see if it's back. Hopes up, hopes dashed, it's a demoralizing cycle.

"Trust me," Jay said, through gritted teeth as he dragged a heavy coffee table away from the grand fireplace, "it will be fun."

"You're not serious," Robson complained. "Talent Night? Like in *Dirty Dancing*? This is a corporate retreat, not a flea-bag resort in the Catskills."

"Well, I love the idea," Charlotte said, gripping the arm of the long, red leather sofa. Parker positioned herself on the opposite end and together they dragged the unwieldly piece of furniture inch by inch away from the 'stage' in front of the fireplace. Once they got it off the carpet and onto the hardwood floor it skimmed easily across the room.

"I agree," Parker said, her eyes scanning the room,

looking for a place to stash the sofa. "Talent Night will be a great way for corporate teams to bond at the end of a long day. Charlotte, where are we taking this thing?"

"There." Katie pointed in Robson's direction. By the time the three women finished rearranging the furniture, Robson was barricaded into his armchair.

"Really Mother," Robson complained, poking his head over the top of the sofa.

She looked at him, coolly. "Robson, if you don't think you're as talented as your sisters you can sit this one out. Pretend you're a member of the audience."

Robson spluttered that he had every intention of participating, he just needed time to figure out what he wanted to do.

"I have an idea." Elise said as Robson crawled over the coffee table jammed next to his chair. "We can do a salsa." She caught my eye. "Robson was the best salsa dancer in our class." It was all I could do to stop my jaw from hitting the floor. The image of Elise tossing her golden hair and Robson snaking around behind her was one I could do without.

Louisa shot me a look that indicated she'd rather attend her own execution than perform, but Jay was surprisingly persuasive and soon our little group—we dubbed ourselves BLV + *One*—was huddled in a corner dreaming up ways to showcase our collective talents.

Robson, being the competitive sod that he is, insisted the performances be judged and ranked from one to ten with ten being the best score. Katie declared she would be the judge and her first official act was to award the kids a handicap, five points each like in golf.

After a few false starts BLV + *One* settled on a skit from an old *Dick Van Dyke Show*—the one where the cast pretends they're playing an instrument, drums, piccolos, trombones and tubas, while singing a silly song. AJ was particularly pleased when he *wah-wahed* his pretend trombone and everyone hooted and clapped.

Teddy and Amelia took first place in the under-twelve category as well as overall best-in-show for throwing a ball back and forth across the makeshift stage until Teddy dropped it. To be fair, Amelia's aim was wildly erratic. Much to my delight BLV + *One* beat Robson's solemn recitation of *O Captain! My Captain!* Not only was Robson's delivery pretentious, but the line about the captain lying cold and dead on the deck struck too close to home.

The silliness of Talent Night seemed to calm the family. The children drew their parents into a board game, Parker and Charlotte chatted quietly at the bar, and Katie snuggled into a large squishy armchair with a small book. I couldn't make out the title, but it had an ornate blue cover, reminding me of the marbled end paper you'd find in a first edition by Dickens.

I decided to grab the opportunity to ask Jay about the CCTV footage and was rising from my chair when Louisa touched my arm and asked if I could join her in her room.

"Now?"

By then Jay was huddled with Charlotte and Parker at the bar, they were having what looked like an intense conversation.

"I have something to show you," Louisa said.

"Fine, but it better not be a dead mouse."

One day we'd come home from work to find Quincy in the middle of the living room, his head on his paws, staring sadly at the intact body of a dead mouse. Louisa said it caught a glimpse of the bull terrier and died of fright, but I figured Quincy chased it around the house until it keeled over, dead of a heart attack. Bull terriers are terrific rat hunters. I didn't relax until the exterminator declared our house vermin-free.

Louisa looked at me aghast. "Why would I show you a dead mouse? You hate mice."

"Just wanted to be sure."

I threaded my way through the obstacle course that was her room and still managed to stub my toe on her suitcase which was lying open on the floor at the foot of her bed. At home, her room is immaculate, including her floor to ceiling bookshelf which is packed with the strangest assortment of bric-a-brac I've ever seen. She collects antique medical equipment; once she ordered a syringe set off the internet and it arrived complete with a tiny vial of strychnine. This kicked off her interest in poisons. Like I said, strange.

Louisa pushed a stash of pinecones wrapped in a face cloth to the side of her desk and retrieved a slim, leather-bound binder. The words *Welcome to Mirror Ranch* were embossed in gold on the cover. The guest information directory.

She bounced onto her bed and patted the bedspread beside her. After we plumped up the pillows and propped ourselves up against the headboard she said, "Every room has a guest book. I'll bet you twenty bucks you haven't glanced at yours."

"I have," I said. Whenever she challenges me like that I become defiant. But she was right. I hadn't opened my copy of the guest book. "It's full of the usual bumf." This wasn't a complete lie. I *had* clicked on the Mirror Ranch website when Madeline booked our reservations. The photos of the Lodge warmed by the setting sun and smiling guests horseback riding along dappled forest paths and Lucky the Pig—apparently pig walking is a thing—convinced me that Madeline had picked the right place.

Louisa gave me a skeptical look. She didn't believe me. "When you get back to your room, check to see if your book is the same as mine." Her finger slipped between the pages, marking her place.

"Why?"

"I should have bet you fifty bucks."

"I'll buy you a chocolate bar. Now show me what you're talking about."

She flipped the binder open to the *About Us* page. Like its online counterpart it stated that Mirror Ranch was an MMG property, operated by Charlotte Moore and Sanjay Azeem. At the bottom of the page in tiny print was a short blurb explaining that MMG was an IT and consulting company with government and private sector clients around the world. The online version of this page noted that MMG's latest acquisition had been a crypto security company. I remembered that transaction, it roiled the news cycle for a couple of days because the takeover target sold surveillance technology to authoritarian governments in the Middle East. This kicked off a flurry of op-eds about morality in business. A topic that always makes me laugh.

Louisa turned to the next page. "Let's just see who's who in the zoo." I glanced at the glossy photo of Charlie, smiling benevolently for the camera before letting my eye drift down to Charlie's bio.

"Oh, oh." I pulled the binder out of Louisa's hand and peered at the words scribbled across the glossy paper in a tiny hand:

Mr. Moore is a liar and a cheat. The tax man should check out his secret bank account in Panama.

"Oh, Louisa, that's not good."

Charlie sent all his clients to Mirror Ranch for their

off-site meetings. Parker said it was his way of appeasing Charlotte after he'd fired Jay. Perhaps someone wasn't happy with MMG's services. Nevertheless, smearing Charlie's reputation in a guest services book seemed like a juvenile way to make your point. Wouldn't it be better to simply demand a refund?

I passed the guest book back to Louisa. "We should let Charlotte know, in case there are more like this."

"Maybe it's a family member." she said.

"They called him Mr. Moore."

"Could be a disgruntled employee—"

That was as far as she got.

CHAPTER 40

The air vibrated, smelling thick and acrid. First came an unbearably bright flash. Then the ear-splitting crack as if the roof was being ripped off. Instinctively I started to count. Flash-to-bang. Zero seconds.

Another brilliant flash; another violent crash. Zero seconds. The lightning was right on top of us.

"We have to get out of here! Louisa! Go! Go!" I pushed her across the bed. Away from the window. The ceiling light exploded. Everything went black. "Jesus! Go!"

Then another flash. Another boom. And the sound of wood cracking.

The window exploded. Something huge and wet and heavy scraped across my back, scratching my arms, tangling my hair. The wind roared into the room, deep, hard and powerful.

Louisa was crawling. I was right behind her. We rolled off the bed, landing with a thud in the narrow space between the bed and the wall. Outside thunder rumbled. Flash to bang five seconds. Lightning one mile away.

I hauled her to her feet. Tripping over each other, we ricocheted along the wall, searching for the door. She found the doorknob first and yanked the door open. Stumbling into the pitch black corridor and colliding with AJ. His face ghoulish in the harsh light from his phone. Louisa staggered against me, stumbled, and AJ caught her and dragged her out of the open doorway. Away from the wind and the flying glass.

I shouted, "A bloody big tree came through the bloody window!"

"Are you okay?" AJ shouted in my ear over the sound of thunder, rumbling farther away.

"What happened? Are you guys all right?" Keith raced down the hall. The beam of his phone light jittering along the black wall. Behind him came Jay carrying a large, bright lamp. Light and shadow raking over us as AJ plucked a sparkling shard of glass out of my hair.

CHAPTER 41

Jay's lamp swung in agitated circles as he shouted instructions from the top of the staircase. "Everybody downstairs. Let's go. Go, go, go!"

Downstairs in the coal black lobby, the children whimpered, their disembodied cries heart-rending in the thick and heavy air.

I grabbed Louisa's arm, yelling, "Are you sure you're all right?" It was quieter now, there was no need to shout, but I couldn't stop myself. I wanted desperately to hug her. But I was covered in glass and afraid she'd turn into a pin cushion.

"I'm fine, what about you? You took the brunt of it."

"It's all part of the big sister's job description."

Gripping the railing, with Keith and AJ hustling us along, we crept downstairs.

"You lost your magnificent tree," I said, thinking about the massive black pine laying broken across her bed. It shot through the window with such speed.

"The bomb cyclone is supposed to be over by now. That's what Madeline said." Louisa's tone implied the rogue tree was somehow Madeline's fault.

"Madeline said it lasts 24 hours. That means it ended last night. This must be a bad thunderstorm, apparently staged for your sole benefit."

That made her giggle.

"Will you two stop talking and keep moving!" AJ hustled us along like an Australian sheep dog yipping at its flock.

We clung to the stair railing, putting one hesitant foot in front of the other while the thunder rolled away in the distance.

Then with a tremendous *whoosh* the generators kicked in; the deer horn chandeliers sparked back to life and the Tiffany lamps scattered around the lobby glowed red, green, and blue. Blinking, I stopped at the bottom of the stairs to get my bearings.

Huddled in front of the stone fireplace were Elise and the children, Robson stood in the entry to the kitchen with a look of panic on his face while Charlotte struggled to push past him.

"Where's Mom?" Charlotte's voice was shrill.

"Here." That was Parker. "It's okay, I've got her." She gripped Katie's elbow, guiding her around the bar stools and into the centre of the lobby. "She's fine, aren't you Mom?"

"Charlotte." Katie's tone was agitated. "We have to check the horses. They will be terrified."

"Mom, I—"

"Charlotte, Shadow will tear his stall apart, you know he will."

Parker passed Katie over to Charlotte who rubbed her back, telling her quietly that they would go down and tend to the horses very soon. "I promise, Mom."

And that was the moment Robson chose to assert his authority. Barking orders like a deranged drill sergeant he demanded Jay seal up the doors and the windows, before turning on Katie, yelling that only an idiot would go outside in weather like this. Charlotte cut him off in midsentence with a torrent of obscenities that would stop a rhino in its tracks.

"All right, all right, that's enough." Jay sounded remarkably calm. "Robson, I suggest you join your family on the couch. They need you." He pointed to Elise who was perched on the edge of the red leather sofa with her arms tightly wrapped around her hollow-eyed children.

Robson's mouth dropped open. *The impertinence.* When Jay's grim expression did not change, Robson demanded to know Bernard's whereabouts, complaining it was Bernard's duty to protect the family. *Duty? The man's a chef, not a bodyguard.*

"Bernard and Opal are up in the staff building where they belong." Jay fired back. "They know the drill. Shelter in place until the storm blows over. Robson, I strongly suggest you make yourself useful by staying out of my way."

I'll say this for Jay, he knows how to take charge in an emergency. In less than ten minutes everyone was gathered in front of the large stone fireplace listening as Jay assured us that the Lodge was built like Fort Knox and we were perfectly safe. What we'd just experienced was not the bomb cyclone, but a thunder shower. "They can be pretty intense down here in the valley."

Everyone was going to sleep in the lobby, he said, just to be on the safe side. Tomorrow Jay would check all the trees close to the Lodge to make sure they hadn't been damaged by the storm. Just because they were standing didn't mean they wouldn't come flying through a window on a violent gust of wind.

Louisa and I went into the kitchen to check each other

for glass splinters while Charlotte hustled around the room dispensing sleeping bags and air mattresses.

When Parker clicked her lighter, kindling the fire in the fireplace, Amelia clapped and everyone relaxed as the small wavering flame took hold.

Jay huddled with Keith and AJ, then spoke to Charlotte who disappeared down the hall, returning with three raincoats.

"Thanks babe." Jay smiled at Charlotte, "we've got to board up Louisa's window." They pulled on their jackets and disappeared into the rainy night.

Charlotte put the kettle on while the rest of us gathered around the fire. In thirty minutes Keith and AJ returned lugging a large tarp between them. It sagged like an overloaded fishing net, heavy with the weight of saws and hammers and other tools.

"Where's Jay?" Charlotte's eyes darted to the kitchen door.

AJ's shoes squeaked on the hardwood floor. "Right behind me," he said, not breaking stride, "with a cart full of plywood to seal up the window."

Keith grunted as he changed his grip on the old tarp. "First things first. We've got to get that tree out of there."

The kitchen door banged open and Jay appeared, pushing a narrow, unwieldy cart loaded with sheets of wood. Pellets of mud fell from the cart's rubber tires leaving a speckled black trail across the hardwood floor. The Moore sisters and Louisa and I gathered round the cart, unclipping the bungie cords and picking up the wooden sheets and carrying them upstairs where we leaned them against the wall in the corridor.

Inside Louisa's destroyed room Keith and AJ had hung a utility lantern from the top of the bathroom door. It cast hard shadows across the black pine which lay in a sinister heap on top of her bed. Reminding me of the chaos after the Great Flood, only this time the room smelled of wet pine needles not sewage.

When we returned downstairs, Robson was still parked in his armchair staring blankly at his wife as if he couldn't quite comprehend what had happened. Elise crooned to her children and whispered in their ears. It seemed to be working. Their tears had stopped.

Little Teddy lifted his head off his mother's shoulder and glanced around the room. "I'm not afraid," he said in a whisper, his lower lip quivering.

Robson shuddered, glancing around as if he didn't know who had spoken.

"Daddy, I'm not afraid," Teddy said it again louder. His face glowed in the dancing light of the fire.

"Damn right, Teddy." Robson said, rising from his chair and wandering over to the fireplace where he began to pace. "Damn right."

Overhead something bumped across the roof and landed with a sodden thud on the paved terrace. The storm had dislodged some cedar shakes and they were falling to the ground one by one.

The noise seemed to frighten Robson who froze in front of the fireplace and stared up at the ceiling. "We have to get away from here."

On the sofa, Amelia sat bolt upright. She turned to Elise and said, "It's Grandpa. He's mad we put him in the freezer. He wants to come out and sit with us by the nice warm fire."

She slipped off the sofa and darted toward the kitchen.

"Amelia!" Her mother screamed after her.

Louisa stepped forward, scooped the little girl off the

floor and carried her back to her mother, telling her that Grandpa was fine.

Parker put another log on the fire, then came over to stand next to me. After asking how I was doing she said, "I'm so sorry about this. But don't worry, we've got everything under control."

Looking back I wondered whether those innocent words were too much for the gods. Because they certainly weren't done with us yet.

Elise and I were strolling through the garden at their house in Mount Royal. She was upset about the ancient crab apple tree. Robson chopped it down to make room for his fitness studio.

Robson was twelve when he became obsessed with fitness, ordering magic potions online and working out as if he were training for the Olympics. But all the exercise in the world wouldn't bulk him up or make him six inches taller. He was a little boy who grew up to be a little man.

I was assuring Elise that the Japanese maple would fill in soon when Teddy hurtled out of the fitness studio, screaming bloody blue murder.

Mamma, mamma, he threw himself into Elise's arms, his wrestling singlet sliding off his skinny shoulders. Daddy tried to kill me.

Robson ambled up behind his son, telling us to ignore the boy, he was overreacting.

It turned out Robson and Teddy were practicing wrestling. Robson was determined to toughen up his son, who was as small and slight as he'd been as a boy, and enrolled Teddy in a variety of sports, baseball, fencing, tennis. Teddy hated them all. He wanted to try dance or music. As far as Robson was concerned, that was out of the question.

All he needs is more practice, Robson said. But Teddy was afraid of being knocked about. So Robson decided to show Teddy there was nothing to be afraid of. He put the boy in a choke hold and kept squeezing until Teddy went limp.

Elise was horrified. Teddy why didn't you tap out?

I did, the boy sobbed, but Daddy wouldn't release me.

Robson shrugged. It would toughen the boy up. He'd learn that the worst thing that could possibly happen to you wasn't that bad after all.

Teddy threw his headgear to the ground and screamed, I hate you.

Robson laughed and strolled across the lawn back to the fitness studio to finish his workout.

CHAPTER 42

Wednesday

Dawn came softly the next morning. The rain had stopped and an orange sun shone through wispy cotton candy clouds. In the woods the birds were trilling in the treetops, celebrating the miracle of a new day.

Katie and the kids were outside on a quest to ensure Lucky the pig and the chickens hadn't been blown to the land of Oz, Bernard was busy hauling heavy black bags of garbage—the meat in the big bar fridge had gone off—out to the dumpster. And Charlotte was sorting through the pots in the kitchen, picking the biggest ones to take up a rickety ladder to the attic—the roof had sprung a leak—while Jay was on the roof hammering down tarps to protect the bare spots until he could replace the missing cedar shakes.

When Jay gave AJ and Keith permission to use his chain saw the guys raced out the door to chop up fallen branches. There's nothing like a chain saw to keep a man out of your hair for a couple of hours, my mother used to say.

I was standing in the middle of Louisa's wrecked room. We were debating the merits of duct tape versus masking tape: as in which is better at pulling glass splinters out of sodden clothing. I was not happy about it. Although upon reflection it was preferable to being downstairs where Parker and Robson almost came to blows over who had first dibs on the rotary phone.

Louisa tried to lighten my mood. "You must admit, it's better than digging the sludge out of the basement after the flood. At least the room smells of fresh air and crushed pine needles."

"Yeah, like a man's deodorant instead of a sewer."

"Based on my limited experience"—she held up a duct-taped fist, prickly shards of glass glistened like alien fur—"duct tape is pretty good."

"For the record, I still think this is a bad idea." I picked at the roll of duct tape, trying to find the end. "The shards are too fine, you'll slice yourself to ribbons the minute you pull that sweater over your head. Have I mentioned that you wouldn't be in this mess if you'd put your clothes away properly in the first place?"

She rolled her eyes to the ceiling, then peeled the duct tape off her fist and gently smoothed the sweater with her open palm.

"Voila! Ow!" Tiny pin pricks of blood flared on the edge of her palm. "Damn." She marched into the bathroom and emerged with tweezers, leaning on the doorframe under the utility lamp to pick the splinters out of her flesh.

"It's ruined. All of my clothes are ruined." She was blinking rapidly now, trying not to cry.

When Louisa was small she had a terrible temper and regularly flung her Barbies across the room. Mom said she'd grow out of it and she did. She doesn't chuck things to the floor anymore but has on occasion thumped books down so hard it makes your teeth rattle. This would not be the time to say: *I told you so.*

"Okay, here's what we'll do." When Louisa gets like this, she needs a plan B. We dumped everything into garbage bags and decided to make this the drycleaner's problem.

It wasn't until after we'd hauled the garbage bags downstairs and stashed them in the trunk of Louisa's car that I realized the guest services book accusing Charlie of having a secret bank account in Panama was missing.

CHAPTER 43

Charlie had been dead for more than three days. Our cells and Wi-Fi were spotty and I was losing my mind. It wasn't so bad during the day—if you ignored Bernard picking through the food and scowling as he carted the graying meat and the flaccid vegetables out to the dumpster—but we were so programmed to internet connectivity that the lack of TVs and laptops and iPhones weighed heavily on us in the evenings. Someone could have started World War III and we'd never know.

Louisa, AJ and I were lolling on the red leather sofa in front of the stone fireplace staring at the blaze as if it were the latest movie streaming on Netflix. Louisa pulled herself upright long enough to glance at her cell phone.

"Still no service. God, I miss the internet." She flopped back into the couch cushions.

My sister had a wonderful relationship with the internet. She loved it and it loved her. Unlike me. The last time Microsoft updated my laptop, I lost a day. It took Louisa a couple of hours to fix it. She said I'd inherited the digital version of my mom's ability to stop time. Mom couldn't wear a watch, whether it was a cheap Swatch or a fancy Birks, the thing was dead within a week.

AJ groaned, rotating his shoulders as he stretched his legs out in front of the fire.

"Oh you poor boy," I tsked. "one day chopping wood and you're exhausted. You're getting soft in your old age."

He shook his head and smiled but didn't reply.

Charlotte received sporadic updates, non-news really, from the police on the rotary phone, but it didn't change the fact that we were trapped here. I made a mental note to never ignore anything Madeline says. Ever.

"We're losing the fire." Louisa gave AJ a winsome smile. He groaned and heaved himself off the sofa and threw another log on the blaze.

At the other end of the lobby we could hear Robson bickering with Jay. Tonight's topic was Jay's supposed lack of emergency preparedness.

"That's a clear violation of the terms of your loan agreement, Jay, don't you forget it." They were sitting across from each other at the dining room table. Robson was half out of his chair and waving his finger in Jay's face. "I'm getting out of this fleabag hotel—"

Jay caught Robson's hand and squeezed, forcing Robson to sit down. "Robson, I wouldn't push my luck if I were you." Wisely, Charlotte swept into the room and asked Jay to help her with something in the kitchen.

"They're going to kill each other if we don't get out of here soon." The heat from the fireplace made me sleepy and my words sounded like they were spoken by someone else.

"I wonder why she stayed with him," Louisa said. "Katie, I mean."

"Are you kidding." AJ laughed. "He's a multi-billionaire. Why wouldn't stay with him?"

"I wouldn't stay with someone I didn't love, even if he were a multi-billionaire." The part of my brain that wasn't asleep told me I didn't want to get into a conversation about love with AJ. The dozy part of my brain kept on talking. "Can you imagine the misery of waking up every morning and seeing the face of someone you despise across from you at the breakfast table."

AJ wiggled his toes, he was wearing orange puffin socks, he's got the largest collection of weird socks I've ever seen. "Robson and his dad seemed to be perfectly aligned."

What a random comment, the not quite asleep part of my brain said.

AJ lifted his arms and rested them along the back of the sofa. "Although I'd say he's more ruthless than Charlie, much quicker to play the power card. Me: big boss. You: minion." AJ made an *oof, oof* sound like a big gorilla.

I'd worked with lots of CEOs and noticed that the best ones didn't whip out the power card unless it was absolutely necessary. The thought melted away before I could put it into words.

Somewhere on the edge of my perception I heard AJ say, "According to Opal, Mirror Ranch saved Bernard's life."

What?

I was mulling this over when Keith's voice floated into the conversation. Saying something about Sleeping Beauty. Oh, that must be Louisa. She's asleep. I tried to take a peek but my eyes wouldn't open.

"Everyone's too tired to haul their sorry asses upstairs to bed." AJ's voice.

I managed to open one eye and lean forward to see Louisa. Her head was tipped to one side and her mouth was slightly open. She was making a soft susurrating sound. She'd kill me if I said she was snoring.

I whispered to AJ, "Looks like you're going to be stuck here for a while."

He whispered back, "That's all right, there's no place I'd rather be."

CHAPTER 44

Hours later in the thick dark night, I heard a noise. A low aggressive growl. Louisa's bedside clock read: 11:22 p.m. She'd refused to move to a different room after the pine tree incident and was now in the next bed, bleating softly like a lamb.

The sound was gruff and harsh. Not Louisa. Low, angry voices coming from downstairs.

Instantly I was fully awake. Swinging my legs over the side of the bed, I hauled a terry robe off the hook on the bathroom door and crept out into the corridor. Below me in the dimly lit bar, Robson and Bernard were arguing. Easing myself down onto the top step I heard Robson call Bernard a liar and a thief.

"Bernie, don't try that shit on me. Once an addict, always an addict. You saw your chance and you took it. You're going to hawk it for drugs, am I right?" Something metal banged down on the polished mahogany bar, underscoring Robson's words. "I'll say this for you, you've got good taste. That's top quality Arabian silver. It's actually worth something."

"No." Bernard's voice was low and strained. "For the last time, I didn't steal it." The sound of their footsteps faded into the kitchen. Then Bernard's voice. "You got what you wanted, now get the fuck out of my kitchen."

Robson gave a cruel laugh. "Your kitchen? This is my kitchen. And my bar and my lobby. Mirror Ranch belongs to me. You work for me, Bernie, and don't you forget it."

"The fuck I do," Bernard shot back. "Charlotte's my boss. You have no say here."

Robson sighed as if he were talking to a dimwitted child. "I don't know what garbage she's been feeding you but MMG loaned her the money and I can call that loan any time I want. Enjoy your wilderness experience while it lasts because you won't be here much longer." With that Robson marched out of the kitchen and returned to the bar.

I froze. I could see him clearly. Could he see me? He groaned like an old man when he bent down and hefted a box of booze up onto the counter. Bottles clinked as he rifled through them, yanking them out one by one and setting them on the counter until he found what he was looking for. A drawer squeaked open. He was pawing through the cutlery.

"Where's the bloody funnel? Bernie, I'm talking to you. Answer me." No response from the kitchen. "This flask better be filled with Macallan when I pick it up tomorrow or consider yourself fired. Do I make myself clear?"

Still nothing from Bernard.

"Stupid little shit." Robson grumbled under his breath as he stalked across the lobby heading for the base of the staircase.

I scrambled to my feet and hurried back into the corridor, turning left down the hall to my room. When I twisted the doorknob, it was locked. Of course it was locked. The trusty automatic door closer had done its job, silently shutting the door behind me when I crept out.

The door to Louisa's destroyed room was ajar—Jay was airing it out—and I darted inside, flattening myself against the wall behind the door. I knew Robson couldn't possibly see me, but to my eyes my white terry robe shone like a light house beacon, making me very nervous. Robson trudged up the stairs, sounding more winded than he should for a man of his age, and plodded slowly down the corridor to his room. The door clicked open and he disappeared inside.

Five minutes passed before I stepped back into the corridor and tapped lightly on the door to my room, waiting and waiting for Louisa to wake up and let me in.

CHAPTER 45

Thursday

Any news?" Keith asked Charlotte the next morning. She and Jay had just returned from checking the grounds. The damage to the horse trails and hiking paths in the north-west quadrant was worse than Jay anticipated. He'd have to hire outside help to repair them in time for the summer crowd. According to Jay, it would be a costly, difficult job. And he'd be damned if he was going to ask Robson for a loan. On the upside, he'd fixed the Wi-Fi.

"Nothing new," Charlotte said to Keith, "the road crews are working overtime, but the cops were noncommittal. They said they'd get here as quick as they can."

Bernard placed a cup of milky coffee in front of Keith. We'd been here so long Bernard and Opal knew all our preferences.

"Working overtime, my ass," Robson grumbled as he entered the kitchen. "What's the number? Those idiots don't know who they're messing with."

"Be my guest," Charlotte handed him her phone. Robson stalked out of the kitchen and a minute later we could hear him demanding someone's badge number and the name of their supervisor. A couple of minutes after that he was back. He flung Charlotte's phone down on the counter and went back upstairs. Evidently the cops knew exactly who they were dealing with and they didn't care.

The sense of irritation left by Robson's temper tantrum quickly dissipated in the commotion created by Katie and the children. They devoured their cereal and darted over to the coat hooks by the kitchen door, eager to rush down to the barn and teach Shadow a new trick. If Mickey Mouse had invited them to tour Disneyland they wouldn't have been more excited. The kids squabbled over who Shadow liked the best while Katie patiently buttoned up Amelia's jacket and helped Teddy find his boots before they slammed out the back door.

I found myself smiling as I crossed the lobby on my way back up to my room, marvelling at the outsized impact two small children can have. The sun filled the lobby, warming the hardwood floor and glittering off the bottles arrayed on top of the bar and I noticed that the silver flask was gone.

CHAPTER 46

When Louisa and I were small, one of Dad's favourite clients, a chicken farmer, went through a rough patch and Dad agreed to accept payment in kind. Mom wasn't thrilled about it, you couldn't go to the store, slap a chicken breast on the counter and walk out with a new pair of shoes, she said. But she agreed there was no point in driving the poor man into bankruptcy. Every weekend, Louisa and I would go with my dad to collect 'payment,' so I thought I knew everything there was to know about chicken farming…until Charlotte showed Louisa and me the coop Jay built. State-of-the-art didn't begin to describe it.

It looked like an oversized shed on stilts. Charlotte showed us the nesting boxes, the removable nesting bars—all at the same height to avoid dominance displays, apparently chickens, like people, were competitive—a deep litter composting process (whatever that was) and an ingenious little automatic door that opened at sunrise and closed at sunset.

"It doesn't smell as bad as I thought it would," Louisa said when Charlotte opened the nesting cubbies which were empty, all the chickens were running around outside on the grass.

"It doesn't smell at all!" Charlotte handed my sister a small bag of chicken feed. "These little beauties are free range, we do not run a battery chicken farm."

About fifteen red, black and white chickens chased after Louisa as she strolled along the wire fence enclosing the chicken yard.

"Stay clear of the electric fence," Charlotte called after her. "The shock won't kill you but you'll feel it. It's enough to keep the foxes and racoons at bay."

Charlotte said predators were a constant concern and she was thinking of getting a dog for additional protection, but Jay was balking. "Bernard says he'll take full responsibility for the dog. He grew up in an apartment in New York City and always wanted one.

"Jay won't admit it but dogs make him nervous," Charlotte said as she opened a ventilation window even wider. "That's another reason why Mirror Ranch will never become one of Robson's 'self-sustaining doomsday farms.' Jay would go nuts with Dobermans and German Shepards patrolling the perimeter." I wondered whether Jay would have any choice in the matter. As far as I could tell Robson had made up his mind.

"—has grandiose plans to put us one step above the competition." Charlotte was listing some of Jay's more outrageous expansion plans. "Maybe even a mini cattle drive for the authentic cowboy experience. Honestly," she said with a laugh, "I don't know where he gets these silly ideas."

The chickens scooted away from Louisa and over to me when I pulled a Kleenex out of my pocket. They were kind of cute, peeping and fluttering all around us.

The rooster let out a series of loud squawks and the

hens turned like a troop of soldiers and rushed back to the chicken coop and huddled in the dark, shady space underneath. Charlotte glanced around, saying McCabe (the rooster) must have spotted a predator.

"Can't you talk Jay into something more reasonable?" Louisa turned her empty feed bag inside out to show the chickens there was nothing left. "Like skeet shooting or cooking classes?"

"We *are* talking about running cooking classes. Bernard is a wonderful teacher, much more patient than I am. He says he'd be up for it, he's also keen on bee keeping."

Louisa glanced at me and smiled. When I was ten our Aunt Helen—she was ancient and lived alone in a tiny house on sprawling lot on the outskirts of town—introduced us to her bees. She plopped netted hats on our heads and we crept up on her two beehives as if we were crossing a mine field. We'd be fine, she said, as we didn't flail around. Good advice in any emergency. She cut us a chunk of honeycomb and we spent the rest of the afternoon sitting at her kitchen table sucking it dry.

As we approached the gate, the chickens rushed out from under the shed to say goodbye. On our way back up the hill to the Lodge, Louisa asked Charlotte if she could take one of the horses up to Dragon Falls.

"Absolutely not. Even experienced riders like Mom get into trouble up there. The horses don't like to go anywhere near the gorge."

"Can't say I blame them," I said, remembering the treacherous path through the dark woods and how quickly AJ and I had lost our way.

"Mom loves this place," Charlotte said, shielding her eyes and squinting up into the sky. Overhead an eagle circled and I could hear McCabe, the rooster, raise the alarm. "It's magical. You wouldn't know it to look at her now, but she used to have a serious drinking problem. That was the price she paid to be Mrs. Charlie Moore."

Charlotte's jaw tightened as she described how Charlie treated Katie. "He drove her so hard. She wasn't just a wife and a mother, she was an MMG ambassador. He loved to show her off, parading her around in front of his cronies night after night at charity balls and client dinners. She was so beautiful back then and had a bit of notoriety from her time in Hollywood."

Charlotte could tell from our blank expressions we had no idea what she was talking about. "Oh yes, Mom was an actress when Dad met her, a minor celebrity back in the day. She didn't have a big career—she married Dad before that could happen—just bit parts with some big name stars like Paul Newman and Kirk Douglas and Jane Fonda. She'd tell the most amazing stories, like Scheherazade. Dad's friends couldn't get enough of her."

What people don't realize about Scheherazade is it's a story about revenge. A cruel Sultan found his wife in bed with another man and beheaded them both. Then he married a fresh virgin every day and beheaded her every night, eventually racking up 1000 dead wives before he married Scheherazade. She was a clever woman and told a story a night for 1000 nights to save herself from being slaughtered. On the 1001st night she had no more stories to tell, but by then the Sultan had fallen in love and decided to spare her life.

Sure, it's a story about a brilliant, bewitching woman, but it's also a story about a cruel sadistic man.

JOURNAL

———

Christ, it's not as if I was asking for a divorce.

Charlotte wanted me to spend more time with them at Mirror Ranch. I loved the idea but Charlie wouldn't hear of it. He needed me here in the City. Doing my job, glued to his side, the gracious Katie Moore, hostess nonpareil.

He started with flattery. You've still got it, babe.

Of course I've still got it. I don't need him to tell me that. Thick red hair, killer cheekbones, firm jawline. The eyelids may droop a little, but in a nice Charlotte Rampling kind of way.

I've always had it. First in Hollywood and then in my finest role as Charlie Moore's wife.

When flattery didn't work he tried to gaslight me with my meds. Saying if he didn't keep an eye on me, God knows what I'd put in my mouth.

That's when I lost my temper and grabbed the phone to call Charlotte.

He ripped it out of my hand and threw it across the room. It shattered against the fireplace and broke.

Fuck you, I said. I can always buy a new phone.

Then he took away my car keys, telling the staff I was

overwrought and needed my rest. Under no circumstances was I to leave the house without him at my side.

This is ridiculous. I am not a prisoner in my own home. I must get away from him. One way or another I will get away from him.

CHAPTER 47

They looked like wild-eyed cherubs, the children, as they clattered through the double doors. Panting and making a big show of running up the trail from the stable to the Lodge. Behind them came Katie, dutifully picking their coats up off the floor and shoving their boots to one side so the next person coming through the door wouldn't trip and fall flat on their face.

"Children," she said with fond sternness, "wash up and ask Bernard what he's serving for lunch."

Amelia raced past me, then stopped, doubling back to show me 'something special.' In her grubby little hand was a mud-caked whistle. She'd found it on the ground by the stables.

"Grandma says the pea ball is stuck." She waved it in my face. "Want to blow it?"

"Ah, no. It's covered in mud."

She laughed. "You can't. It's broken." And rushed upstairs to hide it in her room.

Teddy explained it was Shadow's training whistle. He mimicked the horse whinnying and rearing up on his hind legs. "When Grandma whistles, he comes running. Just like a dog!"

By then Amelia was back, skipping and spinning her way into the kitchen, with Teddy chasing after her to keep her from getting the 'best' stool. Bernard poured out two glasses of apple juice and set down two plates of triangle-cut sandwiches. How he could concentrate with those two buzzing around was beyond me.

Once she was sure the children were settled, Katie moved over to the fireplace and tossed another log into the flame, sending a shower of sparks into the air. "That will keep them quiet for a little while," she said, almost to herself.

Louisa and I were sitting at the bar, she was trying to tempt me into a card game. When I declined she asked Katie if she'd like to play cribbage.

"No," Katie replied, "all that counting, it's too confusing."

Robson, who was slumped in an armchair scrolling on his phone, snorted. "Everything's too confusing for you nowadays, isn't that right, Mother. I have to wonder how much longer you'll be able to keep Shadow. He's a big brute of a horse, he needs a firm hand." Katie's face hardened but she didn't reply.

Robson rose to his feet and ambled into the kitchen. He stopped in the doorway and made a show of sniffing the air. "Christ, Bernard the food is rotting, you're supposed to be a famous chef, can't you smell it?" Then he shouted at the kids, telling them to speed it up. "I want you upstairs and packed in five minutes."

"Packed?" Katie followed Robson into the kitchen. "What on earth for?"

The children cast their wary eyes on their father when he joined them at the kitchen island. "Finish up." His tone was firm. "We're going back to the city."

Katie touched his arm. "Robson, the roads are impass-able; the police said so."

He shook her off without looking at her. "Amelia, Teddy, time to go. Do *not* make me say it twice."

By then Katie had maneuvered herself between Robson and the children. She was taller than he was and despite her age, was still a formidable presence.

Amelia tugged on Katie's arm. "Can we stay, Grandma? Please?"

"Of course you can stay, darling." She patted Amelia on the head and both children turned their solemn eyes on their father. Grandma had spoken. The matter was settled.

"For Christ's sake." Robson grabbed Teddy's shoulder and roughly hauled him off his stool. The boy lost his balance, knocking his juice glass flying. A sticky stream of apple juice flowed across the white tiles. Quickly, Bernard pulled a washcloth out of a drawer, dampened it, and bent down to mop up the mess.

"You too, Amelia," her father said, "Move it."

The little girl slid off her stool and hid behind her grandmother. In a clear determined voice she said, "No. I'm not going with you."

"Bloody hell." Robson was bellowing now. "Mother, I'll thank you to mind your own fucking business. Kids, move it. Now!"

The children ran to Bernard who looked down at them. Helpless.

But Katie stood firm, determined to reason with her son. "Robson, whatever you have to do in the city, it can't be as important as the children's safety. You'll be stuck on the highway between here and God-knows-where if you leave now. Wait until the roads are cleared, please."

"I don't give a fuck about the state of the roads," Robson

replied with a smirk. "You may recall, or maybe you don't, your memory is pretty pathetic these days, we flew in and we'll be flying out."

That's right, I thought, Robson had flown his family to Mirror Ranch in a small Cessna. It was parked at the hanger a half a mile away.

"That tiny plane? The winds are tricky in the valley, especially after a storm. You of all people should know that." Katie struggled to keep her voice level. "If you must go, leave the children here with me, for their sakes. Please, Robson."

"They're my children," he snapped. "They will do as I say. They're going. End of discussion."

That's when it happened. Katie stepped back, lifted her hand, and slapped Robson hard across the face. The sharp, quick sound echoed in the tiled kitchen. There was a moment of shocked silence, then Katie said, "You're a disgusting man. Worse than your father."

She called out to Bernard, demanding to know where Charlotte was. "And Jay, I want them both here, now." To do what, I wondered, nail Robson's feet to the floor so he couldn't leave?

Robson blinked at her, one hand cupping his cheek. Then glared at his children who were trying to make themselves small behind Bernard, and roared, "Get the fuck upstairs!"

They flew out of the kitchen and up the staircase like frightened rabbits and he stalked out after them.

Twenty minutes later his family was back in the lobby. Elise looked shattered, avoiding eye contact as she struggled with two wheelie bags, hers and Robson's larger one. The children were pale, clutching their tiny backpacks to their chests. Robson went straight to the reception desk and began to rifle through the drawers. "Where's the key to the suv?" he demanded. It was unclear who he was talking to.

Louisa looked at me, aghast. "This is insane, we have to do something."

"Like what? If Keith and AJ were here—where the hell are they anyway—they could tackle him, but Louisa, look at him. If his own mother and wife can't stop him, he certainly won't listen to us."

In the kitchen, Katie was speaking rapidly to Bernard, her movements were stiff and jerky. He gave a curt nod and came into the lobby where he joined Robson behind the reception desk. Reaching into a small box next to the rotary phone, he pulled out a key and offered to drive the family to the hanger. That way, he explained, he could drive the Escalade back after he'd dropped them off.

Robson snatched the key out of Bernard's hand, he abhorred that piece of crap car, but no one was driving the suv but him. If Bernard wanted to come along to drive the vehicle back to the Lodge, that was fine with him.

Bernard nodded and followed Robson to the front door. With a bang the double doors opened and Robson said, "Let's go."

Elise yanked at the rollie bags and the big one, Robson's got caught on the leg of the coffee table. She left it there and maneuvered her own bag out the double doors. By the time Robson retrieved it she and the children were straggling across the parking lot.

I prayed the Escalade's windows had been damaged by the storm, anything to make it impossible to drive, but the engine turned over and in a flurry of flying gravel, they were gone.

JOURNAL

Mother, you look pale, did you forget your meds again? Honestly, Mother, you'd forget your head if it wasn't screwed on tight.

Robson stopped calling me Mom, let alone Mommy, when he was eleven. Charlie said it was about time the boy started showing some independence. But Charlie didn't hear how Robson said it when his father was not around.

Mother. At eleven he said it slowly, as if the syllables were marbles in his mouth. But as he grew into his teen and became an adult the word slid off his tongue, coloured by impudence, condescension, and resentment.

Particularly when I asked too many questions at our Board meetings or voted with Parker and Charlotte, against him and Charlie. Mother, use your head for heaven's sake!

I thought I'd fall off his radar after I moved to Mirror Ranch, but every time he comes here he gets more aggressive.

Mother, you're too weak to control that horse. It might have to be put down.

Mother, you're so forgetful. Are you sure you're not suffering from dementia?

Mother...Mother...Mother...

Who the hell does he think he's talking to.

CHAPTER 48

By the time Charlotte and Jay returned to the Lodge, Katie was barely coherent.

"Charlotte, he's insane. You know the winds around here. They're so unpredictable. The last time he pulled a stunt like this he flipped the plane on the runway. Oh Charlotte, he's going to crash and kill them all. I just know it." Katie was talking very fast and wringing her hands. "I don't care what happens to him, I really don't. He's a grown man, he'll have brought this on himself. But how can he do that to his own children?"

Charlotte wrapped her arms around her mother who was wailing by now. She caught Jay's eye, and tipped her head toward a kitchen cupboard, and was mouthing *Get her meds* when Parker came down the stairs. At the sight of her weeping mother she stopped.

"What's happening? Charlotte, what's going on?"

"It's about bloody time you showed up," Charlotte snapped. Jay came to her side and passed her a handful of pills. She took them and told her husband to go after Robson. "Knock him out if you have to. Drag him back here. I'll take care of Mom."

"No!" Katie smacked the pills out of Charlotte's hand. "No one is going to 'take care of Mom.'" She shrugged Charlotte's hand off her shoulder, refusing to 'have a lie-down' until she knew the children were safe. "In Calgary or the Lodge, I don't care!" Her arms were crossed and her eyes were dark with fury, only a madman would buck her now.

Jay rummaged in the registration desk and pulled out his car keys. "Will you be okay?" he called to Charlotte who was murmuring to Katie and did not respond.

"Everyone stop. Please." Parker's hands were up, she looked helpless and resigned. "It's too late. Even if you could catch him Jay, you won't be able to stop him." She'd worked with Robson long enough to know that when he got like this, he was like a Sherman tank, nothing would deter him from his mission, however stupid and ill-considered it might be.

"I refuse to accept that." Katie marched into the lobby, shouting that Jay had to leave at once. Jay paused, then dropped the keys back into the drawer and declared Parker was right, it was too late. Robson had a significant head start. No one could catch him now.

Opal materialized at Charlotte's elbow and gently suggested everyone could use a nice cup of tea. We gathered around the kitchen island and watched Opal boil the water, our eyes bouncing from the clock and the front door, back and forth, as we waited for Bernard to return.

The sky darkened and it started to rain. Keith and AJ stomped in through the lobby doors, flapping their jackets and pulling off their rubber boots. They'd been chopping up broken trees and the hard work whet their appetites, they couldn't wait for lunch.

It took them a moment to realize something was terribly wrong.

By the time Charlotte finished retelling the story, Katie was crying so hard she could hardly breathe.

———

Two hours later the lobby doors burst open and the children staggered into the room. For a moment I thought Bernard had been able to talk some sense into Robson after all, but then Amelia began to wail.

CHAPTER 49

Katie leapt off the sofa and fell to her knees in front of Amelia, clutching the child's damp little body to her own. "Thank God you're safe! Oh thank God you're both safe!" She touched Teddy's pale face and brushed Amelia's damp hair off her forehead. The little girl's bottom lip quivered and she sobbed even louder.

"Darling, darling, what is it? Tell Grandma what's wrong."

"Daddy." Amelia gulped through her tears. "Daddy—"

Bernard appeared in the doorway. His face was grim. "Katie, take the kids into the kitchen." His eyes searched the room until he spotted Jay. With a flick of the wrist he motioned, *outside,* and the two men went back out to the parking lot. We followed them.

The Escalade was parked at a crazy angle in the parking lot, its doors wide open, its windshield wipers clicking back and forth. Elise was hunched in the front passenger seat, her head in her hands, weeping. Louisa and I helped her climb out of the SUV and took her into the kitchen where she threw her arms around her sobbing children. Katie hovered over them, looking helpless and confused.

We returned to the lobby and started shoving armchairs and end tables out of the way, clearing a path from the front door to the red leather sofa. Parker and Charlotte held the double doors open.

"You'd think we'd be better at this by now." I didn't realize I'd said it out loud until Louisa shushed me with an elbow to the ribs.

The guys had a dreadful time getting Robson's body through the lobby doors. He was a slight man, but still a floppy, dead weight and it took some effort to maneuver his passage through the lobby.

The children watched, horrified, from the kitchen. If we'd had our wits about us we would have sent them upstairs *before* we opened the back of the suv and dragged Robson out, then we could have taken him straight to the cooler and deposited him next to his dad, but it didn't occur to us at the time. Like I said, you'd think we'd be better at this by now.

Finally after much grunting and muttering—the guys handled Robson as if he'd injured his back and they were trying not to make it worse—they eased Robson's dead weight down to the sofa.

And I had a random thought: If that was my sofa I'd ditch it because I'd never be able to look at it again without thinking about dead people.

Raised voices came from the kitchen. Katie insisted on seeing her son. Reluctantly Charlotte and Parker stood aside, allowing Katie to approach the body. Silently, she gazed down at Robson as if he were already embalmed and on display in a shiny, new casket.

"His eyes are closed." Her tone was flat and she said no more before turning on her heel and returning to the kitchen. I caught a glimpse of her face. Blank. As if she'd confronted a lamp post not her dead son.

A few minutes later, the Moore women gathered around the children and shepherded them upstairs. No one glanced at the red leather sofa and what was lying there.

Jay waited until they disappeared into the upstairs corridor before turning to Bernard and saying, "I don't understand. What happened?"

Bernard's eyes flicked to the kitchen where Opal was staring out the back window, a tea towel in her hand, then settled on Robson lying dead on the sofa. "Where's his jacket? Did anyone see his jacket?"

We all turned to stare at the body. Robson lay there like a pasty-faced mannequin, one arm limp across his chest, the other dangling down to the floor. Dishevelled, with his shirt untucked and mud on the knees of his trousers. Robson had been wearing a jacket, green like his eyes, when he dragged his family out of here two hours ago. Where was it now?

Bernard rose and went out through the double doors, jogging across the parking lot and popping open the back of the Escalade. He crawled inside. A minute later he was back. No jacket.

Stiffly, he walked back into the kitchen and spoke to Opal. She pointed to the hooks by the back door. He plucked Robson's green jacket off the wall, squeezed the pockets, then carried it back into the lobby and tossed it down on the registration desk.

Behind us came the murmur of the Moore women, Katie, Parker and Charlotte, as they swept down the wide staircase. None of them looked at the red leather sofa, seemingly repelled by what lay there. Katie gave Bernard a tiny smile and said she was grateful no harm had come to the children.

Someone said we should move the body into the cooler and the lunatic voice in my head muttered that stuffing dead people into coolers seemed to be a regular event around here.

Finally, after the cooler door was tightly sealed and Robson was…what's the right word…*resting* next to his father, we settled around the kitchen island.

"Let's have it," AJ said as he peeled some beer cans out of a six-pack plastic ring and handed them around, "what happened to Robson?"

CHAPTER 50

Bernard's beer remained untouched as he explained how Robson had died. The drive to the small hanger took longer than expected. The high winds from the bomb cyclone blew away the gravel turning the road into a washboard. Robson was driving too fast and would have ripped out the undercarriage on an exposed rock if Bernard hadn't yanked hard on the steering wheel. "That made Robson really mad," he said, "and I kept my hands off the wheel after that."

By midafternoon, they'd reached the hanger. Robson parked the Escalade in front of the office and gave Elise the keys, telling her to wait inside with the children while he readied the plane. Bernard was tasked with clearing the fallen branches and debris off the tarmac.

"The runway was a mess." Bernard toyed with his beer can, so the label went around and around, but didn't drink. "I was almost finished when I heard an almighty crack. Damned if the lodgepole pine right behind me didn't snap off and fall across the runway. It damn near took my head off, it was that close.

"Robson saw the whole thing and came tearing out of

the hanger and we grabbed ahold of some big branches and try to haul that sucker out of the way. But it was a monster and wouldn't budge. It was raining pretty hard by then and we're both getting soaked. That damn tree coulda been welded to the ground for all the good we were doing. It wasn't going anywhere." He gazed down at his palms which were red and streaked with tree gum.

"Robson was getting madder and madder and he sent me back to the hanger to get an axe or a hacksaw or something, but there's nothing in there. Big surprise, it's not Home Depot.

"By then Elise and the kids were back to the SUV. She rolled down her window and yelled at me: *Tell Robson to come back to the car. We're not going anywhere.* That woman was spitting mad and the kids were freaking out in the back seat. So I did what I was told, I said his wife says forget it, we're going back to the Lodge.

"The man goes bat-shit crazy, screaming at me to get off my f-ing ass and do as I'm told. So I grab ahold of the tree and try to haul it away." Bernard's hands were bunched into fists and he jerked them back and forth mimicking how he had yanked on the tree branch. "But that tree's not going anywhere. It didn't matter what that arrogant bastard did." Bernard's face reddened as if he realized he was bad-mouthing the dead.

"And boom. Just like that he does a face plant right into the tree. I figured he slipped or fainted or something." Bernard stole a glance at the cooler. "When he didn't get up I hauled him out of the branches and lay him down on the tarmac. I loosened his collar, like they do on TV to give him air, right? But he wasn't breathing."

Bernard lifted his shoulders in a sad shrug. "Elise is watching from the SUV and comes running. She throws herself onto his body, screaming Robson, Robson, and slapping his face. The guy's head is whipping from side to side. Finally, she realizes he's gone and she helps me haul him back to the suv. And we come home."

Those poor children, I thought, the whole thing played out right before their eyes, like a living nightmare.

There was a long pause as we thought about what Bernard had said.

"What?" Bernard jutted his jaw. He looked angry. "I did everything I could."

"Of course you did," Charlotte said. Calmly, she reassured him. "Of course you did."

Keith cleared his throat and pulled his phone out of his pocket, saying he'd call the police.

"The police?" Bernard looked surprised.

"Yeah, to tell them there's been another death, in case they have to bring another ambulance."

Or whatever it is they use to cart dead bodies around. At this rate they were going to have to bring a bloody caravan.

JOURNAL

Ghosts can enter a room through a keyhole, or so I'm told. The only way to keep them out is to hang a sieve over the doorknob. Protoplasm is a tricky state of being. Ghosts don't like to be riced and diced.

Someone must have held the cooler door open too long, letting Charlie escape.

Now look what he's done, dragged Robson back into the cooler with him.

Got to hand it to you Charlie, that's one hell of a succession plan.

CHAPTER 51

Friday

Parker and Charlotte were talking softly in the reception area when I came down for breakfast the next morning. They looked up, politely asking how I'd slept. I didn't know what to make of it. Robson was lying next to his father in the cooler and yet it was business as usual at Mirror Ranch. The shock from yesterday had disappeared, like the mist rolling off the moors.

It wasn't until midafternoon that I was able to ask Jay whether I could view the CCTV tapes.

"Funny you should ask," he said, "I've been meaning to check the tapes myself but with everything that happened yesterday…" He shrugged.

No kidding.

Jay's office was a small, cramped space with a cluttered L-shaped desk, two mismatched desk chairs on wheels and an old metal stool. On the desk sat a state-of-the-art laptop and two CCTV monitors. The screens were divided into quadrants, The first monitor showed images of the Lodge, front and the back doors, the main entrance to the stable and the conference centre, while the second monitor captured the door to the spa, the archery hut and the airplane hanger.

"Where do you want to start?" Jay asked.

"How about Sunday, the day Charlie died?"

"Sure." Jay fiddled with the joystick as I dragged over the metal stool and positioned myself to his right. He'd just teed up the tape when Charlotte entered. I explained what we were up to and she rolled a desk chair over to Jay's left.

"Any particular time?" Jay asked as he tapped the keyboard.

"Start at the beginning."

12:01 a.m. The time stamp appeared and began to race through the early hours of Sunday morning. There was no moon and the stars were hidden behind heavy clouds, all the quadrants, except the one in front of the conference centre, were illuminated.

Charlotte pointed at the screen. "Jay, the conference centre—"

"Yeah, it's on my to-do list."

At 6:30 a.m. Bernard appeared in the camera over the kitchen door. Seconds later the screen flared, he'd turned on the kitchen lights. Two minutes later Opal came through the same entrance. I wondered which path they'd taken. Likely the staff path. It would be quicker, but in the dark more treacherous than the well trod north-south trail.

The time stamp ticked up to 7:30 a.m. and Charlotte emerged from the kitchen and disappeared around the side of the Lodge, returning twenty minutes later. Now, staring at the monitor she said, "I was checking the strawberry netting, the birds keep pulling it down."

An hour later Katie hustled out the back door heading to the north-south trail. She disappeared from view until she was picked up by the camera over the stable doors twenty minutes later.

"How come we lose Mom for so long on the trail?" Charlotte asked.

"It's a trade-off," Jay froze the image. "I want maximum coverage at the Lodge. This is a superwide camera, FOV is 180."

"Jay, I hear you talking but I don't know what you're saying."

"Superwide gives me a field of vision of one hundred and eighty degrees. Good coverage, but distorted, like a fisheye lens, nevertheless, it's the sensible choice around the Lodge, the camera at the stables has a narrower field of vision, there's nothing of real value down there."

Charlotte glanced at him. "The horses cost a fortune."

"Yes, but they're big, I think we'd notice if a random stranger tried to sneak Shadow out of the barn."

"Not at night," she retorted.

He let that go, pointing instead to the images of the other buildings. "Here we've got standard angle cameras monitoring the points of egress. Two cameras over the two doors at the Lodge and one each at the conference centre, spa and archery hut because that's where the guests congregate. The view is narrower, but the detail and clarity are better, so if there's a security breach at any of these entrances we've got a good shot of the perpetrators."

Jay sounded like a CCTV salesman, but then again, he was a geek and spying on the guests with state-of-the-art equipment was probably preferable to slogging through the underbrush looking for a broken Wi-Fi cable.

"Okay, she's back." Jay pointed at the monitor.

Katie was leading Shadow out of the barn. She leaned close to his cheek and appeared to be talking to him the way I talk to Quincy before we head out for a run. She swung up into the saddle and they galloped around the side of the barn and disappeared out of camera range.

"She's heading for the meadow by the conference centre," Charlotte said. "She looks happy, doesn't she. Riding is her therapy." I thought it was an interesting observation given that it was hard to make out Katie's expression in the grainy footage.

A few minutes later Katie and Shadow galloped into camera range by the door to the conference centre. Shadow slowed to a trot, then stopped. Katie sat tall in the saddle, looked around, then with a quick movement of her torso, urged Shadow forward. They wheeled past the building, heading in the direction of the windswept meadow.

Nothing happened on the monitor for thirty minutes and I revised my earlier opinion: spying on people wasn't as nearly as exciting as it's cracked up to be. Jay rotated his shoulders and I heard his spine pop. Charlotte stepped out to fetch us some coffee, returning a few minutes later.

"Coffee will be ready in ten minutes, did I miss anything?"

"No," I said, "your mom just came back. She's in the barn with Shadow." We waited a few minutes and Katie reappeared, moving with a fluid grace. She had a good three decades on us, but Louisa and I were so stiff after our ride we could hardly put one foot in front of the other. Katie ambled up the path, disappeared and eventually reappeared in the camera over the front door of the Lodge.

Jay cranked up the speed, Louisa and I burst out of the Lodge like Keystone Kops, walking in double time down to the garden, then returning to the Lodge where we were almost trampled by the children who hurtled past us on their way to the north-south trail. "They were playing a strange game," I said, "if you can tag the other guy, you get to knock them down."

Charlotte laughed. "Those kids are always playing strange games."

The boughs of the pine trees beat the air in double time and the pebbles and pinecones on the path rippled, making it look alive, like a snake.

Jay cranked up the speed again and a few minutes later said, "Hold on, we've got activity." AJ and I appeared on the tape, we were heading up to Dragon Falls. Our Keystone-Kops images laughed and pointed at each other's shoes. I remembered AJ saying my runners were inappropriate and me replying I knew how to take care of myself. An hour later I proved him right by slipping off the path and twisting my ankle.

The minutes raced by until we returned to the Lodge at five-thirty. AJ held the door open and I hobbled inside. The way we moved reminded me of the little man and the little woman who pop out of a German weather house when the barometer changes. Given the bomb cyclone gathering strength overhead, AJ should have been first through the door, carrying a little wooden umbrella to signify bad weather on the horizon.

"Everyone is inside," Charlotte said. "it's dinner time."

The time stamp read *6:35 p.m.*

The sky darkened and the cones of light shining on the CCTV screens became brighter and flecked with rain. The time stamp raced: *7:00 p.m… 7:30 p.m… 8:00 p.m.*

"Wait!" Charlotte touched the image on the screen showing the Lobby door. "Jay, back it up."

CHAPTER 52

Charlotte's wobbly desk chair squeaked as she rolled closer to the monitor. The camera over the lobby doors picked up a dark shadow. It flickered, then faded away.

"Did you see that?" Charlotte asked. We did, but we couldn't make it out.

Twenty minutes later there was movement at the barn door. Charlie blinked up at the camera in the sparkling rain. His walrus mustache glistening with raindrops as he yanked open the barn door and ducked inside.

"Huh," Jay said quietly. "The shadow was Charlie. When he left the dining room, he crossed the terrace, the front door camera almost caught him, but he was stayed out of range. What's he up to?"

"If he got to the barn why didn't he stay there?" Charlotte asked. "The rain was picking up by then. He could have called to let us know he'd taken shelter."

Fat chance, I thought, *Charlie was a modern day Hemingway, a few raindrops falling on his head wouldn't faze him.*

Jay clicked the tape back to normal speed and we watched the white raindrops fall through the cone of white light for what seemed like a very long time.

"Is Dad still in there?" Charlotte asked Jay. "Did he slip out the back?"

"If he did, we wouldn't know, there aren't any camera on the doors at the back."

It crossed my mind that we were waiting for a man who had no idea he'd be dead soon. The glow on the monitor changed, something was happening. In a swirl of wind and rain Charlie burst into view. He was riding Shadow.

Charlotte's breath caught in her throat. "Oh, Mom's not going to like that." As if Charlie were still alive and Katie was going to give him an earful when she saw the tape. "Dad's way too rough with the horses, especially Shadow. He hates it when Shadow defies him."

"Tell me about it," Jay muttered under his breath.

My mind went back to the day after Charlie died. Charlotte had discovered abrasions on Shadow's flank. What had Charlie done to him?

"Jay," I asked, "can you follow them?"

"Yeah, but not for long." He tapped the keyboard. The camera near the kitchen door filled the screen, catching a fleeting glimpse of horse and rider, Jay played it again, slower this time. Charlie's heels jabbed Shadow's sides, forcing the horse father up the trail.

"God, I wish he wouldn't do that," Charlotte said. "It stresses the horses."

Even I who knew nothing about horses could tell Shadow was distressed by the way he moved, stiffly and tossing his head. The time stamp read 9:12 p.m. An hour after Charlie had flounced out the dining room. Six hours before we found his body.

With horse and rider out of view, the screens went quiet. Six cones of light caught the trees writhing in the wind and the rain bucketed out of the sky. The bomb cyclone had Mirror Ranch in its grip.

"Where is he?" Charlotte muttered.

"I can't see anything." Jay replied.

"Stop!" Charlotte tapped the monitor in front of her. The time stamp read 11:35 p.m. "What's that?"

Jay rewound the tape. A whisper of movement flickered in the camera over the kitchen door. Jay replayed it again and again; you could almost but not quite see a shape. It was maddeningly ephemeral, like a wisp of candy floss on your tongue.

"Maybe a raccoon or a fox?" Charlotte asked.

"Could be." Jay replied.

At 1:13 a.m. I saw something. "There! By the barn. Something shimmered in the light." Jay ran it again, slower.

Shadow flashed through the pearly haze of light, distorted in the fisheye lens, then disappeared under the dark mass of the pine tree that stood just outside the barn door.

"Did you see Charlie?" I asked.

Jay rewound the tape. Shadow's silvery body passed backward and forward. Riderless.

"Where's Charlie?" I asked.

"Shadow must have gone around to the back of the barn. Can you see Daddy?" Charlotte glanced anxiously at Jay, then back at the monitors.

"Sorry, babe, I've got nothing." Jay fiddled with a dial, speeding up the tape. Charlie was gone.

Charlotte drew a deep breath. "Somewhere along the north-south trail something spooked Shadow and he bucked Dad off."

"Or," Jay suggested, "Charlie simply fell off. He'd had a lot to drink, Charlotte."

Charlotte nodded slowly. "Whatever possessed Dad take

Shadow out in that weather? He knows Shadow doesn't like thunder. Why couldn't he just leave Shadow alone?"

I had my theories, but this was not the time or place to share them.

The time clock continued to whir until the cameras at the Lodge exploded with light. It was 2:24 a.m. Charlotte had raised the alarm. Every light in the Lodge was lit, every corner of the Lodge had been searched and now everyone was flying out the doors, running along rain slick paths to the stables and convention centre, and the spa and the archery hut frantically searching for Charlie.

Until we found his lifeless body and carried it back down the hill to the Lodge where Katie was blissfully sleeping.

CHAPTER 53

D amn it, Louisa, where are you?" This was typical Louisa. Ever since the pine tree incident that girl had been glued to my side, but now that I was desperate to talk to her she was nowhere to be found.

Even Bernard, who knew more about our comings and goings than Big Brother, had no idea where she'd disappeared to. I paced in front of the river stone fireplace until Amelia hopped off the red leather sofa to inform me, in a very loud whisper, that my sister had gone off with Charlotte to look at the exotic plants in the greenhouse.

"You can't get in. It's locked," Amelia's eyes grew round. "Teddy has a pick-lock kit but even he can't get in."

Exotic plants? Under lock and key?

"Amelia, are these plants poisonous?"

She gave me a solemn nod.

Louisa is the gardener in our family, some of her favourite plants, foxglove and lily of the valley, are poisonous. I've told her many times she must have been a witch in a past life. "A good witch," she'd reply. "There will be no poisonous plants in my garden. I don't care how beautiful they are. Quincy is so stupid he'll eat them and die."

Now Amelia was dancing on her toes. She grabbed my hand, swinging it back and forth. "Let's go for a walk. The fresh air will do us good." It sounded like something an adult would say.

Soon we were heading up the path that would take us to Lucky's house. According to Amelia, the pig liked to go for a stroll every afternoon but the rainy weather had kept him cooped up in his little house. "Poor Lucky, he needs some exercise."

The afternoon sun was warm on our faces as we followed the trail around a small copse of trees, picking our way past the broken branches, their leaves fading and already starting to curl.

Amelia was chattering like a magpie, she'd been accepted into an exclusive private school on the outskirts of the city. Teddy was already enrolled there— "Mommy says he's a troublemaker"—his behavior could have jeopardized Amelia's chances of admission but she'd impressed the intake officer and had secured a spot. "Daddy said Mommy was being silly to worry. I was guaranteed a place."

"Oh, why is that?"

"Daddy built them a brand new music room, they wouldn't dare turn me down."

She skipped ahead of me, singing. "I'm going to the best school with the best people." The kid was only five, already she'd learned the dynamics of money and power.

We rounded a gentle curve in the path. Lucky's house, a well maintained structure that looked like a miniature barn, was just up ahead.

I asked Amelia the question adults always ask little kids when they're trying to make conversation. "What do you want to be when you grow up?"

"I'm going to be a chee-eff," she replied. Hopping up and down waiting for me to catch up to her.

"A chee-eff? What's a chee-eff?"

"Guess!" She twirled around and raced up the path.

"Hmm, does this person work with animals?"

"Nope!"

"In an office?"

"Nope!"

"On the moon?"

She laughed and ran back to me, her thin, red jacket flapping in the breeze, then she stopped and tapped her finger against her chin as if she were giving my last guess serious consideration.

"Nope!" she said, sprinting the last fifteen feet to Lucky's pen where she swung open the squeaky wooden gate. As we entered the pen, Amelia called Lucky's name and told me to get his walking stick out of the shed. When I returned with a long, thin stick with a red tassel on the end, Amelia explained that Lucky was well trained. Charlotte had been taking him for walks since he was little.

"Lucky!" she yelled his name again, and with a fanfare of grunts and snuffles an enormous black pig trotted out from behind the little barn, his ears tipped forward and his funny little tail sticking straight out. I've never been eyeball to eyeball with a pig before, but he looked pleased to see us.

"You can walk him," Amelia said after giving me a short tutorial on how to use the walking stick: A light tap on the cheek meant turn, a tap between the ears meant slow down, and a tap on the back meant speed up.

I glanced at the thin willow stick, then stared at the two hundred pound beast that had survived a wolf attack. "You're sure this will work?"

She skipped ahead of me and Lucky trotted after her.

Soon I got the hang of it. It was like walking Quincy, except Lucky had a delightful sashay and didn't tear off after squirrels or rabbits.

"Do you give up, do you? Huh? Huh?" I still had no idea what a chee-eff was. I begged for one last clue.

"Okay, he works in a kitchen and makes you pancakes in the morning."

"Ah! A chee-eff! Like Bernard the chef."

"Yes, yes, yes." She danced over and reached for the walking stick, waving its tasseled end around in tiny circles. Lucky grunted and sat down.

"Why do you want to be a chef like Bernard?" I asked.

"If I'm a chef I can have all the cakes and cookies I want." Then she frowned. "But not *exactly* like Chef Bernard. I want a house when I grown up."

"Bernard has a lovely house. He lives at the Lodge in this beautiful valley." I stopped to take in the rolling gray-green hills and the ridge of mountains on the horizon, Bernard wasn't kidding when he said Mirror Ranch was one of the most breathtaking places on the planet. "Isn't that right, Lucky," I said to the pig who was now trotting briskly in front of me.

We stopped at the top of the small hillock to give Lucky a rest and Amelia pulled a plastic bag out of her pocket and extracted a large pink marshmallow.

"Sit," she said to the pig. To my surprise he sat…for two seconds, but never mind, he's a pig. His head came forward and he bumped the marshmallow out of Amelia's hand. It landed on the grass and he devoured it as delicately as he could.

"No," Amelia said. "Not this house. I mean before Bernard moved here; he didn't have two pennies to rub together or a roof over his head." Against she sounded like an adult and I reminded myself never to say anything I didn't want repeated in her presence.

Lucky turned his tiny black eyes on me. I opened my hands the way I did with Quincy to indicate I wasn't hiding any marshmallows and he swung his snout back to Amelia, grunting for more.

As we turned back toward Lucky's enclosure, I asked Amelia if she was talking about Bernard's life in New York City and she said Bernard was a bum before he met Auntie Charlotte.

Lucky, all two hundred pounds of him, was picking up speed as he trundled down the hill. I tapped him between the ears with the tasselled stick and he slowed down. This willow stick was amazing.

"How do you know that, Amelia?"

"Daddy said. He doesn't like Bernard; he says Bernard doesn't know his place." Knowing Amelia, she probably went straight to Bernard to report what her daddy thought of him. Discretion wasn't exactly her strong suit. I had a feeling it never would be.

When we reached the pen, Amelia opened the gate and Lucky sauntered back into his enclosure while I returned to his walking stick to the shed. He explored his pen as if he'd never seen it before, churning up the fresh straw and making himself a lovely new bed. Amelia hung over the fence, tickling Lucky's back with a piece of grass, making his skin twitch.

Thoughtfully she glanced up at me and said, "Chef Bernard said even Lucky's house was nicer than some of the places he stayed in." She turned back to the pig. "You'd let Chef Bernard stay with you, wouldn't you, Lucky."

CHAPTER 54

When Ameilia and I returned to the Lodge we were greeted by a jubilant AJ who rushed across the lobby, scooped me off my feet and spun me around as if we were ice dancing.

"Great news!" He was practically yelling in my ear. "We're getting out of here tomorrow! Finally! Can you believe it?"

I pulled my head back to look at him. "I take it the RCMP are coming?"

There was an awkward moment when we realized we were nose to nose and gently he set me down on the hardwood floor. He couldn't keep that goofy grin off his face as he explained the highway maintenance crews had finished clearing the high traffic roads and were working on the Class D's, like the one leading up to Mirror Ranch. They'd be here tomorrow by midafternoon at the latest. I glanced into the kitchen. I couldn't see the cooler from here but still I shuddered.

AJ followed my gaze and said, "They are bringing a medical examiner and they reminded us to stay out of the woods where we found Charlie's body"—every time they talked to Charlotte they'd said that. Who in their right mind would want to revisit the spot where Charlie died? — "As soon as they get our statements we're free to go." His blue eyes sparkled. "Can you believe it! Tomorrow we're going home."

"What about Robson?" I asked.

"What do you mean?"

"Never mind." There were two dead bodies in the cooler, but for some reason no one seemed too concerned about how Robson died.

I glanced around the lobby. "Where is everybody?"

Other than the sound of Opal and Bernard warbling to a golden oldie on the radio, the lobby was deserted. Even Amelia had disappeared.

AJ tilted his head toward the staircase. "Upstairs packing."

———

"Let's go, let's go." Louisa clapped her hands and pointed to her watch. "Time's a wasting." She hurled my rollie bag onto my bed and started pawing through a dresser drawer.

"Leave it. I'll do it." Every time Louisa packs for me something goes missing. "Louisa, can I ask you something—"

"You wouldn't believe Charlotte's greenhouse." She cut me off to rhapsodize about the large translucent structure than ran across the bottom of the kitchen garden. It sounded like a space-aged temple, arched and sleek and constructed of polycarbonate which, she informed me, was better than glass when it came to flying debris.

When Charlotte and Louisa had entered the greenhouse, they noticed the musty smell of wet sawdust. "One of the vents snapped off in the storm and the interior gutter that recycles water was cracked. Charlotte almost lost her mind, worried that the miniature cashew trees would be waterlogged."

"She's growing cashews?"

"Yeah, isn't that cool."

"Wait." I closed a low drawer and sat back on my heels. "Aren't cashews toxic?"

I remembered Bernard's signature salad. He said it was Charlie's favourite dish, but Charlie was feeling out of sorts and wouldn't be joining us for dinner. "The poor guy's been sick for two days." Bernard smiled. "Which means there's all the more for you guys." Fresh greens sprinkled with the best cashews I'd ever tasted. It never occurred to me to ask where they'd come from.

Louisa was rummaging in the dresser, pulling out my socks and stuffing them into a rollie bag, hopefully it was mine.

"Lots of plants are toxic, even irises, if you eat them." Louisa was something of an expert on poisonous plants and had her own little poison library at home. "Look." She pulled out her camera and showed me a photo of the lonely little cashew nut dangling out of the pulpy yellowish fruit.

"The poisonous plants are kept under lock and key. It's the only way to keep the kids out of there." She flicked past more photos reciting their names, foxglove, oleander, nightshade, yew. "They're stunning."

Then she turned and went into the bathroom, emerging with my hairbrush and makeup kit. Gently, I took them out of her hands and returned them to their place on the marble countertop.

"Louisa, listen. Jay showed me the CCTV footage from the night Charlie died. Something strange happened."

""Yeah, Charlie died." She glanced at her watch. "Come on, we're late for dinner."

The mood at dinner was disconcerting, like a foreign film that's been poorly dubbed. We talked about our relief that the police were finally coming, but there was an underlying sense of foreboding. How were we going to explain our behavior over the last few days? Charlie and Robson were stone cold dead in the cooler and we'd been carrying on as if they were away on a business trip, filling our days with hiking, board games and walking the pig. In retrospect, it seemed a little odd.

Despite our dwindling provisions, Bernard had outdone himself. He was determined to clear everything out the pantry before the food order arrived.

"Bernard, so help me, if you give us food poisoning," Parker said, eyeing the forkful of tamale casserole she raised to her lips.

Charlotte laughed. "Better you than our paying guests."

Despite the gallows humour we ate with gusto and I realized that consciously or unconsciously we'd been curbing our appetites, not quite sure if the police would show up before the food ran out.

I turned to Parker and said, "I'll bet you'll be glad to see the back of us. Your family needs time to grieve properly."

She pulled her eyes away from Katie who was laughing at Teddy's knock-knock joke. Shaking her head, she said, "We'll be all right. There's so much I have to do to make things right."

Without thinking how it would sound, I said the next

dumb thing that popped into my head. "I expect that'll be easier now that Charlie and Robson are gone."

A peculiar look crossed her face, horrified at what I'd said I fell all over myself trying to apologize.

She smiled as she reached for the cream jug. "It's all right. Evie. Everyone's nerves are shot. Don't worry about it." When she picked up the creamer she noticed it was empty. I took it from her, saying I'd go to the kitchen and refill it.

Bernard was standing just outside the backdoor, smoking a cigarette. He dropped it to the ground and snuffed it out the minute he saw me.

"Here, let me get that," he said as he took the creamer from my hand and walked over to the cooler. It wasn't until the door popped open that he realized his mistake. He gave an embarrassed chuckle and shut the door.

"You'd think I'd know by now that there's nothing in there."

Nothing but two dead men. Who were making me very nervous.

JOURNAL

*F*ive years ago Charlie decided we needed a bigger apartment. We're talking about our place in New York City. It was huge for two people, but apparently a 5,000 square foot unit in the best building in town was no longer suitable for a man of his stature.

He bought the unit next door to ours. The renovations took two years. Mitchell, the designer, and I made three trips to Europe picking out furniture and accessories. Charlie wanted it done right. And it was. Our apartment was featured in Architectural Digest.

I learned a lot from Mitchell and his staff, but the person who taught me the most was the locksmith who installed a state of the art safe in Charlie's study.

Over the course of a boozy afternoon—the safe had arrived but he couldn't install it because the painters were touching up the lacquer on the other side of the wall—he showed me how to override the passcode if I ever needed to get inside the safe. I'd told him that Charlie thought I was an airhead and to save myself embarrassment I'd be ever so grateful if he could help me out. That wasn't true of course.

It was Charlie's safe, he would never give me the passcode but the locksmith didn't need to know that.

A couple of months later after a trip to Lucerne, Charlie breezed into his study and locked the door. He emerged, all smiles. Like the old Charlie I'd married. After he left for work I used the locksmith's override to check the contents of the safe.

I found some strange banking documents.

A little bit of Googling proved to be illuminating. Charlie had opened two bank accounts in Panama.

I would not have known how much money was in those accounts but for Charlie's handwritten notes, also in the safe. For a financial genius, the man's a simpleton when it comes to personal security.

Hundreds of millions of dollars were hidden away from the tax man's prying eye.

I copied the account numbers. One day they'll come in handy.

CHAPTER 55

Thanks to Louisa it took us more than an hour to get ready for bed. She did such a grand job of packing that she couldn't find her pyjama bottoms or her makeup bag. God forbid she go to bed without putting on her moisturizer.

She also managed to pack up my watch. She denied it, reminding me that the little loop on the leather strap was worn out; it probably broke and the watch could be anywhere on Mirror Ranch's 640 acres.

"Damn it, Louisa," I snapped, "stop telling me it's lost and help me find it."

Without a word she went into the bathroom and pulled out all the towels stacked on the glass shelf behind the large marble tub.

I glanced around the room. If I were a small slim black Birks watch were would I hide? My eyes fell on my nightstand. The top drawer was ajar. Maybe Opal found it and tucked it into the drawer for safe keeping.

One yank on the drawer did nothing. It was jammed, half open, half closed. Squeezing my hand through a three inch gap I spread my fingers, feeling around. Bingo! The slender leather strap curled around my little finger. Grasping it, pincer-like, I was inching it out of the drawer when my fingers brushed against something else.

"What on earth are you doing?" Louisa was watching me from the bathroom door. By then I was on my knees, one hand braced against the nightstand, the other stuck in the narrow drawer.

"I've got it; but there's something else in here." Working slowly I was able to prise it out of the drawer.

"Probably a Gideon Bible," she said.

"Ha ha."

I was eight when I heard *Rocky Racoon* on the radio for the first time and instantly became a hardcore Beatles fan. When we went on vacation I'd turn our hotel room upside down searching for a Gideon Bible, convinced it would contain a secret code or something. Why else would the Beatles mention that specific bible in a song. It took me years to admit the reference was simply Paul McCartney being clever.

When I finally plucked the book out of the drawer I could see it wasn't a bible at all. Small, slim, with a distinctive marbled cover like a vintage book. Sepia coloured pages covered with tightly spaced handwriting. Little bits of prose interspersed with drawings and lists.

My cell phone rang. The noise startled me and I dropped the book onto the hardwood floor. A few sepia pages fluttered out. Louisa scooped them up, saying, "Who on earth is calling you at this time of night?"

CHAPTER 56

Who else?" I muttered as Louisa sorted through the loose sepia pages, trying to reinsert them in the little book in their proper places. I showed her the Caller ID. *Madeline*.

Clearing my throat I picked up the call. "Madeline, it's late. This better be good."

"No need to bite my head off," she replied.

"Sorry, it's been a harrowing week, everyone is at the end of their tether. But the cops are coming tomorrow, this will all be over soon." Leaning back against the headboard I put the phone on speaker. "So, Madeline, what can I do for you at this ungodly hour?"

Our bedroom filled with the shrill sound of Rupert the cockatiel screeching at the love birds. He was calling them nasty names. Madeline must be in the conservatory.

"Listen" she talked a little louder to be heard over the menagerie, "I don't want to alarm you—"

Louisa scrambled off her bed and grabbed my phone, shouting into it. "What happened? Is Quincy all right?"

In the background Quincy started to bark.

"Shh Quincy," Madeline scolded the dog. "I'm talking to Mommy."

Louisa laughed, yelling to Quincy that Mommy would be home soon and Madeline said she'd better hurry because Quincy was off his food—something I found hard to believe—and was pining for Mommy to come home.

With an exasperated sigh I wrestled the phone out of Louisa's grasp and waved her back onto her bed.

"Madeline, the reason for your call is…?"

Louisa picked up the little book, frowning at the pages as she inserted them.

Shimmying off the bed, I walked over to the balcony and gazed out the window. "Okay, I'm not alarmed. I'm half dead with lack of sleep. What is it?"

Below me and off to the left the terrace gleamed in the moonlight. The moon was so bright it painted the trees silver. This place must be spectacular in the winter.

Madeline said the day after the news of Charlie's death had been confirmed, MMG's share price tanked. The stock market, being a jittery beast, couldn't handle the uncertainty of a prolonged legal battle between Parker and Robson for control of the company. Then, miracle of miracles, Robson died. Goodbye litigation, hello Parker, the new CEO. MMG's share price shot through the roof.

"The market loves Parker. She's smart and level-headed. Investors trust her way more than they trusted Robson. However,"—here Madeline paused for dramatic effect, I didn't try to hurry her along, there's no point— "rumours are flying that the deaths weren't accidental."

"Which death?"

"Both of them."

"Oh, come on, this was just an unfortunate series of events." As I said it the vague dread I'd been feeling about the two bodies in the cooler crystalized. Like that moment of awful certainty when an owl swoops down on a mouse and the mouse knows it's game over.

She let out a languid laugh and I could picture her sitting in her peacock chair under the cascading pink bougainvillea with a martini glass in one hand and a love bird in the other.

"*An unfortunate series of events*? Evie, this isn't Lemony Snicket. Charlie died. That triggered the Arrangement making Robson his successor, then Robson died, and suddenly there's nothing standing between Parker and the throne. She's going to become one of the richest, most powerful women in North America. And some people think that's a little suspicious."

"Which people?"

"The people who say one death is an accident, but two are not."

I came back from the window and perched on the edge of my bed. "That's just nasty speculation." The little voice that rolls around in my head reminded me that Madeline's grapevine is studded with powerful men, including police chiefs.

Louisa glanced up at me, the tiny worry line between her eyebrows deepened. She closed the marbled book and set it on my nightstand. "We need to talk about this." She said it in a whisper but Madeline caught her words.

"Hi Louisa, what do we need to talk about?"

Louisa grimaced, *should I tell her?* I shook my head. *Absolutely not.*

Madeline refused to get off the line until I promised to call her tomorrow with an update. At that point I was so tired I would have told her anything to make her go away. But given the look on Louisa's face, the one thing that would not be feature in tomorrow's update was whatever was contained in that tiny book.

CHAPTER 57

It looked innocuous. Barely bigger than the palm of my hand, covered with marbled paper, swirls of brown and orange and gold; the brown leather spine embossed with a gold fleur-de-lis. On the inside front cover was a bookplate on which was written: **This Book Belongs To** but there was no name inserted on the line below.

Louisa sat cross-legged on the edge of her bed facing me. Her pyjama T-shirt slid off one shoulder when she reached over and tapped the book with her finger.

"Evie, you have to read this." Her eyes were troubled.

"Isn't it just to-do lists and notes-to-self stuff?" Mom kept diaries, dozens of odd-sized little books, filled with the details of her daily life. Some were mundane, the others made our eyeballs pop out. Louisa and I stashed them a box in the basement after she died; not a brilliant idea as it turned out, they were destroyed in the Great Flood.

"It's much more than that," Louisa said. "I can't tell when the entries were written, but it's pretty obvious who wrote them."

Curious, I picked up the little book. The loose pages stuck out a little bit and I tried not to dislodge them. It looked familiar. I'd seen one just like it recently, except that one was covered with blue and green marbled paper.

"It's Katie's diary."

She nodded.

"What's it doing in my room?"

"Charlotte moved Katie out of your room to put us all together at this end of the hall. She must have left it behind."

Louisa took the diary from me and glanced at the first page. "I didn't mean to read it—the entries, they're so personal—but when I read what was on those loose pages, well…"

She closed the book. The gold fleur-de-lis on the leather spine gleamed in the light from the bedside lamp. "Given everything that's happened…oh, Evie you have to read it."

She passed it to me and slumped down in her bed. An hour later when I switched off my light, Louisa was asleep and I decided not to wake her. I needed time to sort out my thoughts.

The only thing I knew for certain was this: Diaries are precious things, they must be protected no matter what.

CHAPTER 58

Saturday

A scream that sounded like a cat being strangled rose from the kitchen. Louisa and I hurtled down the stairs, taking them two at a time. We flew through the doorway to find Amelia face down on the white tiled floor with Teddy straddling her, his hands clutching the straps of her backpack. Her back arched as he tried to rip the bag off her thin shoulders.

Bernard raced across the kitchen and grabbed Teddy around the waist and shook him, hard, but Teddy refused to let go of the backpack and Amelia flopped up and down like an angry rag doll.

"I mean it, Teddy," Bernard said through gritted teeth, "Let go of your sister. Now!"

Teddy opened his hands and Amelia dropped to the floor, cracking her forehead hard on the tiles. She yelped, Bernard cupped her head and Teddy wriggled out of his grasp.

"It's not fair," he shouted as he ran to the kitchen island and hoisted himself up onto a stool. "She got the whistle. It's not fair."

Bernard pulled Amelia to her feet, smoothed her white cotton dress and checked her forehead. "Cupcake, you're going to have a nice big goose egg there." The bruise on her forehead was already starting to swell. "Are you feeling okay?"

She nodded, but when he tried to slip the backpack off her shoulders, she pulled away. Bernard said she couldn't eat properly with the heavy bag weighing her down and she agreed to let him hang it on one of the hooks by the back door.

With a murderous glare at Teddy, Amelia stalked over to the other end of the island and pulled herself up onto a stool.

I scanned the room, we could grab the small table at the far end of the kitchen or load up some trays and cart them out to the bar. The only place I didn't want to eat was at the island with two carping children.

I opted for the small table. Bernard caught my eye and said he'd be by with a carafe as soon as the coffee finished brewing.

Teddy squinched up his eyes and whispered loudly at his sister. "I'm telling Mom."

"Finders keepers," she shot back to him.

"It's my bottle," he replied.

She ignored him, watching Opal emerge from the pantry with a box of cereal. Bernard, who was halfway out the door on his way to the bar fridge, froze in midstride. He turned sharply and frowned at Amelia.

"Bottle?" he asked. "Amelia, what bottle?"

Teddy piped up. "Grandpa's silver bottle. It's mine now.

I'm the male heir." Good Lord, the kid was only eight. Was succession the only thing this family ever talked about?

Bernard retuned to the island, rested his hands on the edge of the table and leaned closer to Amelia. "You found Char—Grandpa's bottle? Where?"

She looked out the back window, tapping her spoon on the table while Opal finished pouring milk into her bowl.

"Amelia." Bernard took the spoon out of her hand, set it down on the table and folded his arms across his chest. "I asked you a question. Where did you find the bottle?"

She crossed her small arms, mirroring his stance. "In the car when Daddy got sick. He doesn't want it anymore." I shot a horrified glance at Louisa. Amelia was referring to that appalling journey back from the hanger the day Robson died on the runway.

Bernard continued to stare at her. She averted her eyes and said, quietly. "It fell out of Daddy's pocket…and I put it in my backpack."

My first thought was of a magpie. Shiny whistles in the dirt, sliver flasks rolling around in the backseat of the suv. Nothing escaped Amelia's sharp eye.

With Bernard's attention focused on his sister, Teddy made a break for it. He hopped off his stool and raced for Amelia's backpack which was still hanging on the hook next to the backdoor. Amelia scrambled off her stool, tearing after him, but Bernard was quicker than both of them. He reached the backdoor in four long strides, yanked the backpack off the hook, and held it high above their heads. "For Christ's sake," he shouted. "Leave it alone!"

The children watched in stunned silence as he unzipped the roomy pocket, removed the silver flask, uncapped it and set it in the large metal sink. Steaming hot water gushed from the tap and a steady stream of dish soap filled the air with tiny soap bubbles. The flask bumped along the bottom of the sink until it was submerged in hot foamy water.

Bernard's face was flushed when he pulled two stools out from under the kitchen island and ordered the kids to sit down. Meekly, they took their seats, their eyes following him around the room as he circled the island and sat down facing them.

"Now, listen to me very carefully," he said, eyes darting from one to the other. "Did either of you drink from the bottle?" They both shook their heads. "Teddy, Amelia, I want an honest answer. This is very important. Did you drink from the bottle?"

"No!" Amelia shouted, pushing herself off her stool. "Booze stinks. Grandma says it's disgusting." Then with all the dignity she could muster, her little goose egg turning purple, she marched out of the room.

Teddy shook his head, grumbling under his breath. "It's my bottle."

Bernard returned to the sink and swooshed the bottle around in the steaming hot water. That he didn't scald his hands amazed me. Over his shoulder he said, "Teddy, it's no one's bottle. Now shut up and finish your breakfast."

From the startled look on Teddy's face, it was obvious he'd never been spoken to in this manner by anyone, let alone a servant. He jumped off his stool and stomped into the lobby, bellowing for his mother.

Bernard pulled the flask out of the deep sink and carried it, dripping wet, out to the dumpster. We could hear the heavy metal lid groan when he heaved it open. The flask clattered against the sides of the bin then disappeared under the trash. When Bernard returned to the kitchen, he dragged a mop out of a utility cupboard and carefully cleaned up the trail of water droplets running from the sink to the backdoor.

Louisa turned to me and whispered, "What a lot of fuss. Has everyone around here lost their minds?"

Madeline's voice played in my head. Lemony Snicket. And I shuddered.

CHAPTER 59

"This beats a beer bath any day." I pivoted in the saddle to glance at the guys, taking care not to fall off Diablo's back in the process. Keith and AJ, both accomplished riders, moseyed up on either side of me and I felt like a character in a western movie, any minute now they'd start calling me "*Miss Evie*."

This would be our last day at Mirror Ranch and Keith—who owns a large acreage south of Calgary—was keen to explore the grasslands in the eastern corner of the massive property. Even Charlotte, a marketer by training, couldn't overstate the beauty of the rolling green meadows, the dark evergreen thickets, and the ridge of blue-black mountains, hazy in the distance.

"Race you to the aspens." I pointed to the grove of trees on the other side of the meadow.

"Not a chance," Keith said. "You just learned how to trot properly five minutes ago"—actually it was an hour ago, Keith put Diablo and me through our paces before we set out on our ride— "he's a smart horse; I'll not have you banging around on his back giving him mixed signals."

Diablo nickered in agreement and we trotted across the

meadow at a leisurely pace. A large bird dropped out of the sky, diving into the tall grass and a minute later, soaring up into the blue with a small writhing creature in its claws.

When we reached the edge of the aspen grove we dismounted, walking the horses to the top of a small hillock where we spread our jackets on the grass and settled in to admire the view, a panorama so transparent the earth melted into the sky.

Nature is beautiful. And incredibly noisy. The cacophony of birds and the buzz of insects almost drowned out the whispers in my head: *Forget about it. Put it out of your mind.* Almost, but not quite. Katie wrote the entries in the marbled diary, detailing the abuse she suffered from her husband and later her son. Now, both men were dead. How could I put it out of my mind?

Beside me AJ pulled a stiff blade of grass out of the ground, puffed out his cheeks and let out a sharp, piercing whistle.

"Hey there, farm boy, can you teach me how to do that?"

"The person I should be teaching is Amelia. That poor kid spent hours cleaning her whistle, she almost popped a lung trying to make a sound. She got nada."

He glanced at the blue-gray horizon. "Isn't this place amazing. Dragons in the gorge, lucky pigs"—he pulled another long squeaky blade of grass out of the soil— "bomb cyclones and bodies in the cooler."

"Oh AJ, you started so well, then you ruined it."

"Speaking of ruining it." Keith gave a little cough. "There's something I need to tell you." The morning sun wasn't bright, but he was squinting, as if uncomfortable with what he was about to say.

Don't you dare bring up Charlie Moore's offer. How could

he let Charlie believe the firm would consider joining MMG without talking to us first?

Fixing my eyes on him I said, "Nope, we're not discussing anything business-related; not until we get back to the city. You heard AJ, bomb cyclones and bodies in the cooler. We're running on coffee and adrenaline. We're in no condition to have a reasonable discussion about anything."

AJ brought his knees up to his chest, linking his hands loosely around them. "She's right Keith, I can barely tell you what day it is." He looked at me. "It's Sunday, right?"

"Saturday," I replied.

"See. The last thing I want to talk about is Charlie Moore's offer."

Keith raised his hands as if he was prepared to concede, then said, "I understand that. I'm not suggesting we make a decision today."

"Good, let's talk about something else." I scanned the woods to our right. "AJ have you found any good fishing holes lately?" Little clods of dirt sprinkled onto my shoes and I stopped ripping clumps of grass out of the ground.

"No, listen," Keith's voice changed in tone. "You need to hear me out."

Something tripped in my brain, a red flag. This was serious. "Someone's sick." It came out as a statement, not a question, and it caught Keith by surprise.

He turned to me. "As a matter of fact, that's correct. Wendy and I are expecting another child—"

"Oh Keith, that's fantastic!" I knew he and Wendy had been trying for a while. Claire was nine and dying to have a little sister or a little brother.

"Wendy's been diagnosed with hyperemesis gravidarum," he continued.

"Oh no!" I reached over to him and touched his arm.

"Hyper what?" AJ said.

"It's that condition Kate Middleton had when she was pregnant. Severe nausea, vomiting, weight loss. It's quite rare, but it can be very serious," I said.

AJ gave me a look: *How do you know these things?* Louisa and I follow the Royal Family, our dad was British after all, and Louisa is a nurse, how could I *not* know these things.

Keith explained that Wendy's trip to Victoria had been a disaster. She'd wanted to reassure her mother that while her condition was serious it was manageable, but she'd been so sick the whole time that her mother insisted on moving in with them for the duration of the pregnancy.

"Wendy loves her mom, but they can't be under the same roof for more than a week without someone blowing up. The prospect of her staying with us for six months; that's out of the question.

"To cut to the chase, I'm going to reduce my hours and work from home so I can be there for Wendy and Claire. Obviously this will have a serious impact on the firm. For one thing it means I can't do any more big hearings."

He sighed and ran his fingers through his hair. "It's ironic. We came to Mirror Ranch to figure out whether to grow the firm or stand pat and now I'm telling you I'm shrinking my billable hours and reducing the firm's revenue. There's no way you two can carry half my workload as well as your own. That's why Charlie Moore's offer made sense."

"Don't be ridiculous," I got to my feet, yanked my jacket off the ground and flapped it hard. Grass and dirt flew everywhere. "I can't understand why you told Charlie about this before you told us. We can work it out. There was no need to get Charlie Moore involved in the first place."

"It just happened. I ran into him one afternoon and we got to talking." Keith looked sheepish.

"We got to talking? Really?"

Later when I told Louisa about it she said I was overreacting, but at the time I felt betrayed. I trusted Keith and I thought he trusted me. What was he doing yapping about our future, my future, to Charlie-bloody-Moore?

I flapped my jacket harder, startling the horses, and Keith and AJ scrambled to their feet. Everyone became very busy saddling up. And it fell to AJ, the perennial peacemaker, to help us move past that uncomfortable moment.

"Hey man," AJ said to Keith, "Evie and I are flexible. We can work around your schedule. We can hire an articling student or a junior associate. We can find a way."

Keith's horse snorted as he gently tugged on its reins. "I figured you'd say that, but we have to be realistic. Regulatory hearings go on for months, millions of dollars are at stake. You guys can't do your own jobs and mine as well. Charlie and I got to talking and the next thing I knew he's making an offer. We'd join MMG as advisors overseeing the work of dozens, eventually hundreds, of regulatory lawyers."

"Oh for heaven's sake, Keith." I couldn't stop myself. "If you want to play the silver-haired senior advisor you can do it at BLV as easily as you can do it at MMG. You didn't even give us a chance to work through it." *Why do rich guys get first crack at everything?*

AJ shot me a warning look and said, "Listen you two. We're tired. We're not thinking straight. We don't need to decide anything right now. Bomb cyclones and bodies in the cooler, remember."

He paused and gave us the most endearing smile in his repertoire. "All I know is you two are the best lawyers I've ever worked with and I'm confident we can work this out. Now let's park this conversation until we get back to the office, okay?"

We wheeled our horses around to return to the Ranch. Keith rode a few paces ahead and AJ trotted along next to me. I shot him a grateful smile. "Thanks for defusing that."

He nodded and said, "The cops will be here soon"—I still had no idea what I was going to say to them about Katie's journal—"if we get lucky they'll wrap up their interviews quickly and we'll be back in the city by nightfall."

We didn't get lucky.

CHAPTER 60

When I returned to our room I found Louisa sitting in the sun on the balcony. Her chair tilted back and her feet up on the railing. She was wearing a gauzy dress and looked like a nymph ready to climb a sunbeam. She stirred when she saw me and nodded at a plate of sandwiches.

"This is lunch. Cheese and onion sandwiches. Bernard's scraping the bottom of the barrel."

As she passed me a sandwich her smile faded. "What are we going to do about Katie's journal? Do we tell the cops?" The small, marbled journal lay in her lap.

My heart skipped a beat. "Why would we tell the cops anything?"

She looked up at me, puzzled. "You read it. She hated him. That's relevant, isn't it?"

As if to prove her point she flipped the book open to a random page. A pink Post-It note fluttered onto the deck. She picked it up and passed it to me. It was covered with a torrent of words as if the sepia page to which it had been affixed wasn't big enough to contain Katie's fury.

"That's a perfect example." Her jaw was tight. "Where Charlie brings three drunk executives home after a closing dinner. And forces Katie, his movie star wife, to reenact a scene from a B-grade horror flick where she's ravaged by a swamp monster. It was disgusting."

Louisa took the Post-It note from me and stuck it back into the diary. "What kind of man does that?"

"A powerful, immoral man," I said, "the world is full of them." My mind went back to my first corporate deal at Gates. The senior partner warned me to stay clear of the lawyer representing the other side. A jowly, pompous old man. In the middle of the signing process, he called his office and ordered his assistant to bring over a document he'd 'forgotten.' Fifteen minutes later a willowy blond sashayed into the conference room with the missing document under her arm. Later I learned this pig of a man had three beautiful assistants that he trotted out at every closing, as if they were his personal harem.

"Decades of that kind of abuse would scar anyone," Louisa said. "No wonder she turned to booze." The diary snapped shut and she set it on the small table. "I don't know when she started keeping a journal, but she had to do something or she'd have lost her mind."

———

We found Charlotte and Parker on the terrace. They were drinking margaritas. It was warm and the air finally smelled of summer. They were having an intense conversation and didn't hear us step through the French doors. Charlotte was asking Parker if they should prep Katie for her interview with the police. Parker replied it wouldn't be a good idea. After a lifetime with Charlie, Katie hated being told what to do.

"How about this, then," Charlotte said, "we tell the cops Mom can't be interviewed because she has mental issues."

"God no, the last thing we want to do is give the cops the impression she's unstable."

"Sorry," I said. "May we join you?"

Charlotte turned such a deep shade of red it looked like she was running a fever. Parker smiled and motioned for us to join them around the low wooden table. Glancing at the outdoor bar, she offered to make us a cocktail.

"That's fine, thanks," I said, then asked how Katie was coping with the loss of her son so soon after the death of her husband.

"Okay, I guess," Parker replied. "Mom's pretty private about her feelings."

Louisa gave a polite cough. "We need to show you something." And passed the marbled diary to Charlotte.

"Where'd you find it? Mom's been looking for—did you read it?"

Louisa told her that I'd found it in the nightstand in my room. "We didn't realize what it was."

Charlotte glanced at Parker. "Of course, that's Mom's favourite room when we don't have guests. I should never have moved her."

"Some of the pages fell out." Louisa said. "As I put them back in the book, well, I couldn't help noticing..."

"We both read it," I said. "I'm sorry."

"What's the big deal?" Parker's eyes bounced from me to Louisa to Charlotte. "What is it?"

Silently, Charlotte passed the journal to her sister. Parker scanned a few pages, then closed the little book. "Oh my God, Charlotte."

The hum of honeybees darting through the wisteria filled the silence. Parker started to speak but was distracted by a small blue butterfly flitting around the rim of her margarita glass. The air was very still, as if time had stopped.

"You had a lot on your mind." Charlotte sighed and sat back in her chair. She took a long drink of her margarita then explained that about a year ago she was overwhelmed with worry about Katie's wellbeing.

"I hadn't seen her in months. Dad refused to let her come to the Ranch without him and of course he was always too busy to come with her. She was very agitated in our phone calls. Finally I'd had enough. I popped in one day when he was out of town, packed up her things and brought her back with me.

"Parker, she was such a mess, so confused, and so very angry." Charlotte blinked rapidly, fighting back tears.

"Angry at who? Dad?"

"Dad and Robson. The stories she told about those two would curl your hair...and at you and me."

"Us? Why? What did we do?"

"She accused us of abandoning her. Leaving her to fend for herself with those two vultures."

Charlotte drew a deep, steadying breath before continuing. "I almost sent her back to Dad when she said that. She'd abandoned me years ago and yet I was to blame? Dad went ballistic when he found out she was gone and threatened to sue me if I didn't return her immediately."

Parker snorted. "He can't sue you. He doesn't have guardianship over her...oh wait, that's it, isn't it. He wanted to keep her close so he could control her and how she voted her shares."

"Nothing came of it." Charlotte said. "I took her to see my doctor, they rebalanced her meds and after a few weeks she settled down."

Charlotte lifted her margarita glass and took another

small sip. Her face softened. "You should have seen her when we got Shadow. She could have bought the finest Arabian on the planet but she had her heart set on Shadow. I thought he'd be too big for her, much too strong, but they bonded instantly. Well, you've seen her with him, she's happy and content."

With Shadow yes, but not with Charlie...or Robson. Images raced through my mind: Katie knocking a bottle of wine into Charlie's lap and slapping Robson so hard it echoed across the room. She was furious with them both.

Charlotte rose and walked to the edge of the terrace, stepping out of the shade of the wisteria-covered pergola to stare at the greenhouse. It sparkled like a crystal at the end of the garden.

"Mirror Ranch is her home now. She's free to do whatever she wants here. Then Dad showed up three weeks ago and she lost her bearings." When Charlotte returned to her chair she was wearing a tight smile. "Well, he can't hurt her now. And neither can Robson."

She turned to Louisa and me. "Did you read the entry about Snowy?"

I nodded. Katie had given Parker a tiny white kitten on her eighth birthday. The next day Snowy disappeared and Katie thought Robson had strangled it out of spite. They found the kitten two days later, locked into a basement cupboard, hungry but unharmed.

"I'd forgotten about Snowy," Parker said, quietly. "That happened thirty years ago."

Was that when Katie started to suspect her son was a psychopath?

"Enough of this gloomy talk," Charlotte said with a cheerful smile. "Mom's here now. Jay and I will take good care of her—"

"Charlotte," Parker interrupted, "if you need any help, financial or otherwise, I'm here for you, just tell me what you need."

The look that crossed Charlotte's face was so sad it would freeze the sun. She took a deep breath and said, "All I need is for everyone to leave Mom alone. She's safe here. No one is going to take her away from me, never again."

They were laughing and crying and patting their pockets for tissues when Jay burst onto the terrace. "Thank God I found you." He froze at the sight of their tear-stained faces. "What is it? What's wrong?"

"Nothing," said Charlotte with a wide grin. "We're fine. Everything is fine."

Jay raked his fingers through his thick black hair and said he'd just received a call from the police. "They'll be here any minute now. We have to get our stories straight."

CHAPTER 61

Parker scooped up Katie's diary and followed Jay and Charlotte out into the lobby. Louisa touched me arm. "We didn't discuss whether to tell the cops about the diary or not."

We hustled across the dining room, but before we could catch up to Parker and Charlotte, the main doors next to reception swung open and a rich, baritone voice called out, "Hello?" The police had arrived.

Soon everyone was milling around in front of the reception desk. The RCMP officer with the splendid voice introduced himself and his younger partner but their names flew right out of my head. To me they would always be Young Cop and Old Cop—not that he was old, he was just older than the young cop. Behind them came two people carrying large kitbags, medical examiners of some sort.

Charlotte stepped forward, her hand extended, and introduced herself to Old Cop.

"The bodies are in the cooler," she said, leading the police and the medical examiners into the kitchen. The rest of us followed dutifully behind them like children trailing the Pied Piper.

The RCMP officers swung open the cooler door and stepped inside while the medical examiners zipped themselves into protective gear before ducking in after them.

We lingered in the kitchen staring at the closed cooler door. Not knowing whether to stay or go. What's the protocol here?

Ten minutes later the two cops reappeared. Old Cop politely ushered us out of the kitchen, suggesting we make ourselves comfortable in the lobby. Obediently, we filed out and arranged ourselves on the sofa and in the armchairs scattered about in front of the massive stone fireplace.

He and his partner crossed the lobby and entered the dining room. They moved to the middle of the long mahogany table and sat down side by side. Young Cop pulled a note pad out of his jacket pocket and lay it on the table, nodding while Old Cop talked to him quietly. Watching them through the glass doors felt surreal, as if we were watching a movie.

Amelia's tiny voice broke the silence. "Are you crying?" She was curled up in her mother's lap, staring at her grandmother who was sitting next to them.

"No darling girl, I'm just tired," Katie replied as she brushed a tear from the corner of her eye.

The young cop opened the dining room doors and told Elise they would not be interviewing the children.

At this, Charlotte leapt to her feet and asked if she and her mother could go first. "As you can imagine, this has been harrowing for my mother." Charlotte glanced down at Katie who was tucking a crumpled Kleenex into her sleeve. "Mom and I were in the Lodge all night with Elise and the kids. We weren't part of the search party. There isn't much we can tell you about Charlie's—Dad's—death."

The cop agreed and stepped to one side, swinging the

dining room doors open to allow them to pass, then quietly clicking them shut again. Through the glass we could see Katie and Charlotte seat themselves opposite the two policemen. Katie glanced at the empty chair at the top of the table where Charlie used to sit and shuddered. A sudden quick movement. Or maybe it was a shadow flickering across the terrace, a trick of the light.

Their voices were low and although we couldn't hear what they were saying Louisa whispered that judging by their demeanor, the cops seemed to be treating Katie and Charlotte with kindness.

When the women emerged thirty minutes later, Katie's lips were firmly pressed together and Charlotte stared straight ahead as she ushered her mother upstairs to her room.

Slowly, the interviews progressed. Opal brought us hot tea and fresh baked scones. Bernard's pantry was bare, but like a magician he'd whipped up something to sooth our troubled souls.

While we waited to be interviewed, I texted Madeline to say the interviews were progressing and we'd be home later tonight.

She replied:

Dream on. It's 2:00 pm now. There's no way you're getting out of there tonight.

If she were here, we'd be on our way in an hour. Once when we heading to a concert, she was stopped for speeding. She flashed a dazzling smile, apologized, and mentioned she was late for an appointment. The next thing I knew the cop tore up her speeding ticket and offered to escort us—sirens wailing—to our destination.

Gradually the group waiting to be interviewed grew

smaller and the group released from the dining room into the kitchen grew larger.

"Evie Valentine, Parker Moore, please." Young Cop's voice was jarring. They'd grouped us into the teams we'd formed when we set off to search for Charlie.

Parker and I took our seats opposite the two RCMP officers. Old Cop gave us a benign smile. His voice, warm and comforting, melted my apprehension. *Be careful* the voice in my head rang with alarm. *Don't let your guard down.*

Young Cop scribbled notes, lifting his head only to ask for clarification.

At the end of our interview Old Cop asked whether there was anything we'd like to add to the information we'd already provided. A look passed between Parker and me, we hadn't had a chance to, as Jay said, get our stories straight.

I knew (and the cops did not) that Charlie had two personas, the warm, gregarious facade he presented to the outside world and the cruel and vicious man he was with his family. Never speak ill of the dead, especially if it will harm the living.

"No," I said, "there's nothing I'd like to add."

CHAPTER 62

Louisa and Jay were the last to be interviewed. They'd found Charlie's body, so it stood to reason the police would take some time with their statements, still it seemed to me they were stuck in the dining room for an awfully long time. By the time Louisa finally appeared in the kitchen doorway I was desperate to talk to her but Charlotte reached her first.

"Where's Jay?" Charlotte whispered.

"He's taking the cops to his office. To show them the CCTV tapes," Louisa replied.

I felt a flash of guilt. I'd completely forgotten to mention the tapes. I pulled Louisa away from Charlotte and the excited babble in the kitchen. "Did you tell them about Katie's diary?"

She shook her head. "No, did you?"

"No, it's not relevant…if Charlie's death was accidental."

That was a mighty big if, but even if Katie despised her abusive husband, until someone determined that Charlie's death wasn't an accident, there was no need to mention Katie's journal or the countless other journals that were, no doubt, stashed in secret corners of the Lodge. The monster who lived in those diaries could still, in the hands of an over-zealous cop, make Katie's life a living hell.

Louisa eyed me carefully. "And if he *didn't* die accidently? What then?"

"We'll cross that bridge when we come to it."

Someone placed a hand on my shoulder and I jumped. AJ looked at me, then at Louisa and said, "You two look like you're plotting to overthrow the government."

"We are," I said, praying he hadn't overheard us. "We're replacing the patriarchy with a matriarchy. Meet Empress Louisa," I said with a bow and a flutter of my hands.

AJ laughed and said, "Don't get me started."

Amelia squealed in protest at the other end of the kitchen as Keith peeled her off his hip and passed her to her mother. He'd been packing her around a lot since Robson died.

When Keith joined us I asked how the kids were doing.

A shadow passed over his face. "Amelia is too young to understand what's going on. She knows her dad and grandfather are dead, but she still thinks they'll come back someday. Teddy on the other hand realizes death is final but emotionally he's struggling to come to grips with it. It doesn't help that Elise is totally overwhelmed by everything and not much use to either of them." This, I thought, was why people say you should have to pass a test before becoming a parent.

Bernard called everyone into the kitchen where he'd set out a buffet on the kitchen island, soups, salads, rolls and sandwiches. Dutifully, we joined the Moores in the queue and were making half-hearted jokes and small talk when the cooler door popped open. Almost giving me a heart attack. I'd forgotten about the two people from the medical examiner's office.

We watched in silence as the first stretcher made its way

across the lobby and down into the parking lot where it was loaded into the back of a van. A few minutes later the second stretcher appeared and repeated the same sad trek.

The van doors slammed with a dull thud and the cops and the medical examiners huddled together for a few minutes in the parking lot before the medical examiners slid into the front seat of the van and drove across the gravel lot to the access road.

The cops returned to the lobby and stood in the entrance to the kitchen. Old Cop scanned the room until he caught Charlotte's eye. He beckoned. When she joined them, Old Cop said a few words. She shook her head. A minute later she was at my side.

"The cops aren't letting anyone leave until tomorrow morning."

Jay came down the hall from his office and handed the cops a memory stick—the CCTV tapes—then came over to join his wife. "Charlotte, what's happening?"

She turned to him and said, "The cops want to examine the spot where we found Dad's body. A reenactment. Tomorrow, in the daylight, when everyone is fresh." She gave us an exhausted smile. "I'm so sorry but it looks like you'll be spending another night at Mirror Ranch."

That's when Jay lost his temper. He marched over to Old Cop and said, "You want to recreate the scene? Like a crime scene? You've got to be kidding me." His voice boomed across the kitchen.

Bernard, who'd been lugging a heavy soup pot over to the buffet stopped in his tracks. His easy grin fading from his lips. Opal put her hand over her mouth, too late to cover the words, *oh no.* The only one who didn't react was Katie.

"Now, now, Mr. Azeem, no one said it was a crime scene." Old Cop's voice was deep and rich as he attempted to placate Jay. Young Cop added that reenactments were standard procedure in cases like these.

"Cases like what?" Jay demanded.

Young Cop looked at Old Cop, but neither gave Jay an answer.

CHAPTER 63

The night was warm. Sparks floated up into the velvety sky. We were clustered around the firepit. Tomorrow we'd be going home. No doubt about it. And yet, I felt uneasy.

Keith poked at the fire while Louisa told AJ about a trip we'd taken to the Rothney Astrophysical Observatory. There we'd learned how the sun, moon and stars impacted indigenous culture. Teepees opened to the east to greet the morning sun and the north and south flaps were painted with the seven sons and the six lost boys—the Big Dipper and the Pleiades constellation. The Big Dipper would have come in handy when AJ and I got lost on our way back from Dragon Falls.

Somewhere outside the safe circle of the firepit an owl hooted softly. A predator hunting its prey.

The cops would be gone by noon tomorrow. Bernard's provisions truck would arrive at three o'clock. Would we have enough food for breakfast? When I'm stressed I worry about running out of food. It's a weird obsession. I've never gone hungry in my life.

"—I had the same impression," AJ said to Keith. I looked

across the firepit at the two of them, lolling back in their Adirondack chairs.

"What impression?" I asked.

"That the cops aren't convinced Charlie's death was an accident." Keith poked a long thin stick into the heart of the fire. He was the official keeper of the flame. Every campfire has one.

Let's not go there, please. I glanced over at Louisa for help, but she was staring into the fire not paying attention, and said, "They told Jay the reenactment was standard procedure."

"What else are they going to say?" Keith pulled his pokey stick out of the fire and the flame wobbled and shrank. "They spent an awfully lot of time in my interview trying to nail down who was where and when."

"Did they ask you any questions about Robson?" I desperately wanted to move the conversation away from who might have a motive to kill Charlie.

"Not really," Keith said, "they seemed to be more interested in Charlie than Robson." The others nodded in agreement.

The fire hissed, the logs still damp from the rain, and Keith ambled over to the long wooden box next to the paddock fence, rummaged around and returned with three scraps of wood. These he tossed them on the flame, triggering a furious explosion of sparks. He scooped up a handful of pebbles and sat down on the low brick wall ringing the firepit.

"Okay, we know where everyone was when we found Charlie. Do we know where everyone was the last time we saw him alive?"

Are we really going to do this?

Leaning forward, he dragged a stick through the dirt, drawing a long narrow rectangle.

Apparently so.

"This is the dining room table and these"—he rolled the pebbles around in his hand— "are the Moore family." Keith placed a round white chunk of quartz— 'Charlie'—at the head of the 'table' and arranged Katie and Elise along one side and Parker, Robson, and Charlotte down the other.

"You forgot Jay," I said. "He was running back and forth to the kitchen but eventually sat down next to Charlotte." *If we're going to do this, we'd better get it right.*

Keith dropped a small pink stone next to 'Charlotte' and said, "It's 6:30. Everyone is eating."

"Stop," Louisa said. "What about Bernard and Opal?"

"Bernard is going in and out of the kitchen, Opal is serving the food."

Louisa stared at him, waiting. He picked up two small round pebbles and set them down a few inches away from the 'table' and looked at Louisa. "Happy now?"

"You don't have the kids." AJ jiggled two small pebbles in his hand, clicking them like dice.

Keith rolled his eyes. "I'm pretty sure the kids didn't kill anyone. Right, it's 6:30, dinner time. Food's on the table. Everyone is happy."

"No they're not," I said. "That morning Charlie told Bernard to make a special dinner and everyone assumed he was going to name his successor. Instead he walked out before dessert and left Robson and Parker hanging. Just before that he tore into Jay about the music, he preferred classical to jazz, then he laced into Charlotte when she said she was the owner of Mirror Ranch and any complaints should be directed to her. God, what a prick."

AJ shot me a small smile. "Why don't you tell us how you really feel?"

Keith picked up the white piece of granite, bounced it up and down, then 'walked' it five inches away from the 'table.' Reminding me of when Louisa and I played Barbies, walking them in and out of their pink doll house on long stiff legs.

"Charlie has a temper tantrum, then barges out the patio doors." Keith set the white stone on top of the bricks ringing the firepit.

"But first," Louisa interrupted, "Robson runs after him, he wants to come along but Charlie blows him off. Parker gives Charlie a jacket and he disappears out the terrace doors. It was raining pretty hard by then."

Keith trotted Robson's and Parker's stones away from the table and back again. "Okay, then what?"

AJ said, "Elise and Katie take the kids up to bed."

"No," Louisa said as Keith scooped up the Elise and Katie stones, "first Robson screams at Charlotte for ruining his big night, then Jay almost comes to blows with Robson for yelling at his wife and Charlotte gets so mad she knocks over a chair. Then Jay and Charlotte join Bernard and Opal in the kitchen."

Keith gathered up their stones and set them on the edge of the firepit. He seemed to be enjoying himself moving all these little pebbles around. *Note to self: Get Keith toy soldiers for secret Santa.*

"Okay," AJ said, "and we went upstairs to our rooms."

I pointed at the small round stone still sitting in the dirt at Keith's feet.

"Is that Robson?"

CHAPTER 64

We stared at the small gray stone. The only one left in the 'dining room.'

"We don't know whether Robson followed Charlie outside or went upstairs to bed," I said. "He could be anywhere."

AJ picked up the stone and tossed it from hand to hand. "All of them could be anywhere. Someone could easily have snuck outside the minute we were tucked up in our beds." He sighed. "We really suck at this Colonel-Mustard-in-the-library-with-the-candlestick game."

"We didn't see anyone on the CCTV cameras." I told them about the strange shadow just out of camera range. "It could have been anything, a person, an animal, a trick of the light, anything."

"Okay," AJ said. "Let's try it another way. Who has motive?"

"Are you kidding?" I said. "Everybody has a motive." I counted them off on my fingertips. "One: Charlie abused Katie, physically and mentally, for decades. Two: Charlie betrayed Parker, leading her to believe she had a shot at his job when he'd already promised it to Robson. And three: Charlie was scheming with Robson to take Mirror Ranch away from Charlotte and turn it into a billionaires' bolt hole. All of the Moore women had a motive.

"And when you add Robson to the mix—you saw how angry he was after Charlie failed to name him his successor—they all had a reason to kill Charlie. The big question is: Who had the opportunity?"

I picked up the small stone representing Robson and tossed it into the fire. "As AJ just said, we're crap at this. Let's leave it up to the cops. They're the professionals."

Keith and AJ exchanged a look that made me laugh. Usually they're the ones telling me not to meddle, to let the police do their job.

"All that's left for us now is to join hands and sing Kumbaya," Keith said with a smile.

The flame shifted in the breeze, blanketing us in smoke. Louisa coughed and AJ fanned his hand in front of his face.

"Kumbaya?" he said, "I'd rather do that Dick van Dyke song." He made *wah-wah* noises as he mimed playing a trombone.

"You're just mad the kids won—Christ, what's that?" I shot to my feet and shook my head. "There's a bat in my hair!"

"It's not a bat." AJ grabbed my arm and pulled me down beside him. "Stop jumping around." He sounded as if he was trying to suppress a laugh. "It's just a bug. Stay still."

"Get it off!" I flapped my hands around my head.

Slowly he extricated something from my hair. It fought him every inch of the way. "It's just a little bug." He opened his hand and showed me the biggest moth I'd ever seen. It opened and closed its dusty brown wings, checking the hinges to make sure they still worked, then fluttered off into the night.

I shivered and hung my head down, fluffing my hair with

my fingers to get rid of the creepy feeling that something was crawling around on my scalp. "God, I hate it when that happens."

"Really?" AJ chuckled. "You could have fooled me."

I gave him a smack on the arm and he turned his attention back to the pebbles, picking up three and tossing them from hand to hand like a juggler.

Keith made a show of yawning and I suggested we return to the Lodge before Charlotte locked us out. We doused the fire and made our way back up the path. The crickets creaked like an old washboard and the nightbirds chirped. It was a soft and gentle evening, nothing like the night Charlie died.

Charlotte was turning on the Tiffany table lamps when we got back to the Lodge. She would leave them on all night in case someone needed something from the kitchen, and they filled the dark corners of the room with a comforting rainbow glow.

She told me she'd put the two RCMP officers in rooms at the end of our corridor.

That should have been reassuring news. But their presence made me feel uneasy.

CHAPTER 65

Sunday

The birds sounded like they were rioting in the trees, but it wasn't enough to mask the sound of the older cop's laboured wheezing. We were halfway up the path to the place where Charlie died. It was early morning and the heat was rising.

Old Cop stripped off his jacket, revealing a small patch of sweat under his armpits. Every few minutes, Jay and Louisa assured him we were almost there. Young Cop hung back, sticking close to Parker at the back of the line and asking questions about the stables and the conference centre, what kinds of locks they used, whether the perimeter fencing was secure.

"I don't know," Parker replied, "you'll have to ask Charlotte"—who wasn't on the reenactment trek because she'd stayed behind with Katie on the night Charlie died.

As we climbed up the path I had the strangest feeling that around the next curve we'd find Charlie lying flat on his back in a bed of ferns. A shiver ran up my spine and I forced myself to concentrate on the sound of the older cop's jagged breathing.

Abruptly, we stopped. Old Cop huddled with Jay and Louisa, asking them to describe precisely how they found the body, then called the younger cop over. He loped past us, conferred briefly with Old Cop, then dropped to one knee to examine the site. After a few minutes he stood up, shaking his head. If there had been any physical evidence here, it had been washed away by the storm.

"I thought as much," Old Cop said. He instructed his junior officer to lie down on the pine needle path. Once he confirmed with Jay and Louisa that the younger cop was properly positioned, he turned and waded into the fern-filled hollow a few feet away to address the rest of us.

"That's Charlie." Old Cop pointed at Young Cop, who was no longer visible from where I stood on the path. "I want you to stand exactly where you were when you first saw his body. Raise your hand when you're in position." We fussed a little, arranging and rearranging ourselves until we sorted out our positions, then raised our hands.

The older cop first questioned Jay and Louisa. Under his gentle direction, they became more animated, moving with urgency.

"Jay, what did you see first?"

"Louisa, what happened next?"

Jay reenacted discovering Charlie, dropping to his knees where Charlie had fallen, calling frantically over his shoulder to Louisa. "I've got him! I've got him!"

She ran to Jay's side and knelt beside him. "I touched his neck and I put my cheek close to his lips to see if he was breathing. But he was gone."

She sat back on her heels and told Jay to call the others.

Jay stood and moved back a few feet and mimed pulling his phone out of his pocket and placing the call. And so it went for all of us as we rushed onto the path and jabbered at each other. Even recreating the argument between Keith and Robson about whether they should move the body or stand guard over it until help arrived. Not knowing at the time that help wouldn't come for days.

By then I was off the path, standing in the ditch, up to my knees in ferns and prickly bushes, thinking about how slippery it had been in the relentless rain. And how tired and miserable I'd felt. Behind me I could hear Parker panting, short, harsh puffs. I turned to comfort her, just like I did that night. And realized that the entire time we were there with Charlie's body Parker stayed behind me. Never once approaching him. Making no effort to see her father one last time.

When the older cop had all the information he needed, he released us. Our trek back down to the Lodge was quicker than on the night Charlie died, but just as solemn.

Parker disappeared upstairs while in the kitchen Charlotte badgered Jay and Bernard to tell her exactly what the cops had said. "Do you think they learned anything new?"

Louisa and I joined Keith and AJ who were draped across the armchairs in front of the empty stone fireplace, debating the quickest route to get home. Upstairs there was a thud of a door being slammed shut. The kids were loose in the corridor and heading for the broad staircase.

"Quick!" I said to Louisa. "If we move fast, we can make it to the veranda before they see us."

"Evie-e-e-e!" Amelia shrieked as she trundled down the stairs.

Too late.

She flung herself into my lap and demanded to know where I'd been all morning. Before I could respond, Teddy materialized next to AJ's chair, pleading for a lift home.

AJ's mouth dropped open and he stammered something unintelligible—he's even less accustomed to bossy children than I am—eventually mumbling that there was so much gear in Keith's van there wasn't enough room for a little boy.

Undeterred, Teddy turned to me. "I'll go with you then."

"I'm catching a lift with Louisa. I'm afraid her car is even smaller than Keith's and we have no room at all. Girls pack way more stuff than boys do." It was a terribly stereotypical thing to say, but desperate times call for desperate measures. "I'm sure you'll be more comfortable going home with your mom and Amelia."

Teddy scowled and said he didn't want to go home on the plane. They had to wait for the pilot to arrive, he was driving up in a company car and that would take hours, besides he didn't like the pilot and the plane was loud and bumpy and a horrible ride.

Amelia cupped both hands around my ear and shout-whispered, "Teddy is afraid he's going to die. Just like Daddy."

"I am not!" He puffed out his chest and crossed his arms. "Moores don't get scared. Take it back!" A look passed between AJ and me. *The poor little guy is terrified.*

Amelia began to chant: "Teddy is a scaredy-cat, Teddy is a scaredy-cat!"

Teddy's bottom lip trembled and he lunged for Amelia trying to throw her to the ground when from the kitchen came a sharp, metallic crash.

I rushed past the children into the kitchen where I found Opal standing by the Aga with a red quilted oven mitt in her hand. She was staring at Bernard who was at the sink, running cold water over his hands. A large metal soup pot lay on its side on the stovetop. A disgusting mess of brown broth and chopped vegetables splashed halfway up the back wall.

Bernard grabbed a tea towel, then looked at Opal. "I can't deal with this right now. Going to get the eggs."

"But your hands," Opal protested while Bernard steamed out the back door.

AJ came up behind me. "What happened?"

Opal turned her bewildered eyes on us. "He…he dropped the soup pot." She looked down at the over mitt she was clutching. "He burned his hands."

By the time I reached the backdoor Bernard was cutting diagonally across the grass behind the Lodge, heading for the staff path. He stripped off his apron and flung it to the ground. Head down, arms swinging by his sides.

AJ jostled past me into the open doorway. "Should I go after him?"

"No, let me." There was something about the way Bernard moved, sharp, jerky, as if he were fighting for control, that reminded me of the night I heard him arguing with Robson about the flask.

Bernard had a good start on me, but the path was relatively flat and I'm a runner, I was gaining on him.

"Bernard," I shouted. "Wait. Please."

He glanced over his shoulder, his eyes red and angry, but didn't break stride as he veered right to go up the path. Definitely not heading for the chicken coop.

CHAPTER 66

It was the archery hut. Bernard yanked the rain swollen wooden door open and disappeared inside. A moment later I followed, pausing on the threshold to let my eyes adjust to the gloom.

Of all the buildings at Mirror Ranch, this one was the roughest, made of course-grained wooden planks and illuminated by bare lightbulbs. Hesitant shafts of sunlight filtered through two cobwebbed windows and dust motes swirled as Bernard made his way to the wooden table jammed up against the back wall. Behind the table was a peg board from which hung an assortment of sharp and pointy tools. The only two I recognized were a pair of pliers and a reel that looked like it belonged on an old fashioned clothesline.

Bernard leaned against the table and leveled his eyes at me. His mouth was tight and beads of sweat sat high on his forehead. I decided not to crowd him and sat down on a plank bench a few feet away. Allowing my heartbeat to drop back down to normal

"Bernard, what's going on?"

He shrugged, then said, "Why couldn't he just leave us alone?"

"Charlie?"

"And Robson. The son was worse than the father. They could buy anything in the world but it was never enough."

He narrowed his eyes as he squinted up into the rafters. A tiny corner of the roof was turning black. Water damage, it should be cut out before the rot spread.

"She couldn't fight them. It didn't matter how many times Jay ran the numbers—he's smart, that kid, I underestimated him—Mirror Ranch, the resort, would never be as profitable as Mirror Ranch billionaires' bolt hole."

Bernard couldn't tear his eyes away from the black stain spreading across the rafters overhead.

"They can't chuck people out of their homes like they're trash."

His colour was rising, then unexpectedly, he laughed. A cold, harsh laugh. I glanced at him, suddenly wary. He'd picked up a small plastic box of tools, it looked like a set of Allen wrenches, and popped the lid, open and closed, *snick, snick*, then set it back down on the table.

"Robson was always a jackass, but I expected better of Charlie." He gave a derisive snort. "The old man wasn't born with a silver spoon in his mouth. He knew what it was like for the little guy struggling to get ahead only to be knocked down again and again. But he forgot. He got too comfortable living the cushy life."

A tiny smile crossed Bernard's face. "I decided to make his life a little less comfortable. The arrogant bastard. He loves his tomatoes. Has to have them every time he comes. His lordship's wish is my command. But this time I added a little something extra from Charlotte's garden."

"The poison garden? You tried to kill him?" Other than

the cashews, I couldn't remember what else Charlotte was growing out there, but whatever it was, she kept it under lock and key.

"Hell no. I wanted to knock him down a peg, make him really sick, not kill him." Bernard chortled. "He couldn't leave his room for two days."

That's why we didn't see him until dinner on Friday night. But still he managed to crawl out of his sick bed long enough to persuade Keith to join MMG. Never too ill to land a deal.

The smile on Bernard's lips faded when I asked him about the night Charlie died. "You didn't tamper with that meal, did you?" We all ate the same thing…or at least I though we did.

"What? Of course not. I would never monkey with his food with the kids around. They get into everything. Besides, it'd be a waste of time. After the big announcement he'd do what he always does when he screws with somebody, he gets blind drunk and pukes his guts out."

A pensive look crossed his face. "But there was no announcement and he didn't go off on a bender, instead he went out and got himself killed."

"Bernard, what did you do after Charlie stormed out?" I was thinking about all the little pebbles we'd moved around in the dirt. We'd focused on the family, not Bernard and Opal.

"Yeah, that pretty much killed the evening, didn't it. Charlotte and Jay had a rip roaring fight in my kitchen, then went to bed. Opal was so strung out I sent her home. I was loading up the dishwasher when who should sashay into the kitchen, fully dressed and raring to go, but Katie. She didn't like the looks of the weather and she was heading to the barn to check on Shadow."

"Katie? What time was this?" I asked.

"Eleven. Eleven-thirty, something like that. There's no bloody way I'd let her go down to the barn by herself in that weather. So I went with her. We get to the barn, but the bloody horse is gone and Katie goes batshit crazy."

The image on the CCTV footage of Charlie barreling up the trail on Shadow flashed in my mind.

"I told Katie to wait for me in the barn, I'd find Shadow and bring him back. She kept shoving that stupid whistle in my face, telling me he'll come to it, one toot, two toots, she could make that horse dance if she wanted to, but I don't know the signals and finally, she let me go."

Something skittered across the roof overhead and Bernard and I looked up. It sounded heavy as it trundled up one side and down the other. I shuddered.

"The rain is pissing down and the wind is howling like a freaking freight train and somehow over all that racket I hear him. Shadow, up ahead on the path. Charlie's in the saddle yanking on the reins. I get closer and who do I see but Robson, standing on the path, screaming his fool head off. He says he wants answers. What happened? Why no announcement? He's scaring the bejesus out of Shadow who's twitching, getting soaked, while these two assholes are screaming at each other.

"Charlie blows his stack. He drops the reins, leans down and punches Robson in the face. Pretty good jab for an old guy, I gotta say. Then Katie lets loose with that whistle, two sharp blasts, and Shadow rears up. Charlie flies off and Shadow bolts. That damned horse woulda flattened me if I didn't jump in the ditch.

"By the time I get back to the barn, Katie's tucked Shadow into his box. So I take her back to the Lodge and put her to bed."

Something glinted behind his eyes and I wondered what he wasn't telling me.

CHAPTER 67

Bernard pushed himself off the edge of the table. "We'd better get back before your boyfriend sends out a search party."

"Boyfriend? You mean AJ? He's not my boyfriend." I brushed the comment aside trying to focus on what Bernard had just told me.

The swollen door was stuck again and made a horrible screech when it finally popped open. I followed Bernard out into the brilliant sunlight.

The meadow sloped down toward the Lodge. I could see the storm-ravaged roof, now a patchwork of tarps anchored in place by lengths of two-by-fours. A last ditch effort by Jay to cover the holes created by the wind when it ripped off the cedar shakes. From here the Lodge looked shabby.

I picked up a long stick and swacked at the tall grass as I kept pace with Bernard. Seedheads flew left and right as if I'd attacked them with a scythe. Something didn't sit right with Bernard's story.

"Just so I'm clear, at this point you and Katie are back in the Lodge and Charlie and Robson are still out there on the path in the pouring rain. What happened next?"

"You sound just like the old cop," he said, giving me a sardonic look. "I went home to bed and was fast asleep when Charlotte called."

"When did Robson get back to the Lodge?"

Bernard's voice brightened at my question. "Damned if I know." Then he smiled, his black mood lifting. That confirmed it. I'd definitely missed something.

We cut through the meadow to the staff path and were about twenty feet from the Lodge when the kitchen door banged open and Amelia barrelled out flinging herself at Bernard who scooped her up and settled her on his hip. "If you don't slow down, Cupcake, you'll fall flat on your face."

Amelia said it was safe for Bernard to come home now. The police were gone and Auntie Charlotte wasn't mad at him for making a mess in the kitchen. Oh, and the food truck came early and Opal needed help putting everything away.

Amelia fixed me with a stern look. "Auntie Charlotte has paying guests coming in a few days and you people have to go home." From Charlotte's lips to Amelia's ear, the message was loud and clear. Go home.

———————

An hour later our rollie bags were lined up front of the reception desk. Opal packed us a picnic hamper, convinced we'd starve between truck stops; but we weren't going anywhere because Louisa's wretched car wouldn't start.

AJ thought there was something wrong with the distributor. Keith said it was water in the ignition system. Everyone blamed the torrential downpour, but I blamed Louisa who's too cheap to get rid of her junker car. Louisa absolved herself of all responsibility— "It's an act of God.

It's not as if I forgot to fill the gas tank"—I eyed the freshly restocked bar wondering if it was too early for a huge gin and tonic.

When I texted Madeline to tell her we were running a little late (again!) she offered to send Paulo in a helicopter to airdrop caviar and champagne.

To keep your spirits up.

I texted that I missed her, and she made me promise never to go to a dude ranch again.

I was pacing the floor in the lobby when Parker appeared with a jug of lemonade and four glasses and tilted her head in the direction of the wisteria covered terrace. "Come on, it's cool and shady out there." The temperature was rising, soon it would be outside my comfort zone which sits nicely between 18°C and 22°C.

Louisa and Charlotte were lolling on the best patio chairs, the breeze ruffling their hair. When we're not in the middle of a bomb cyclone, the breeze is quite wonderful here, soft and smooth, like peaches, not the sharp, gritty wind we get back home.

Parker filled our glasses and Charlotte proposed a toast to her sister. "Thank you again for your generous support. Jay can't wait to get started."

Parker smiled. "Don't thank me, thank MMG."

"Ah, but you're MMG now. I want you to know we are very grateful."

Seeing my quizzical expression, Charlotte explained that Parker, sorry, MMG, had made a significant investment in Mirror Ranch.

I nodded. "So Jay will get his zip line across Dragon Falls after all?"

"Not quite," Charlotte said with a laugh. She took a long

slow sip of lemonade before continuing. "We're starting small with rustic weddings and overnight camping in the meadow, then we'll work up to fly fishing in a man-made lake. Eventually, I want Mirror Ranch to be open all year round, to be a real dude ranch, not just a corporate retreat. No offence Parker."

"None taken." Parker tore her eyes away from the guys who were still fussing with Louisa's car in the parking lot. Jay had joined them and they were all standing around with their hands on their hips and frowns on their faces.

"We're going to call it Parker Lake, in honour of you." Charlotte tipped her glass at her sister.

Parker laughed. "Wonderful, I'm going to have a big old mosquito infested mud puddle named after me."

Charlotte sat back in her chair with a dreamy look on her face, itemizing all the improvements Jay intended to make. "Cross-country skiing and snowshoeing in the winter, oh and get this, dogsledding. My darling husband is afraid of dogs, I don't think he understands that sled dogs are pack animals, not house pets." She shuddered. "God, if they ever got loose and went after Lucky, they'd tear him and his little house to bits."

I shuddered at the thought of poor innocent Lucky. He was just a baby when wolves slaughtered his entire family. He wouldn't recognize danger if it was staring him in the face.

That's when the penny dropped. I finally understood why Charlie and Robson had to die.

CHAPTER 68

The hood of Louisa's car slammed down with a loud bang, drawing my attention. The guys, looking hot and grumpy, glared at the car as if they could shame it into behaving.

"Hey, Louisa," AJ yelled from the parking lot. "We've got a problem." Behind him Jay and Keith were moving around, picking up various tools and throwing them back into the toolbox. It had to be at least ten degrees hotter down there in the gravel lot than up here on the vine covered terrace.

Louisa and I stood at the edge of the terrace and listened while AJ explained she needed a new distributor cap.

"Fine," Louisa shouted, "let's get one."

"It's not that easy," Jay shouted back. "I can order one for you, but it will take a couple of days to come in. You're welcome to stay with us, but we'll have to move you to a smaller room."

Dismayed Louisa turned to me. "But I have work and Quincy—"

"Jay," Charlotte called out as she and Parker joined us at the edge of the terrace. "The utility shed is packed with junk, can't you MacGyver something together with duct tape and binder twine. It only has to hold together until they get back to Calgary." That would be four hours over twisty country roads and high speed superhighways but by the look on Louisa's face she was prepared to risk it.

Jay shook his head. "We tore the shed apart, trust me if there was a band-aid fix for this, we'd have found it."

I gave Louisa a side hug and said we'd jam ourselves in with Keith and AJ. Madeline would take care of recovering her car. With her connections she could transport a Brink's truck halfway around the world if she had to.

Jay picked up the toolbox and Keith and AJ started rearranging their luggage in the back of Keith's van to make room for our bags. When they were done AJ announced they were heading back to their rooms for a quick shower. Then we'd be off.

Good. That gives me time to talk to Bernard.

———

I found him in the greenhouse, plucking tiny plum tomatoes off their dusty green stalks and placing them in the basket slung over his arm. He was deep in thought when I called his name.

"You're heading off?" he said, arching his back, letting his spine pop. The afternoon sun glinted off the metal bones of the greenhouse, inside the air was hot and still. Way past my comfort zone.

He smiled in that awkward way people do when they've gotten to know each other a little too well under trying circumstances and are no longer sure where their boundaries are.

"Have a safe trip home, Evie." Bernard glanced out the open greenhouse door at the sky, which was a brilliant, robin's egg blue. "Looks like the weather is going to coop-erate for a change."

It's now or never.

"Bernard, can I ask you one more question about the night Charlie died?"

His mouth twitched, but he said sure. I tugged at the front of my T-shirt, flapping it in an effort to cool off.

"You think it's hot in here, you should try the poison garden," he said, glancing at the locked partition that sep-arated Charlotte's poisonous plants from the rest of the greenhouse. "Come on, let's go outside."

I followed him out of the greenhouse and we stood in the cool shade of a sprawling maple tree. The grass was strewn with chipped flowerpots and broken stakes. With the tall caragana border on one side and the massive maple on the other there was no breeze, the air was quiet.

"What's up?" he asked, setting the small bamboo basket down on a peeling blue bench next to the open greenhouse door. The basket tilted and three small, red tomatoes rolled out and dropped to the ground. He picked them up, dusted them off, and put them back in the basket.

"Bernard, why did you go back for the flask?"

"What flask?" His expression remained friendly, but cautious.

I told him I'd overheard his argument with Robson the night before he died. "You two were the last to see Charlie alive. Since Robson didn't have the flask you must have taken it from Charlie."

Bernard's eyes flicked to the narrow opening between the greenhouse walls and the prickly caragana hedge and it occurred to me that no one knew where I was.

CHAPTER 69

Bernard tipped his head to one side, dark eyes searching my face. "Parker said you were smart. What gave me away?"

"Your love for this place."

When he didn't argue, I knew I was right. About everything.

He let out a slow breath. "Yeah, okay, I skipped a few things." After Katie blew the whistle and Shadow bucked Charlie off, the old man lay on the path, one arm clutching Robson's pant leg. "Robson crouched down close to Charlie's head." Bernard blinked a couple of times. "Let me put it this way, Robson had a rock and he sure as hell wasn't giving him mouth to mouth."

"Robson *killed* Charlie?"

"The man was dead as a doornail when we found him, wasn't he?"

Charlie's sodden body splayed across the path flashed into my mind. "Why didn't you tell us where Charlie was? We wasted so much time running all over the countryside in the pouring rain. Maybe we could have saved him."

"Nothing coulda saved him." Bernard shook his head

in disbelief. "You think I'm going to admit I was one of the last people to see Charlie alive. It'd be my word against Robson's. Not a chance."

Bernard had a point.

"Robson hated his old man. Even tried to get Charlie booted out of the company a couple of years ago. The little prince couldn't pull it off. The old man was too powerful and had too many allies."

"How do you know this?"

Bernard gave me a sardonic look. "I'm a servant, remember. Feeding them, cleaning up after them. In and out of the room, but never there.

"Finally the old bugger decides to retire, for real this time. Robson's in seventh heaven. Then at the last minute Charlie changes his mind. So Robson takes him out."

A wasp buzzed around my head. I moved over to the blue bench and sat down. Bernard sat down beside me, leaning back, almost touching the glazed wall. It radiated so much heat, I didn't know how he could stand it.

"Bernard, tell me about the ketamine."

He stared at me dumbfounded.

The morning after we found Charlie, Katie dragged us out to the barn to check on Shadow. The horse was fine except for the abrasions on his flank. Katie insisted Shadow needed a shot of ketamine, but when Charlotte went to administer the dose she realized a vial was missing and thought she'd forgotten to record it properly.

Watching Bernard, I laid out my theory. "Katie discovered the scratches after she used the whistle to call Shadow back to the barn. Keto was Katie's go-to remedy and she told you to fetch some from the tack room."

His eyes hardened and I wondered if he was going to try to deny it, but he didn't.

"Yeah," he said, "it was in the medicine cabinet. By the time I got back downstairs Shadow was calm and Katie was so tired she just wanted to go back to the Lodge."

"So you pocketed the vial. Which was why Charlotte was one vial short the next morning."

An angry buzz sounded in my ear. The wasp was back and, dear God, it landed on my shoulder. It was all I could do not to start flailing.

"It's just a wasp," Bernard said, flicking it off my shoulder and into the greenhouse wall where it bumped along until it reached the corner of the building and flew away.

Satisfied, he turned to me and said, "A man as vicious as Robson has no business bringing children into this world. The kids were suffering, each in their own way. Teddy's already a little jerk. He's afraid of his dad but will do anything to get his attention. That kid is going to be real screwed up if he doesn't get help. But Amelia, she's a little firecracker, she'd buck Robson every step of the way until he broke her." Bernard's voice cracked. "I wasn't going to let that happen.

"So yeah, I took the flask off Charlie's body and the keto from the tack room and made Robson a special cocktail." A thin smile crossed his lips. "Robson caught me fiddling with the flask and told me to fill it with the best rum in the house. Hey, no problem buddy, it's your funeral."

Bernard's eyes wandered past the garden to the Lodge. I followed his gaze. Keith and AJ were standing under the pergola, heads bent over their phones, Louisa paced back and forth across the terrace, casting the occasional glance in my direction.

"What I didn't bank on," Bernard continued, "was Robson deciding to fly the whole family out the next day."

"That's why you insisted on going with them to the hanger."

Bernard nodded. "I was sitting right next to him, I coulda grabbed the wheel if he checked out, but he didn't start sucking on that flask until we reached the hanger. I was shitting myself. What if it kicked in after they took off?"

He pressed his palms together as if he were praying. "Thank God for Mother Nature. The runway was blocked. Robson goes nuts. Tries to drag the pine off the tarmac and, boom! It's all over."

His eyes darkened as he contemplated what was coming next.

"Damned if that bloody flask doesn't fall out of Robson's pocket on our way back and Amelia, that little packrat, stuffs it into her backpack. I've never been so scared in my entire life. Jesus Christ, I coulda killed her."

"But you didn't Bernard. She didn't drink it."

"I know, but she could have."

"Evie!" AJ was standing in the shade of the pergola at the edge of the terrace, he cupped his hands around his mouth and yelled. "We're heading out." Keith and Louisa were next to the van, all of its doors were open. If I was going to do this, I had to do it now.

"Coming!" I shouted back. Then I leaned close to Bernard and whispered in his ear. At first he looked bewildered. Then he smiled.

"Bernard, you understand what I'm saying, right?"

He nodded, then reached into the woven basket and handed me a smooth, warm tomato.

CHAPTER 70

The scramble for seats in Keith's van was quickly settled when Louisa announced she gets car sick and had to ride up front or else.

"I can vouch for that," I said, remembering all the times Dad slammed on the brakes and Mom hauled Louisa out of the backseat so she could throw up on the verge. Eventually they realized Louisa wasn't faking it to get dibs on the front seat. "Come on AJ, get in the back. At least we won't look like two old married couples out for a Sunday drive; men up front and women stuck in the back."

After much clicking of seatbelts and adjusting of rear-view mirrors, Keith was finally ready to roll. Parker and Charlotte stood by the front door, their copper hair gleaming in the sunlight. Smiling and waving. I couldn't shake the feeling they were glad to be rid of us.

As we passed through the main gate I glanced up at the wrought iron sign. The 'N' in *MIRROR RANCH* was missing. I'd meant to tell Jay about it but forgot.

The van picked up speed on the two-lane access road. Rows of baby corn and cauliflower were obliterated, broken vegetation hammered flat by the storm. In the distance, farm machinery droned, preparing the fields, getting ready to start all over again from scratch.

As the telephone poles flashed past the window my mind wandered. Bernard's admission was shocking, but what surprised me even more was my reaction. *I wanted to protect him.* From the law which doesn't always deliver justice.

"Louisa." I raised my voice to be heard over the country music wailing out of the stereo. "How long does ketamine stay in someone's system?"

"What?" We were travelling at a steady eighty-three kilometers an hour—the speed limit is sacrosanct to Keith—and the wind roared past his side window. He insists he needs fresh air to stay awake on long trips. It's a real pain in the wintertime.

"Just curious. How long does ketamine stay in the human body?"

She frowned as she twisted around in her seat to face me. "Anywhere from one to three days. Why?"

"What about a dead body?"

Keith's eyes flicked up to the rear-view mirror. "Ketamine in a dead body? That doesn't sound like a random question."

"No, it's not." Now was as good a time as any. "So guys, I have some news. We've been retained by Bernard. He may have committed a crime and needs a referral—"

"Hold on, hold on," AJ interrupted. "When were we retained? I don't recall anyone waving fistfuls of cash at us."

Keith turned down the music, some poor soul lamenting his sad sack life, and said, "You did that peppercorn thing again, didn't you? In the garden with Bernard."

Louisa looked puzzled. "What peppercorn thing?"

Keith explained the old British court case that said all

you need for a binding contract is valuable consideration; even a single peppercorn would do. AJ laughed and asked what Bernard had given me as consideration, a cucumber, a radish? I pulled the small plum tomato out of my pocket and showed it to him.

Keith groaned and reminded me that Louisa wasn't a lawyer, she wasn't bound by privilege so we couldn't talk freely with her in the car. Her face fell, but then I passed her the tomato and said I'd just hired her as a medical consultant. Smiling, she popped the tiny tomato in her mouth.

"Right," I said, "now that the formalities are out of the way—"

"You think Bernard poisoned one or both of them." Louisa said with a smug look on her face. "That's why he needs a referral to a criminal lawyer. In case he's charged." She's very smart and incredibly intuitive, actually we both are, but I still find it annoying when she beats me to the punch line, even if she's only half right.

"*What*?" Keith hit the brakes, the van shuddered, almost stalled; his foot tapped the gas pedal and the vehicle began to pick up speed. The other two were babbling so fast I could hardly understand what they were saying.

"Let's not jump to conclusions," AJ said. "We don't know for sure how Charlie died."

"We do." I said. "Bernard saw Robson bludgeon Charlie on the path after Shadow bucked him off. And he told me in the garden that he poisoned Robson with ketamine—"

"Shadow?" Keith was getting riled. Still a couple of beats behind. "What's Shadow got to do with this?"

"That would explain the gash on Charlie's forehead," Louisa said, talking over Keith. "And how it got there given we found Charlie flat on his back."

"You're kidding! Bernard poisoned Robson with ketamine?" AJ looked incredulous.

Judging by the angry red blotch on back of Keith's neck, he was not a happy man. I had to slow things down before he exploded in the front seat.

"Let me take you through it…over lunch." Food always makes things better, right? I reached behind me for the picnic hamper and flipped open the lid. Opal had sent us off with a gourmet food basket. "Anybody want a sandwich? A Bernard Special."

Louisa and AJ practically tore the polka dotted sandwich boxes out of my hands, but Keith, still huffy, said he'd prefer to wait. I fiddled with the flaps on the light blue box until it popped open like a flower and flattened out to form a round cardboard plate. Bacon butty. I took a bite.

"Wow, this is fantastic! Keith, are you sure you don't want one? The bacon is nice and crisp; I can't tell what Bernard used for the sauce, maybe HP."

"Or ketamine," AJ said. I shot him a look and tipped my head in Keith's direction. *Don't say that!* AJ gave me a mischievous grin and bit a huge chunk out of his sandwich.

I took them through my conversation with Bernard in the garden, every detail from Bernard finding Charlie and Robson on the path to him stealing the ketamine and mixing it with rum in the silver flask. Then I repeated my question to Louisa: how long would it take for ketamine to disappear from a dead body.

She said she didn't know. "Google it."

"I did, it doesn't make any sense. This AI generated stuff isn't all it's cracked up to be."

From the driver's seat came a long, drawn out sigh. Keith asked for his sandwich and I unpacked it and passed it to him. He set it in his lap, keeping his eyes fixed on the straight-as-an-arrow road ahead.

Finally he spoke. "Forget Google, wait for the medical examiner's report. The findings will determine whether Bernard, or anyone for that matter, is charged."

I poked around in Opal's picnic basket—there had to be a dessert in here somewhere—and found a little cake tin, bright red and gold. When I pried off the lid the aroma of rum balls filled the van. Louisa laughed and said it smelled like Christmas.

Keith caught my eye in the rear-view mirror and raised his right hand, palm up. I passed him the biggest rum ball. "Easy does it, big guy. We don't want you over the limit."

He gave a small smile and set it in his lap and said, "Even if Robson killed Charlie while he lay helpless on the ground, that doesn't help Bernard. If Bernard poisoned Robson with a flask of ketamine, that's premeditated murder."

Louisa interrupted. "It might not have killed him, it depends on the dosage and a number of other things like Robson's general health. Did he have any serious health issues?"

AJ brushed some chocolate sprinkles away from his mouth and said, "The guy was a fitness fanatic, down in the gym"—which was nothing more than a mirrored room with a couple of treadmills and a bicycle— "every morning hogging the equipment. Doctor's orders he said, for his heart."

"This is where we need Louisa's expertise." I leaned forward, peering at her from between the two front seats. "Now you're going to earn your fee, that nice, fat, plum tomato. Would the keto have killed him if he had heart issues?"

"Perhaps. Ketamine poisoning can trigger acute systolic heart failure." Louisa reeled off a bunch of medical terms that meant nothing to me.

"In layman terms, please, Louisa."

"Robson's underlying health issues combined with ketamine laced rum could have killed him, but then again, the cause of death could have been a plain vanilla heart attack triggered by the stress of trying to drag a huge pine off the tarmac. We won't know until the autopsy."

AJ inhaled in mid swallow and started to cough. His face turned red and his eyes filled with tears. I reached over to whack him on the back but he waved me away. Then, coughing fit over, he looked at me. "I see where you're going with this. You're thinking you can't murder a dead man."

"Exactly," I handed AJ my serviette and he wiped his eyes. "If Robson died of a heart attack *before* the ketamine kicked in, assuming it was enough to kill him in the first place, then Bernard didn't murder him, even though he wanted to."

That was my problem. There was a lot of ambiguity, but I believed Bernard was a good man and Charlie and Robson were evil. I wanted Bernard to go free.

Then Louisa asked me a question that damn near stopped my heart.

CHAPTER 71

We were almost through the cloverleaf, drifting across a verge that was littered with shattered trees and fluttering bits of trash, when Louisa popped her head around her headrest and asked, "What if he's lying?"

"Who? Bernard?"

"Yeah. What if Bernard lied to you? What if Robson never left the Lodge that night and when Shadow bucked Charlie off it was Bernard, not Robson, who bashed Charlie's head in with a rock. There's no way to corroborate Bernard's version of events."

My heart skipped a beat. *Had Bernard lied to me?* I stared out the window, focusing on the horizon where the empty sky melted into the dark earth, and thought about it. He'd withheld the truth a couple of times, but not once had he flat out lied to me.

"No." As I said it, I became even more convinced. "I think Bernard was telling the truth."

Louisa clutched the back of her seat and pivoted to see me better, carefully watching my face. Her eyes narrowed. "Out with it. What are you thinking?"

After Charlie and Robson died, something changed with

the Moore women. I interpreted it as an inability to grieve the way other people grieved. Now I realized they weren't grieving at all. Charlie's death was a shock, Robson's death less so. Like bumps in the road the deaths were behind them, the women were free. They were moving on.

"I can't shake the feeling that the Moore women played a part in all this. Let's face it, Charlie and Robson were evil. They made Katie's life a living hell, they were going to kneecap Parker's career and destroy Mirror Ranch which was Charlotte and Jay's dream—"

"And Bernard's home," added Louisa, yanking on her seatbelt which was now tightening around her neck.

"Katie, Parker and Charlotte had barely survived Charlie's abuse. Robson was even worse. How does anyone stop the top 00.01 percent from doing what they want to everyone else?"

I thought back to Katie's journal. She knew Charlie was enslaved by greed. He loved power and would hold onto it forever if he could. She'd watched Robson, a nasty little boy, grow up to become a brutal, privileged man. Father and son were on a collision course. It was only a matter of time.

"They may not have planned it down to the very last detail—some things like the bomb cyclone were random—but the Moore women are smart. They knew Charlie and Robson better than anyone. They knew which buttons to push."

"Whoa." AJ raised his hands. "What on earth are you two talking about?"

Up front, Keith jammed on the brakes. The van veered onto the shoulder before righting itself and easing back into the long line of cars. Bumper to bumper as far as the eye could see. Sunlight bouncing off their windows like shards of sizzling glass.

Anxiously, Louisa peered out the windshield. "Is it an accident?" She'd be out on the hot tarmac rendering first aid in a second, if it was necessary. Keith said he couldn't see anything amiss up ahead.

AJ pulled out his phone to check the traffic update. "Nothing online. It could be the ripple effect after an accident that's cleared."

The van rolled to a stop. Keith pressed a button and all the windows rolled down, filling the car with the sweet smell of grass and large animals. On our right in a sleepy green field, a herd of cows were grazing. They were so close to the fence we could almost touch them.

"How would they pull it off?" Louisa asked me.

"The women? All Parker had to do was tell Robson that Charlie had changed his mind and was going to give her control of MMG after all. She'd certainly worked hard enough for it."

AJ who'd finally caught the drift of our conversation said, "Yeah, but Robson wouldn't take Parker's word for it. He'd hustle back to Charlie and demand to know if it was true."

"Sure," Louisa said, "and Charlie would deny it. Robson would relax, thinking Parker was going to get her comeuppance at Charlie's special dinner, but when Charlie didn't name Robson as his successor, Robson would take that as proof that Charlie had changed his mind and Parker was going to get the job after all."

"Right." I nodded. "When all along Charlie was just messing with them. One last twist of the knife before he gives up control. Can you imagine Robson's state of mind? Another arrogant, privileged, rich kid not getting what he thinks he deserves.

"If Bernard and Katie could get out of the Lodge without

being spotted by the CCTV cameras, then so could Robson. He sneaked out, maybe called Charlie's cell to locate him, then caught up to him on the path and killed him just like Bernard said. After that all Robson had to do was go back to the Lodge and wait for someone to notice Charlie was missing."

"That's cold," AJ said, softly.

I snorted. "Welcome to the shark tank where psychos always get their way."

Ahead of us a car revved its engine and the line started to creep forward. Keith geared up into second, then third.

His eyes caught mine in the rear-view mirror. "Even if you're right about Parker setting up Robson and Robson killing his father, anyone one of them could have poisoned Robson's flask with ketamine. They all had access to the medicine cabinet in the barn."

"True," I said, "but only Bernard had access to the flask. He took it off Charlie's body."

"I can't picture it," AJ said, shaking his head. "Bernard is such a sweet, gentle guy, especially with the kids."

"That's precisely why he did it." I told them about Jay's 'brilliant' idea of holding dogsled races, and Charlotte's worry that if the Huskies got loose they'd tear Lucky to bits. Lucky was too innocent to recognize a dangerous predator when it was staring him in the face.

"Sled dogs?" Keith said from the front seat. "What do sled dogs have to do with this?"

"Unlike Lucky, Bernard is street wise. He can spot danger a million miles away. Charlotte gave him a new start after he'd lost everything in New York City. A home at Mirror Ranch, a job he loved, and, most importantly, a family. Bernard recognized Robson for what he was, a vicious, brutal man, and decided to eliminate him to protect the people he loved."

"Let's not forget," Louisa added, "Bernard saw Robson murder Charlie on the path. He knew the Moore women would never be safe as long as Robson was around."

AJ reached past me into the picnic hamper and rooted around until he pulled out a bottle of pineapple juice. He wiggled it at me and said, "Sorry, Valentine, that's the last of the food. Two more hours to go. You're gonna starve."

I smacked his hand and he dropped the bottle into my lap, then reached behind me and pulled out a second bottle for himself.

After he scrutinized the label he looked up at me and said, "So tell me this. Why did Bernard confess to you? Why didn't he just wait and take his chances with the medical examiner's report? The bodies were out in the elements, then stashed in the cooler, after all that time the forensic evidence would be compromised."

"Because I confronted him with the truth. As you said, he's a sweet guy, perhaps he couldn't handle the guilt. He was devastated when he thought he could have poisoned Amelia. He just threw it out there into the universe and left it up to the universe to decide whether he should be punished."

Louisa pulled her seatbelt away from her body and wriggled around to look at me. She'd been riding sideways for most of this journey and I hoped she wasn't going to get sick all over the place.

"Lucky for Bernard, he came to the right universe. You didn't tell him to turn himself in to the police. You told him about the peppercorn…or in this case the plum tomato."

AJ shook his bottle of juice, popped it open and took a long swig. "Would it bother you if everything happened just the way you said, if the Moore women teed it up, if they set Charlie and Robson at each other's throats, and if Bernard was on his own mission to poison Robson? If they all got away with it in the end?"

I settled back in my seat, no longer straining against the seatbelt to see what was happening up ahead.

"Charlie and Robson were responsible for their own actions, regardless of whether the Moore women egged them on or not. I believe Robson killed Charlie and Bernard tried to kill a dead man. The world is rid of two evil men and the Moore women and Bernard will be able to live out their lives in peace. That's a form of justice, isn't it?"

"Rough justice, perhaps." AJ looked at me for a moment, then smiled. "Are there any rum balls left?"

I passed him the red and gold tin. Inside, resting in their pretty little paper cups, were two rumballs. AJ took one and I took the other and we tapped them together, a little rum ball toast.

Which sent chocolate sprinkles flying everywhere.

JOURNAL

At last, it's arrived. The medical examiner's report.
Findings: inconclusive. As I expected.
The bad kings got what they deserved.
All I had to do was blow the whistle.
Shadow did the rest.

ACKNOWLEDGEMENTS

The lives of the rich and famous are endlessly fascinating (and bizarre). However, for me it's the ordinary people who really matter.

I'd like to thank some of them here.

First, from the bottom of my heart, thank you to my husband, Roy, who's been a constant source of inspiration from the very beginning, and to my daughters, Kelly, a former nurse and Eden, a paralegal, who are always there, day or night, to answer my cockamamie questions.

I'd also like to thank Charlotte Morganti, an amazing writer and a brilliant first reader for her insights.

A special thanks to my sister Rose Marie and her son Brad who spent a delightful week at Echo Valley Ranch & Spa (the inspiration for Mirror Ranch) where nothing calamitous befell them.

Lastly, I'd like to thank you, my readers, for your support and encouragement.

I am so grateful to you all.

ABOUT THE AUTHOR

SUSAN JANE WRIGHT studied anthropology before she became a lawyer. She worked as a litigator in a national law firm then went in-house with a multi-national corporation. Her career has taken her from the boardrooms of Calgary to the streets of Hong Kong.

The Privileged Death is the fifth in the Evie Valentine mystery series. Her earlier books have been bestsellers with *Box of Secrets* being selected as a finalist by the Crime Writers of Canada and *Fortune Favors the Dead* being named the best mystery by the Canadian Book Club Awards.

She lives in Calgary, Alberta. When she's not writing she's travelling with her husband and two daughters. Her favourite vacation was a trip from Prague to London on the Orient Express. One day she'd like to take the train from Venice to Istanbul.